Unicorn vs. Goblins

Another Phoebe and Her Unicorn Adventure

Unicorn vs. Goblins

Another Phoebe and Her Unicorn Adventure

Dana Simpson

Andrews McMeel Publishing®

a division of Andrews McMeel Universal

INTRODUCTION

CORY: You know what I think? We should write about how we found out about Phoebe and why we love her.

POESY: Wait, how DID we find out about Phoebe?

CORY: Don't you remember? I brought the first book home, but I didn't like the cover, so I stuck it on your shelf and forgot about it and then—

POESY: —One day I took it off the shelf. We read it, and we liked it.

CORY: That's what I remember, too, more or less. I came into your room to shout at you to brush your hair for school, and you were reading this great comic book and laughing. I told you to put it down and brush your hair and came back five minutes later, and you were still reading it and laughing.

POESY: There's too many "and"s in that sentence.

CORY: Then I took it away from you. I read it, and I started laughing, too.

POESY: Nah, my description is totally better.

[Let the record show that here, Poesy asked to re-read some of the strips in this volume and took the laptop away from me. I couldn't get it back until Alice distracted her with guacamole, and I took the computer back.]

POESY: I like the part where Phoebe goes to music camp and Marigold makes a friend.

[At this point, Cory asked Poesy to draw a Phoebe and Marigold, on a rocket-skateboard, playing music.]

POESY: You mean a hoverboard.

pheobe   +   Marigold   =   pheobe gold

CORY: It's easy to compare Phoebe to Calvin and Marigold to Hobbes—I did it when I reviewed that first collection ("If Hobbes was a snarky unicorn and Calvin was an awesome little girl"), but Calvin was kind of a creep, especially to little girls. By contrast, Phoebe has a very well-adjusted relationship with the young dudes in her life—and still manages to be funny as heck when they come around.

I love—LOVE—how Dana finesses the way that Phoebe's parents relate to Marigold, too. Calvin's mom and dad rolled their eyes every time Calvin talked with spittle-flecked excitement about his imaginary friend. But Phoebe's parents are cooled out by Marigold's SHIELD OF BORINGNESS, which means that they can react to her as if she were just one of Phoebe's little pals, albeit a pal with a horn, hooves, and magic powers.

But best of all is Marigold. I mean, her last name is HEAVENLY NOSTRILS. Say that aloud with me. HEAVENLY. NOSTRILS. How much fun is that to say?

All the mischief, the pure id and self-centered, delightful sociopathy of youth is evenly divided between Phoebe and Marigold. They're each other's best friends and worst influences.

When *Sesame Street* launched, the show was all kids' jokes. Think of Barney the $#@@{!#* Dinosaur. About as much fun for adults as a fiberglass smoothie. But Jim Henson and the Children's Television Workshop pulled the show and went back to the drawing board, redesigning it so that it had as many adult jokes as kid ones—and so that adults and kids would have a reason to sit and watch together. Whatever value the show had, they reasoned, it would be multiplied if parents and kids shared an experience together, if they had something to talk about after.

The same principle guided the design of Disneyland. Walt Disney was sick of sitting on the sidelines, watching his daughters go around and around the Griffith Park carousel, so he built a theme park full of stuff that kids could bring their grown-ups on. The rest is history.

[Poesy is now singing a Spice Girls song. Where did she learn that?]

There's just enough humor here that sails over kids' heads and lands squarely on their grown-ups to make this an indispensable read for adults, but there's also an infinitude of kid stuff that we both laughed at. I love so many things about this book, but most of all, I love that we read it together.

— Poesy Taylor Doctorow (age 7)

— Cory Doctorow (age 44)

Burbank, California

August 2015

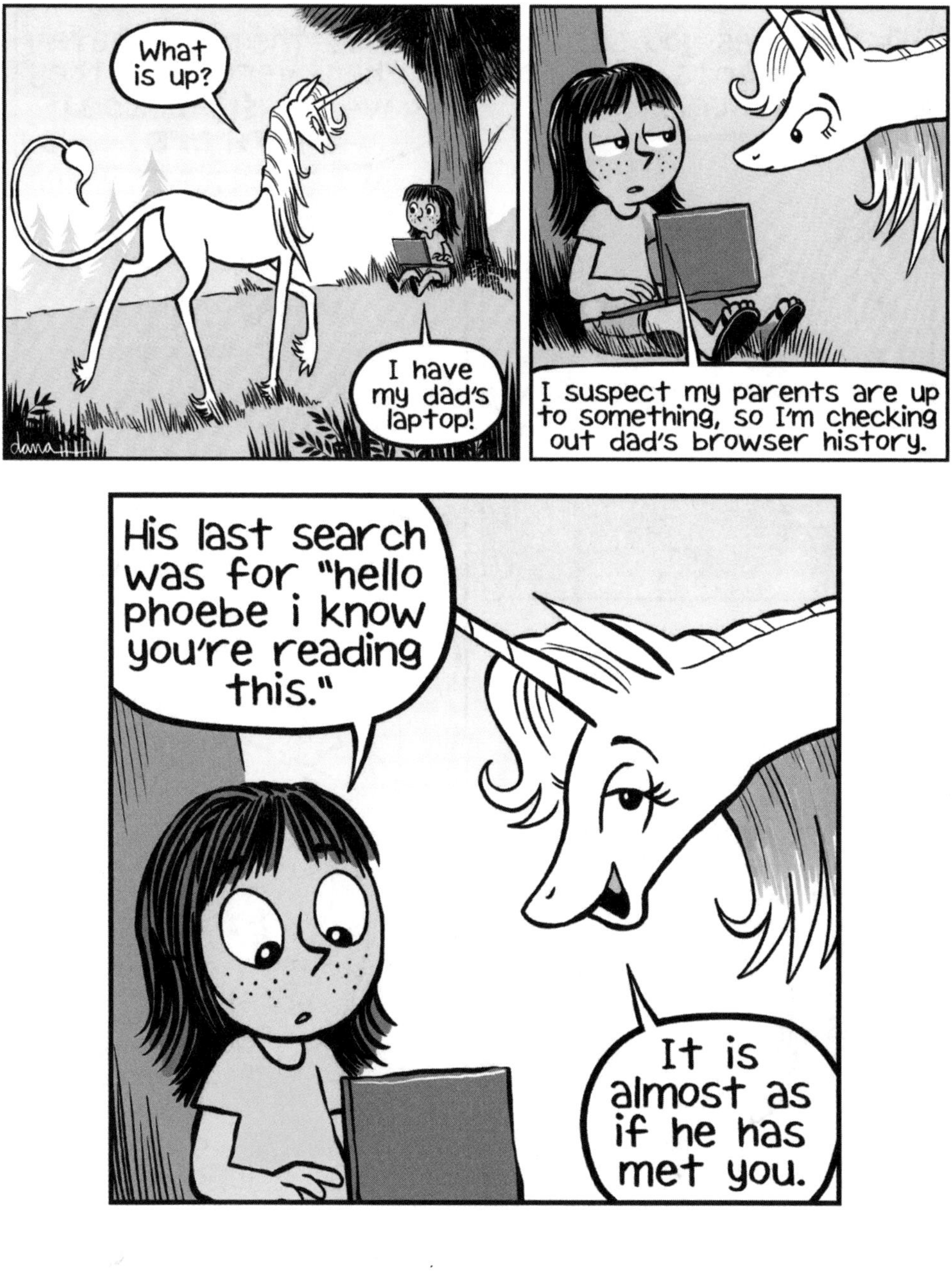
What is up?
I have my dad's laptop!
I suspect my parents are up to something, so I'm checking out dad's browser history.
His last search was for "hello phoebe i know you're reading this."
It is almost as if he has met you.

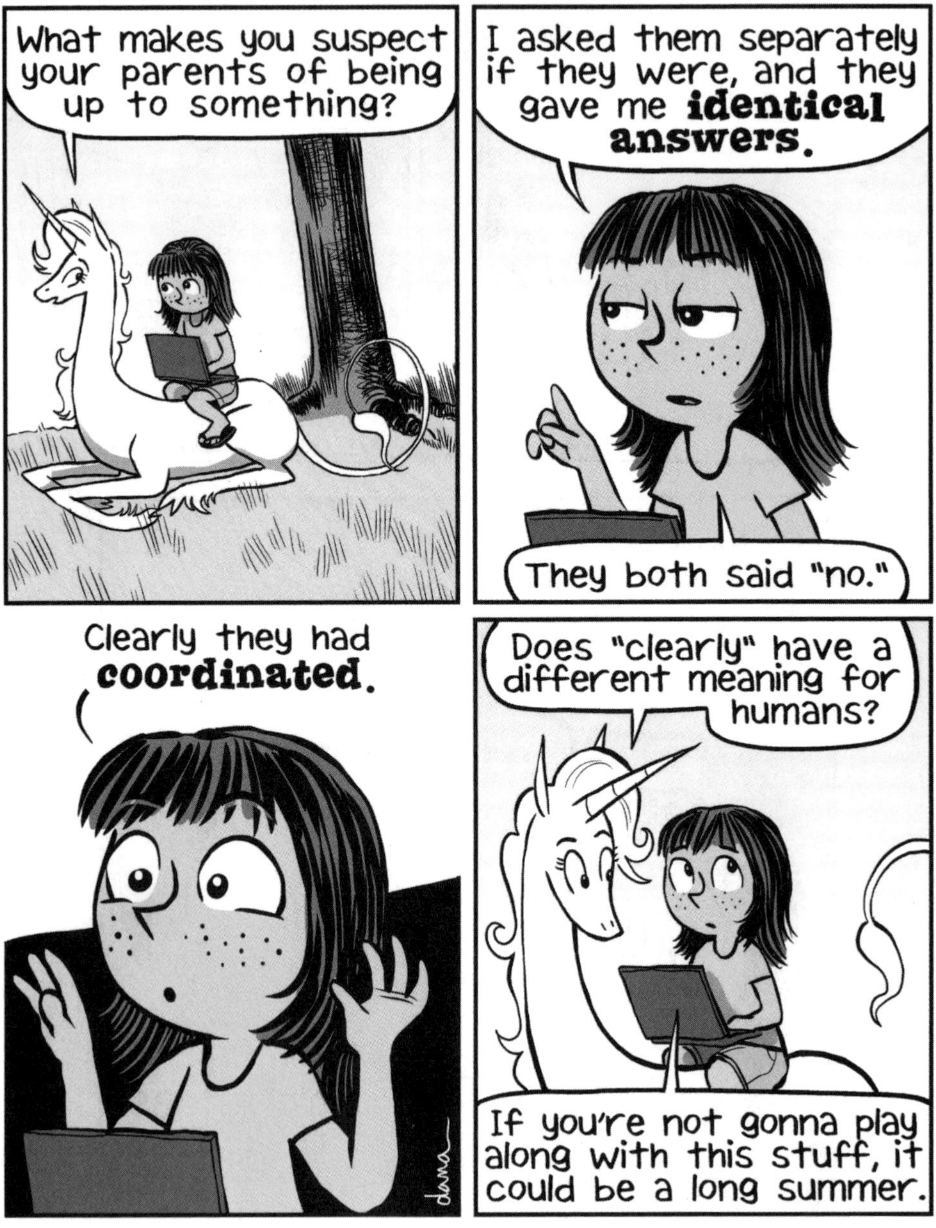
What makes you suspect your parents of being up to something?
I asked them separately if they were, and they gave me **identical answers**.
They both said "no."
Clearly they had **coordinated**.
Does "clearly" have a different meaning for humans?
If you're not gonna play along with this stuff, it could be a long summer.

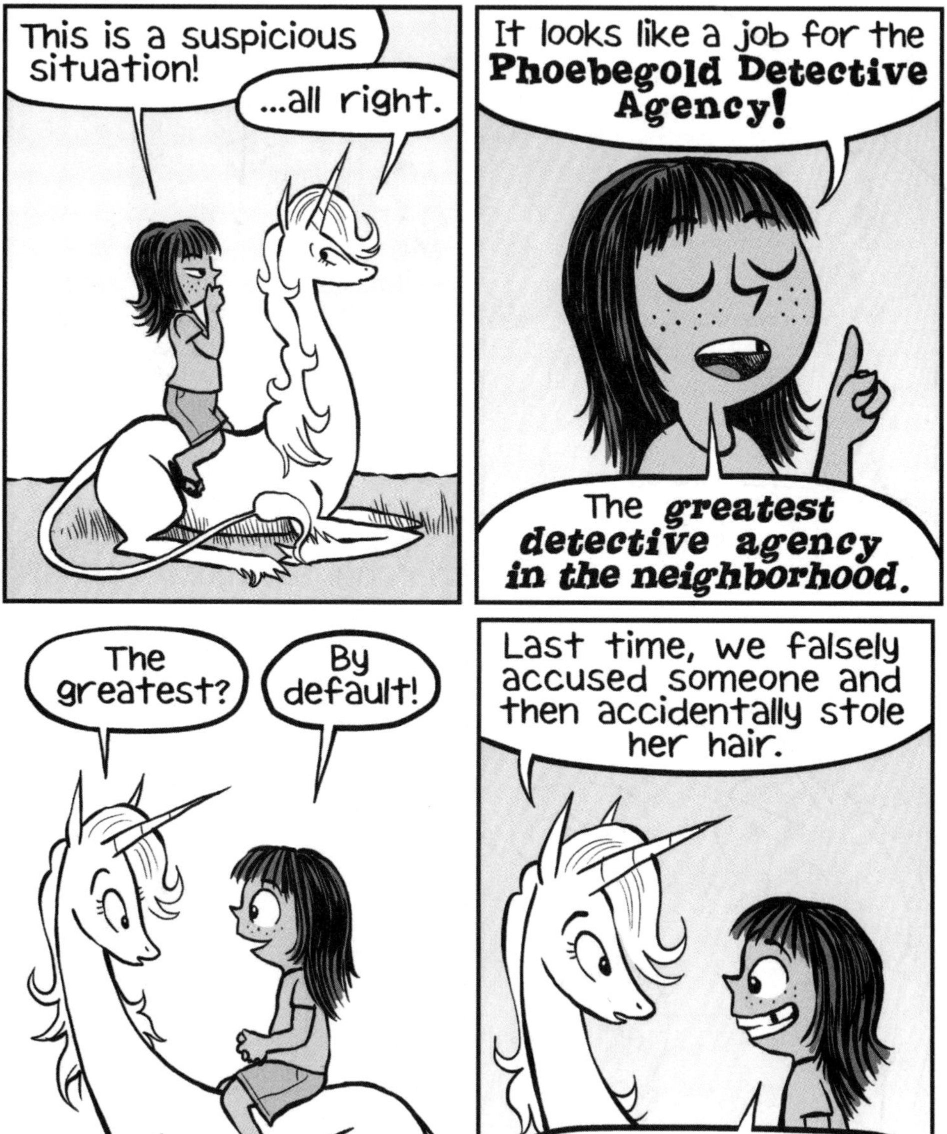
This is a suspicious situation!
...all right.
It looks like a job for the **Phoebegold Detective Agency!**
The ***greatest detective agency in the neighborhood.***
The greatest?
By default!
Last time, we falsely accused someone and then accidentally stole her hair.
That's what's so great about default!
dana

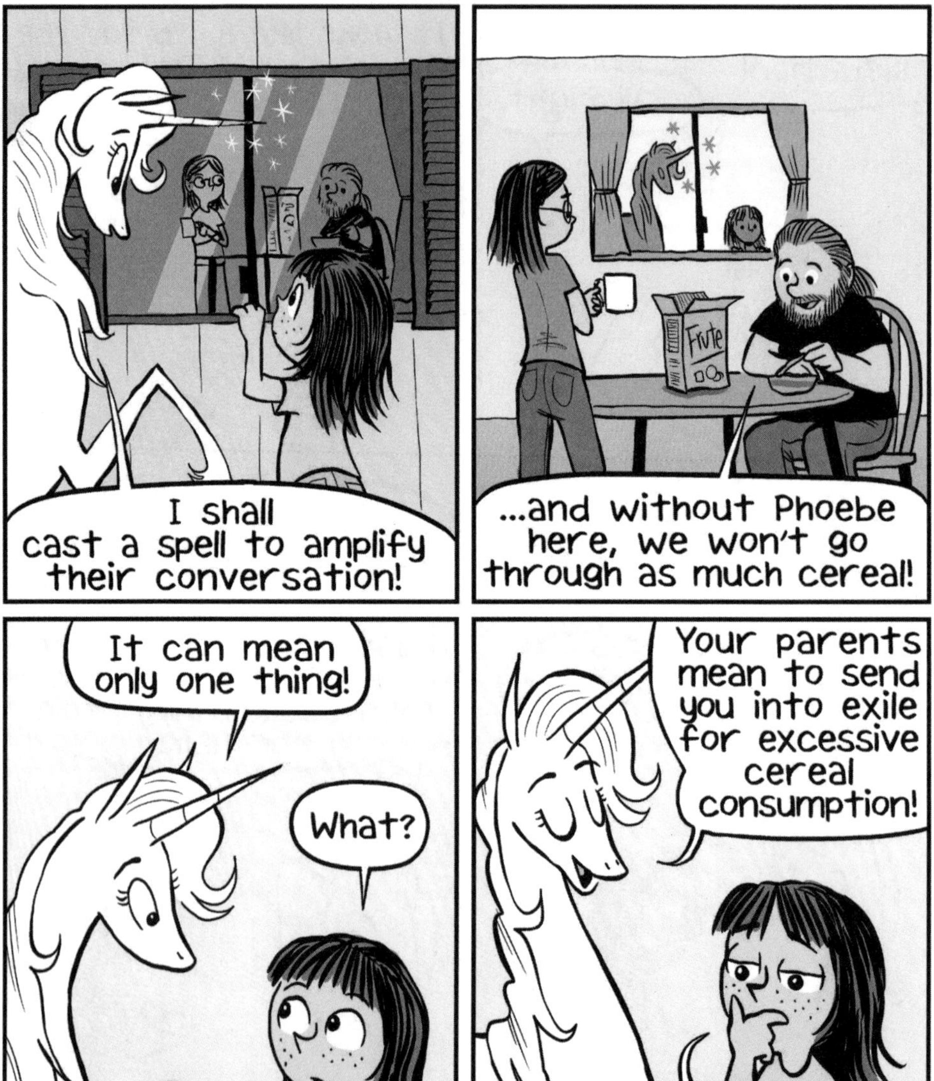
I shall cast a spell to amplify their conversation!
Frute
...and without Phoebe here, we won't go through as much cereal!
It can mean only one thing!
What?
Your parents mean to send you into exile for excessive cereal consumption!
Then we should start playing "law firm" instead of "detective agency."
dana

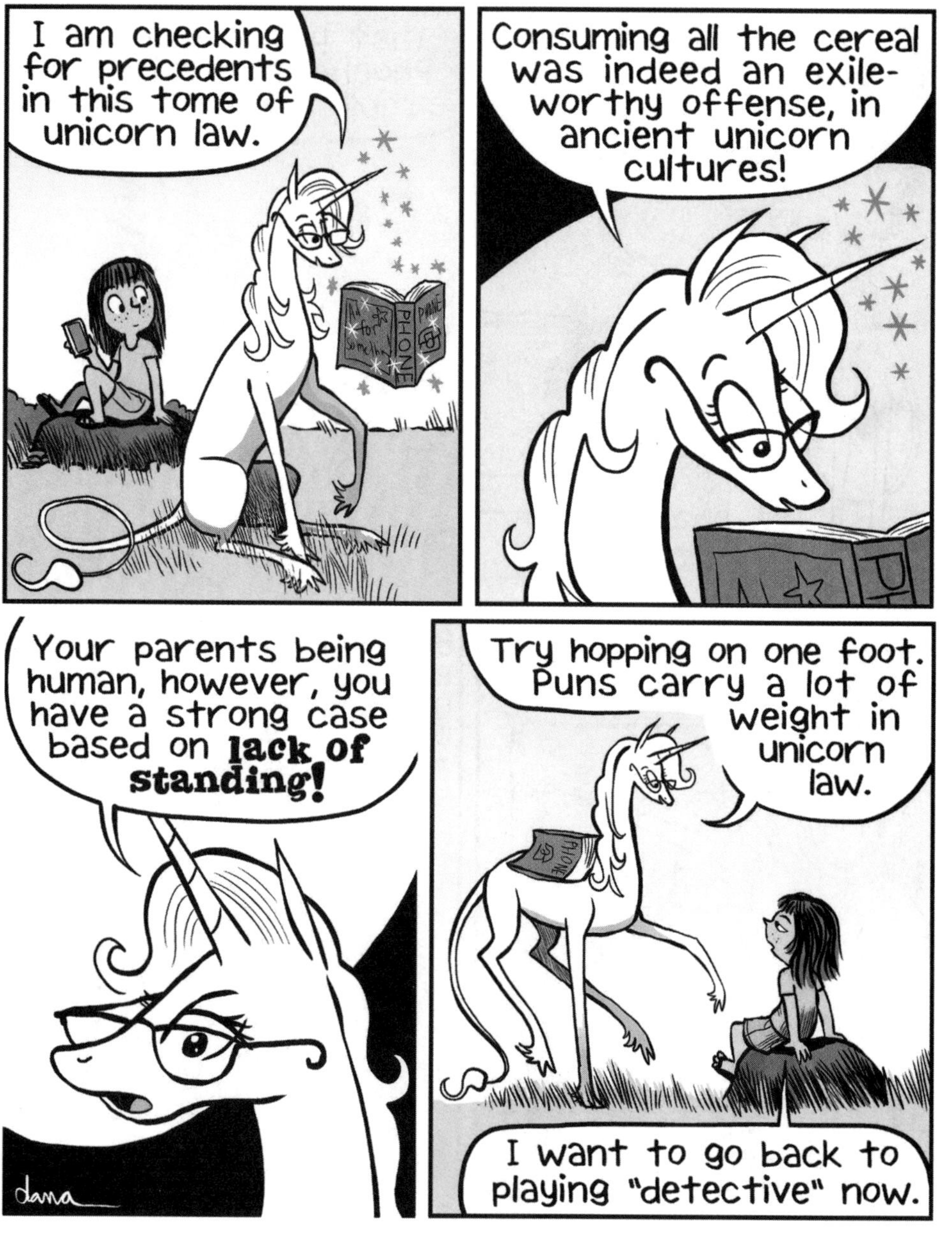
I am checking for precedents in this tome of unicorn law.
PHONE
Consuming all the cereal was indeed an exile-worthy offense, in ancient unicorn cultures!
Your parents being human, however, you have a strong case based on **lack of standing!**
dana
Try hopping on one foot. Puns carry a lot of weight in unicorn law.
PHONE
I want to go back to playing "detective" now.

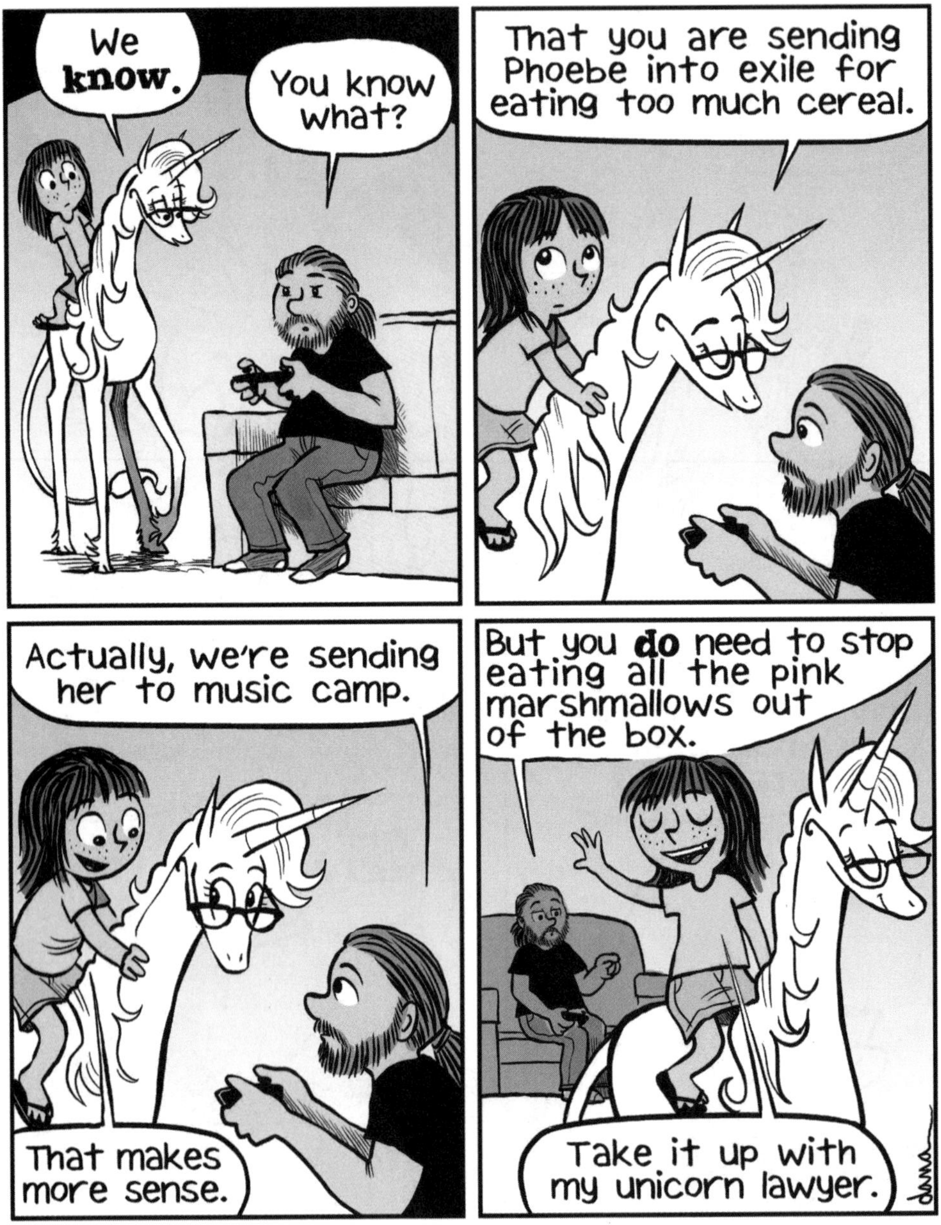
We **know.**
You know what?
That you are sending Phoebe into exile for eating too much cereal.
Actually, we're sending her to music camp.
That makes more sense.
But you **do** need to stop eating all the pink marshmallows out of the box.
Take it up with my unicorn lawyer.
dana

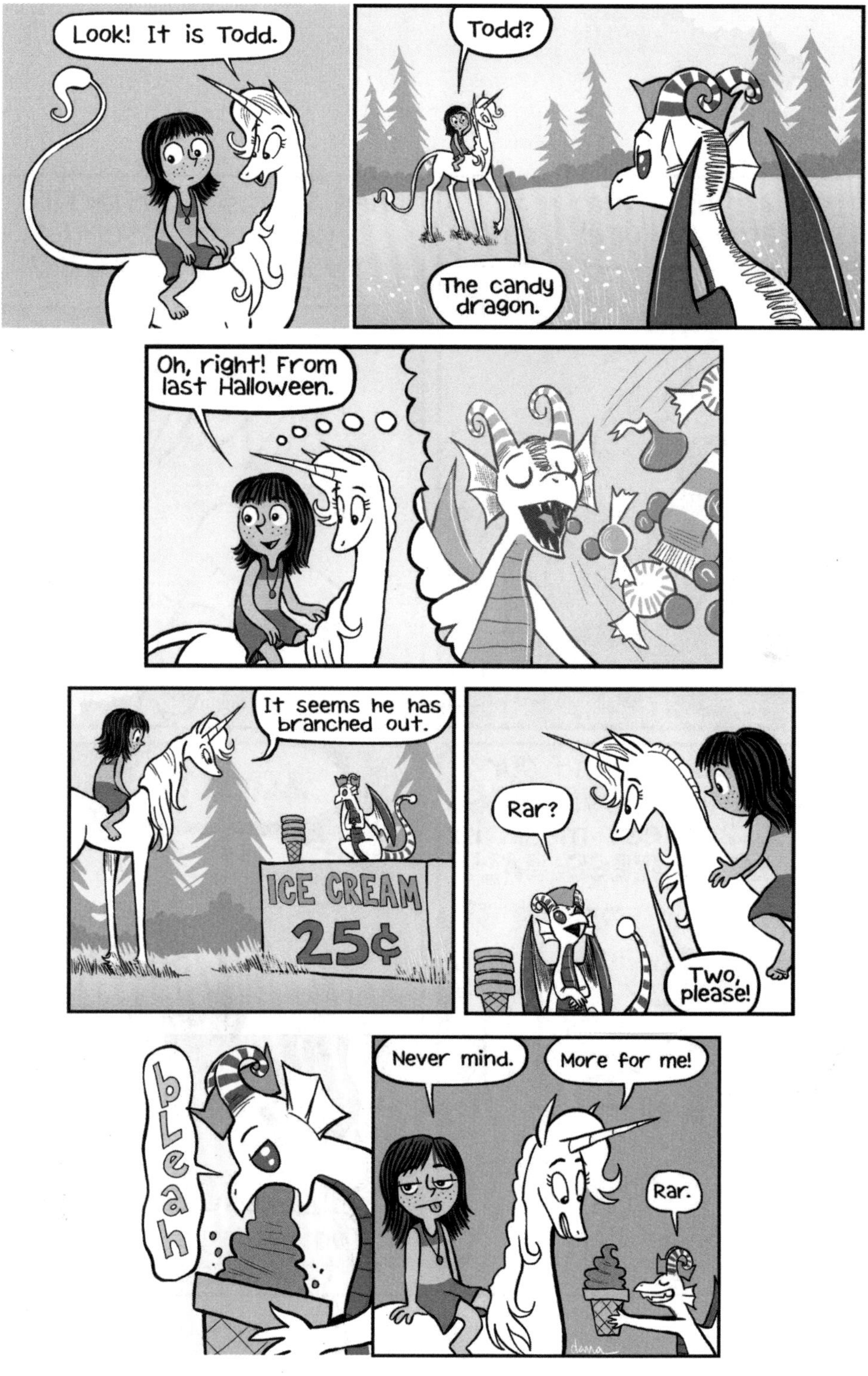

Look! It is Todd.
Todd?
The candy dragon.
Oh, right! From last Halloween.
It seems he has branched out.
ICE CREAM
25¢
Rar?
Two, please!
bleah
Never mind.
More for me!
Rar.

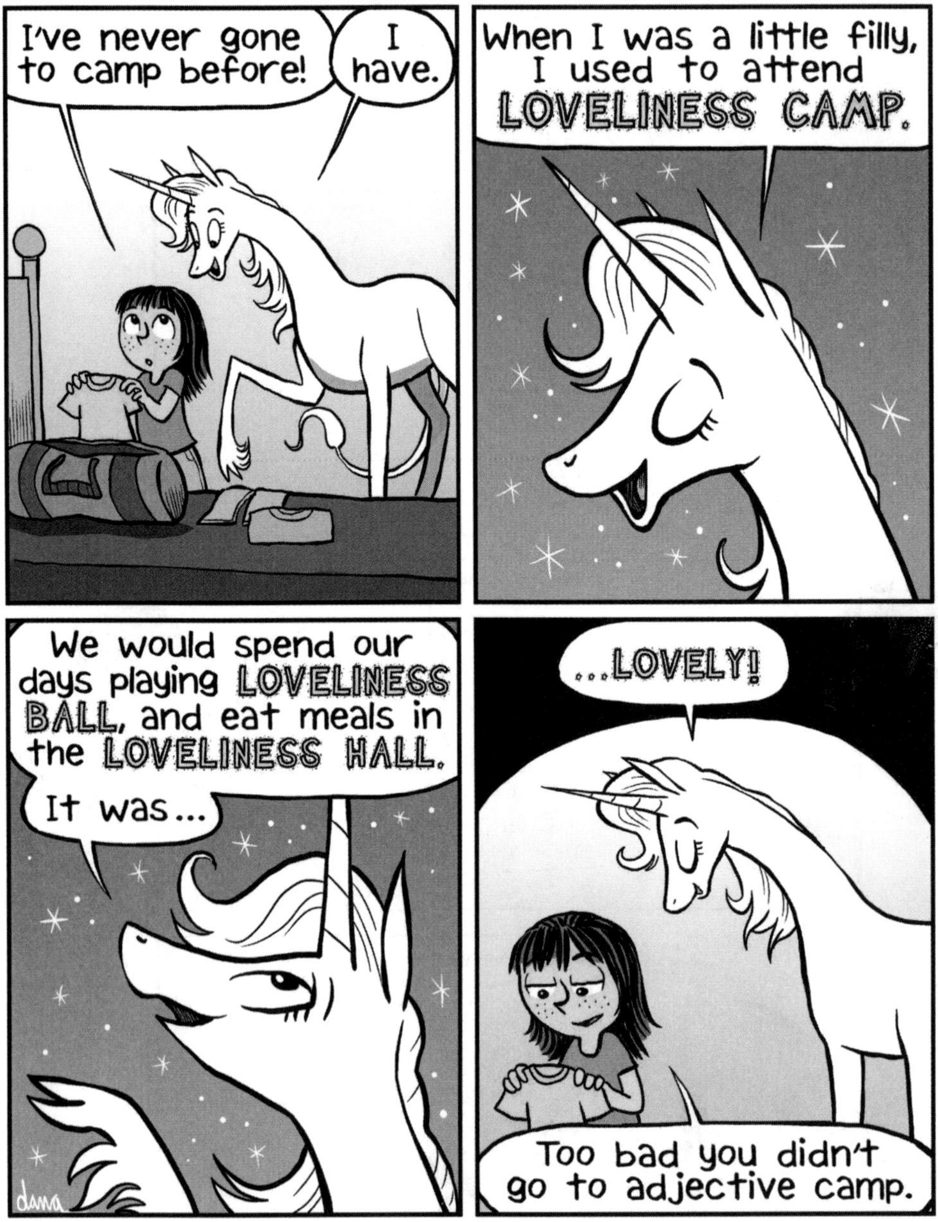
I've never gone to camp before!
I have.
When I was a little filly, I used to attend LOVELINESS CAMP.
We would spend our days playing LOVELINESS BALL, and eat meals in the LOVELINESS HALL.
It was...
...LOVELY!
Too bad you didn't go to adjective camp.
dana

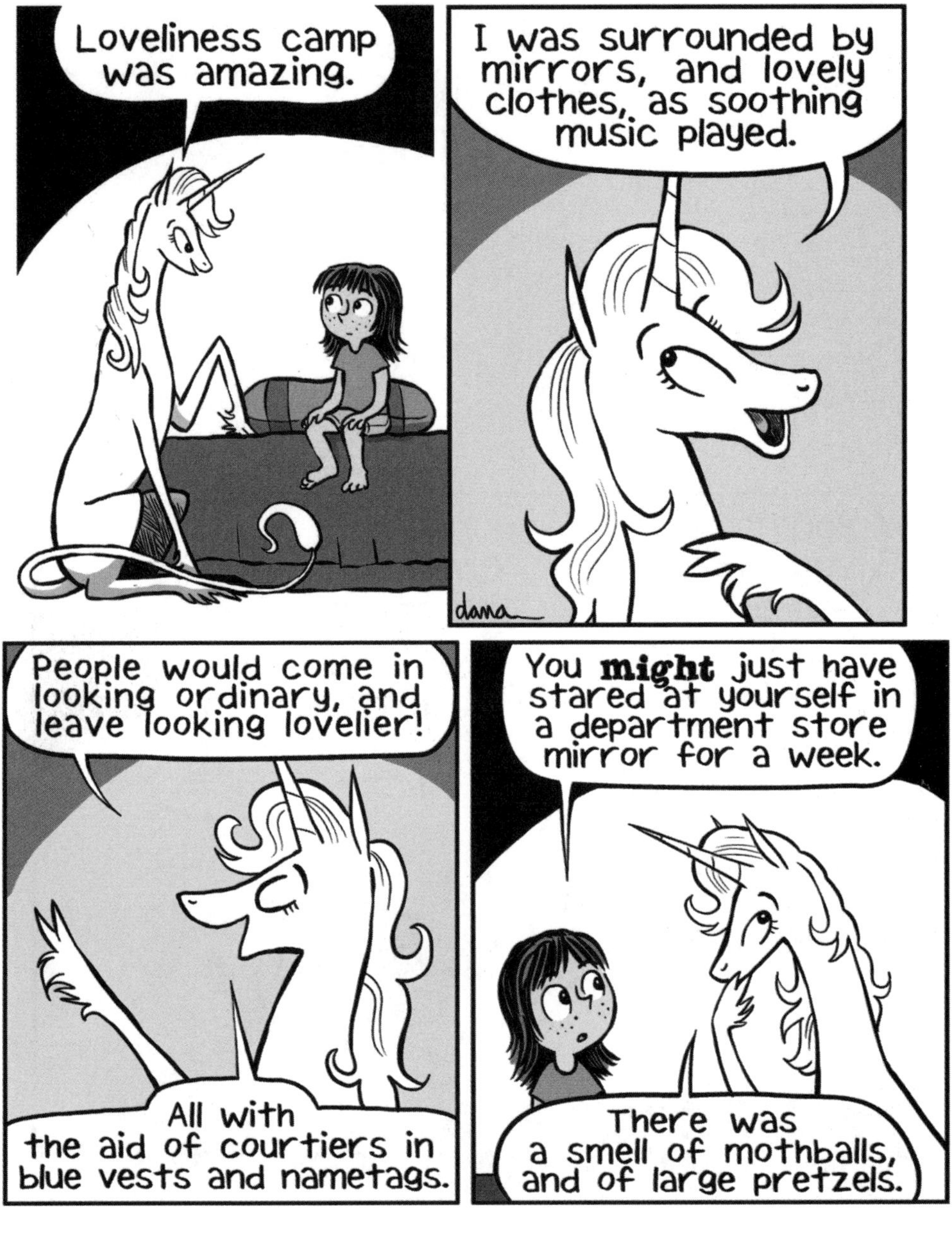
Loveliness camp was amazing.
I was surrounded by mirrors, and lovely clothes, as soothing music played.
dana
People would come in looking ordinary, and leave looking lovelier!
All with the aid of courtiers in blue vests and nametags.
You **might** just have stared at yourself in a department store mirror for a week.
There was a smell of mothballs, and of large pretzels.

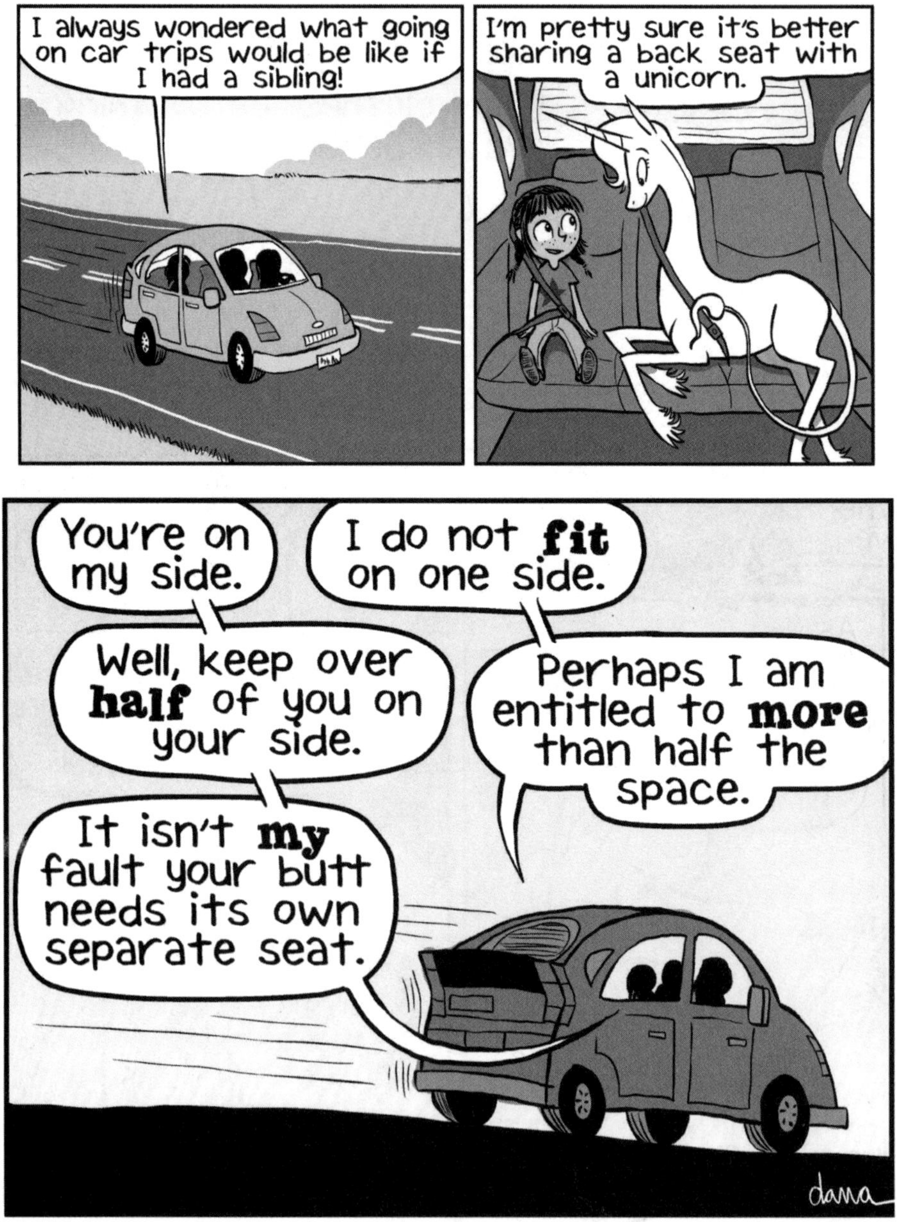
I always wondered what going on car trips would be like if I had a sibling!
I'm pretty sure it's better sharing a back seat with a unicorn.
You're on my side.
I do not **fit** on one side.
Well, keep over **half** of you on your side.
Perhaps I am entitled to **more** than half the space.
It isn't **my** fault your butt needs its own separate seat.
dana

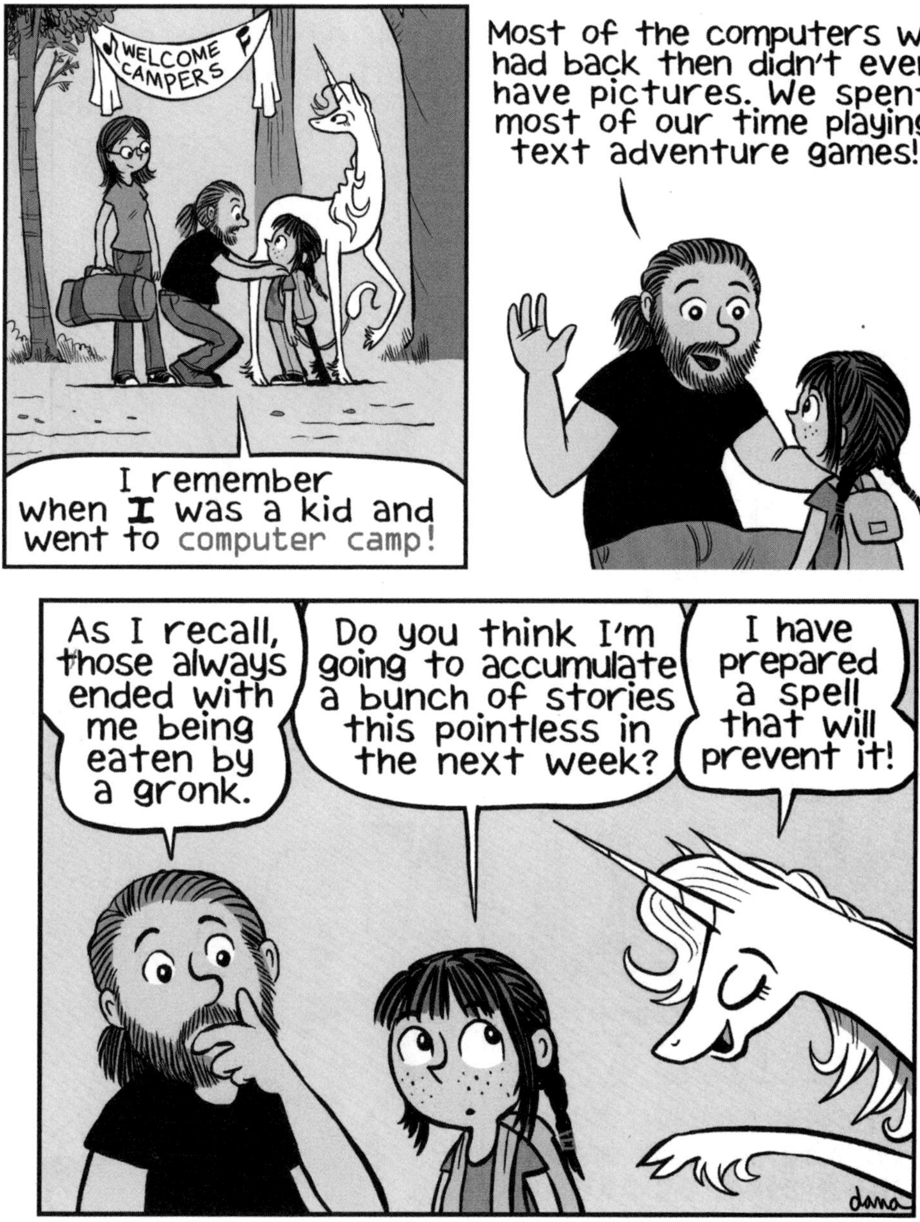
WELCOME CAMPERS
I remember when I was a kid and went to computer camp!
Most of the computers we had back then didn't even have pictures. We spent most of our time playing text adventure games!
As I recall, those always ended with me being eaten by a gronk.
Do you think I'm going to accumulate a bunch of stories this pointless in the next week?
I have prepared a spell that will prevent it!
dana

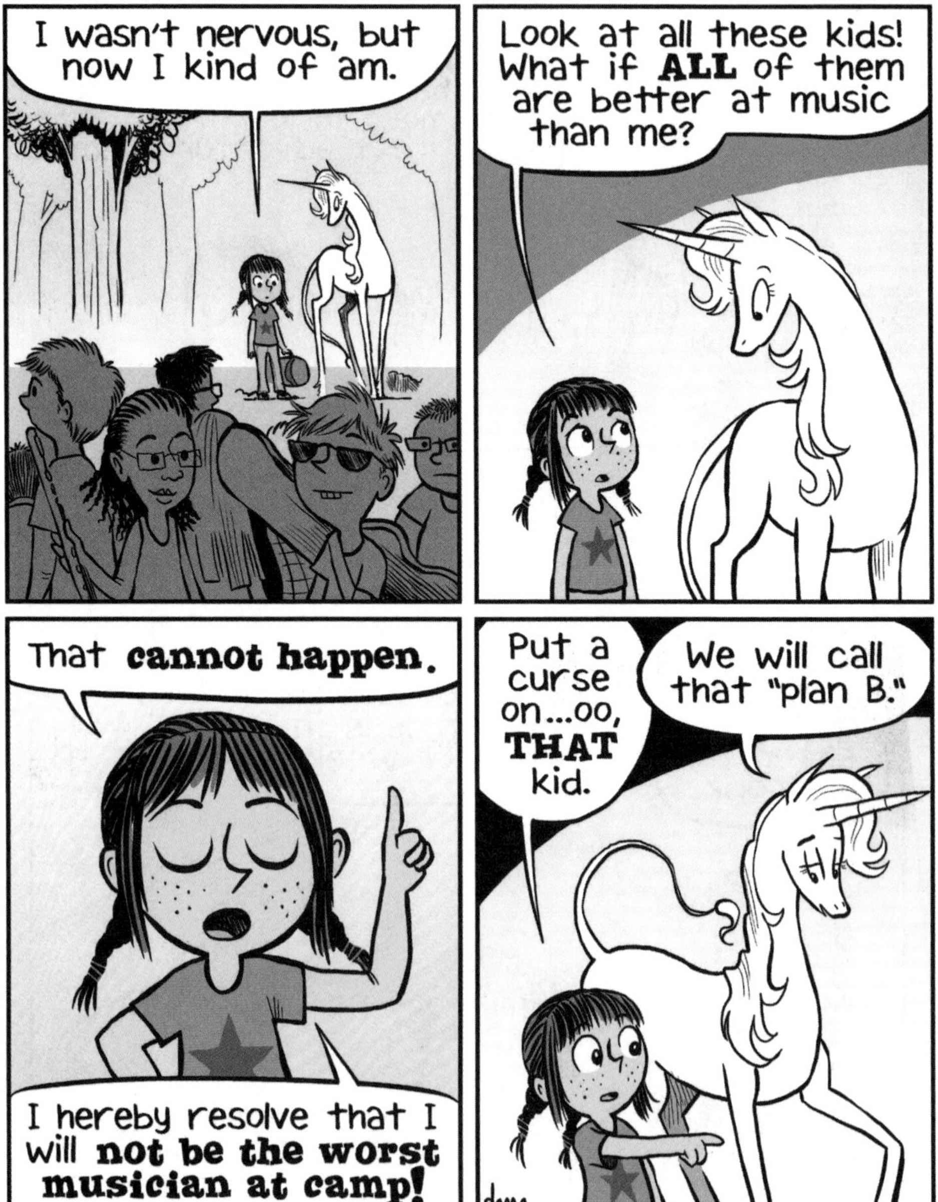
I wasn't nervous, but now I kind of am.
Look at all these kids! What if ALL of them are better at music than me?
That cannot happen.
I hereby resolve that I will not be the worst musician at camp!
Put a curse on...oo, THAT kid.
We will call that "plan B."
dana

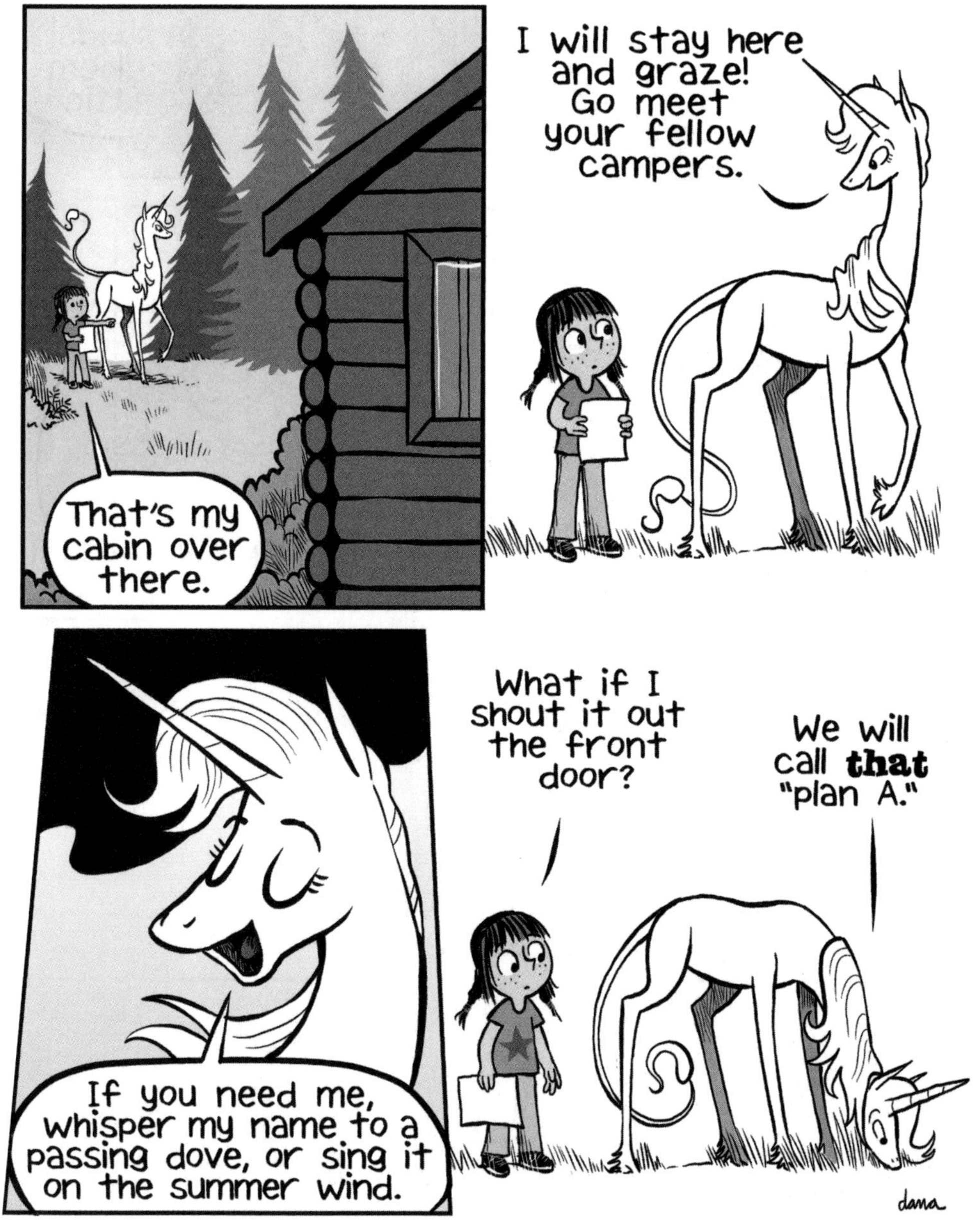
That's my cabin over there.
I will stay here and graze! Go meet your fellow campers.
If you need me, whisper my name to a passing dove, or sing it on the summer wind.
What if I shout it out the front door?
We will call **that** "plan A."
dana

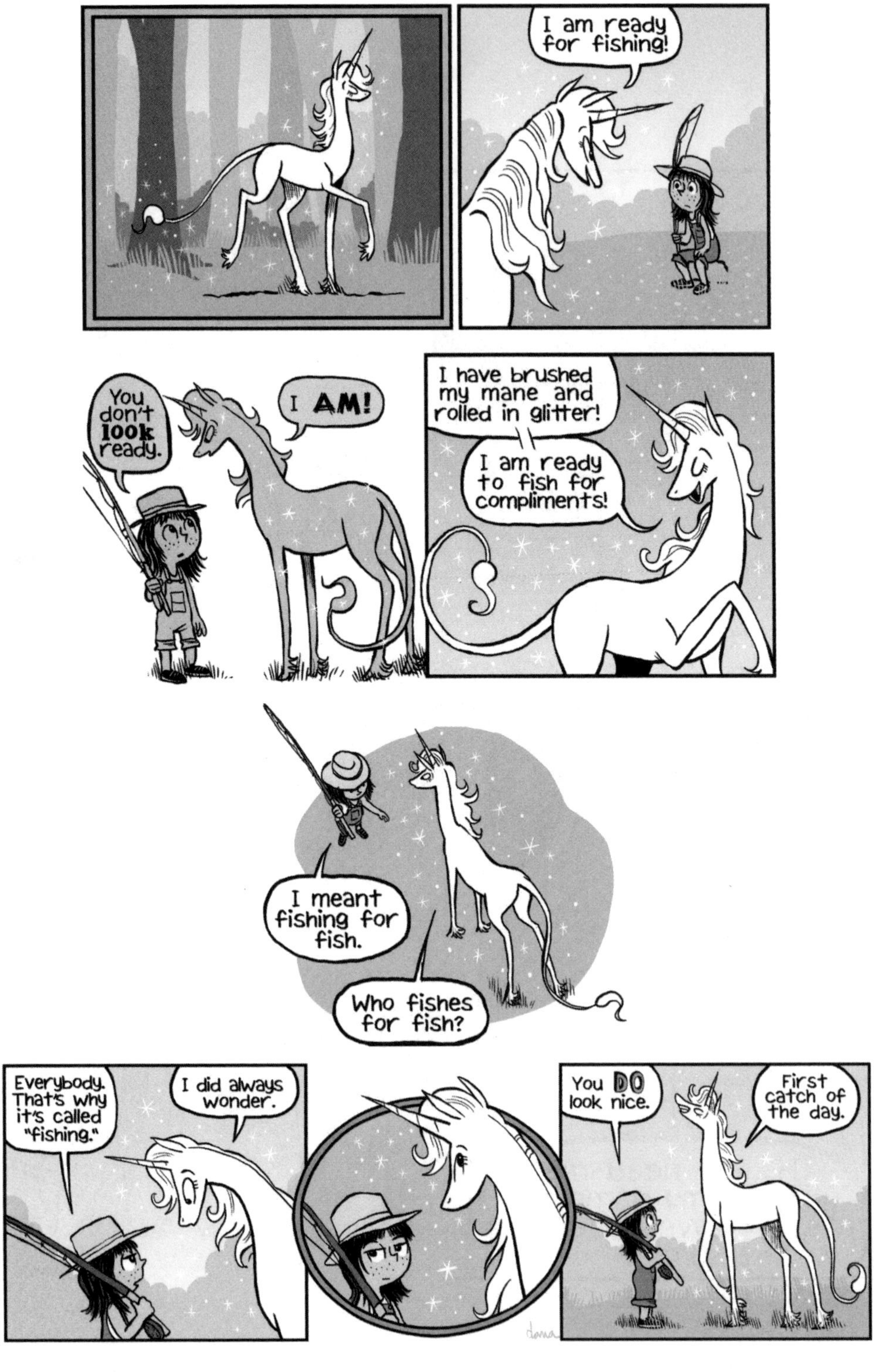
I am ready
for fishing!
You don't look ready.
I AM!
I have brushed my mane and rolled in glitter!
I am ready to fish for compliments!
I meant fishing for fish.
Who fishes for fish?
Everybody. That's why it's called "fishing."
I did always wonder.
You DO look nice.
First catch of the day.

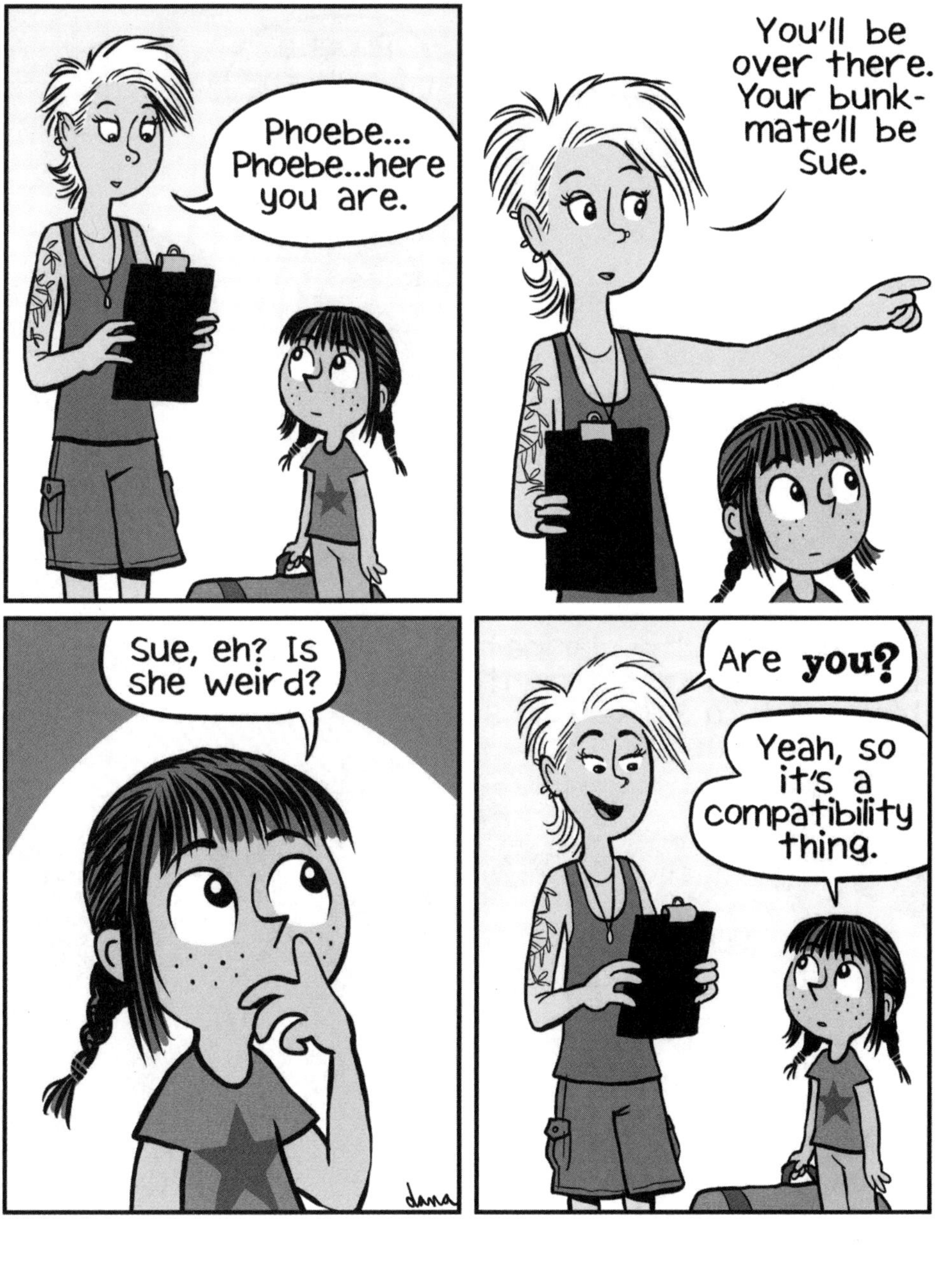
Phoebe... Phoebe...here you are.
You'll be over there. Your bunk-mate'll be Sue.
Sue, eh? Is she weird?
Are **you?**
Yeah, so it's a compatibility thing.
dana

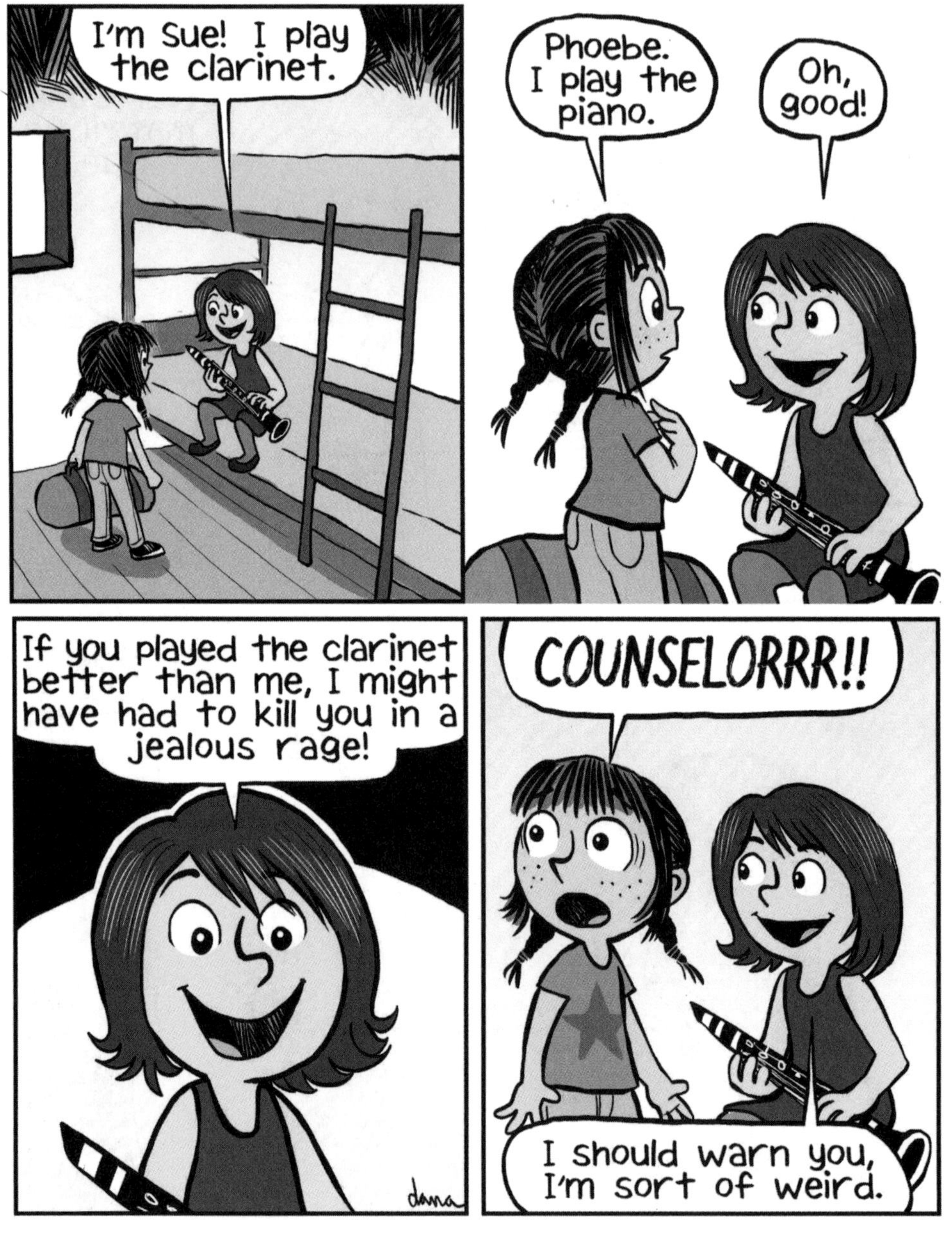
I'm Sue! I play the clarinet.
Phoebe. I play the piano.
Oh, good!
If you played the clarinet better than me, I might have had to kill you in a jealous rage!
dana
COUNSELORRR!!
I should warn you, I'm sort of weird.

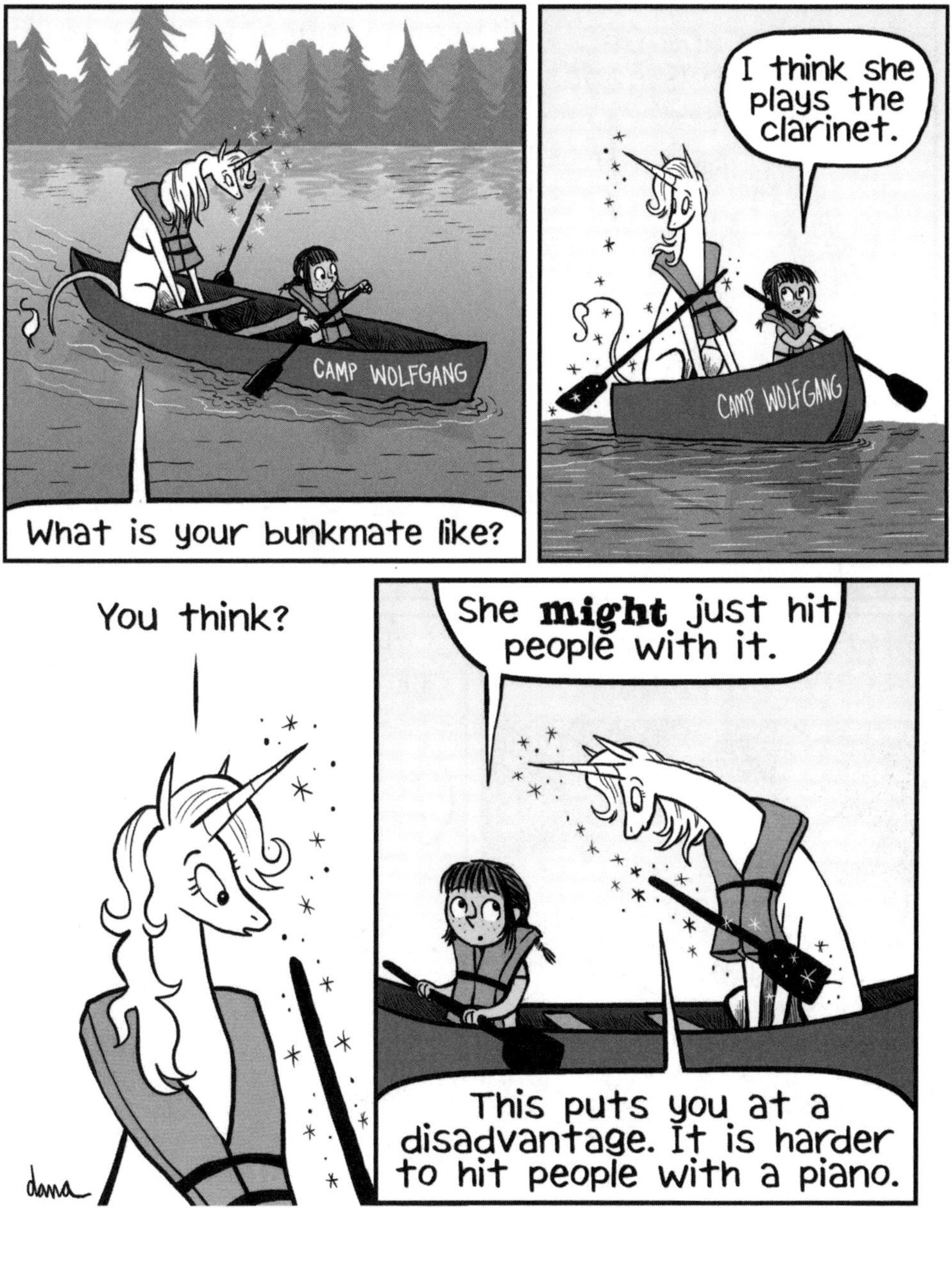
CAMP WOLFGANG
What is your bunkmate like?
I think she plays the clarinet.
CAMP WOLFGANG
You think?
She **might** just hit people with it.
This puts you at a disadvantage. It is harder to hit people with a piano.
dana

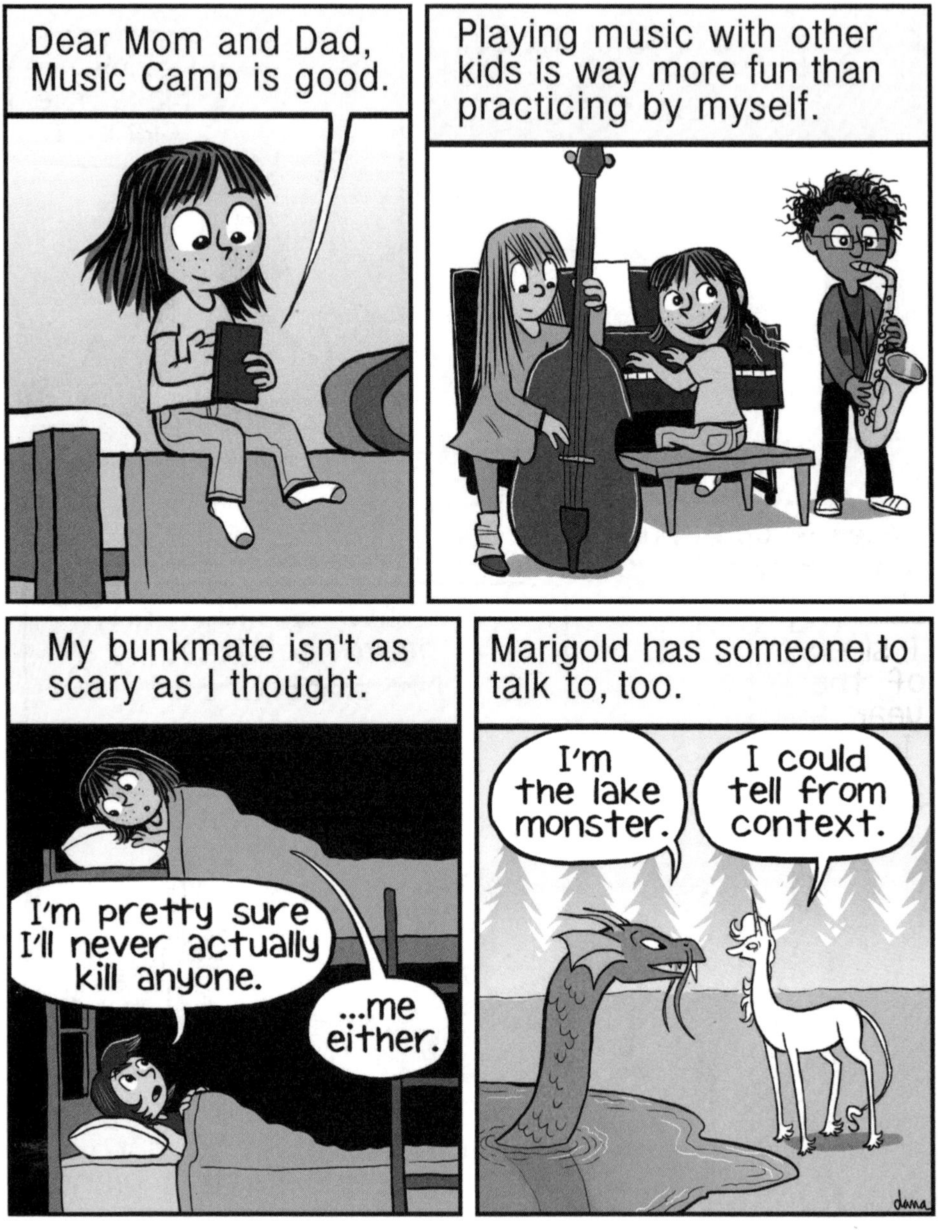
Dear Mom and Dad, Music Camp is good.
Playing music with other kids is way more fun than practicing by myself.
My bunkmate isn't as scary as I thought.
I'm pretty sure I'll never actually kill anyone.
...me either.
Marigold has someone to talk to, too.
I'm the lake monster.
I could tell from context.

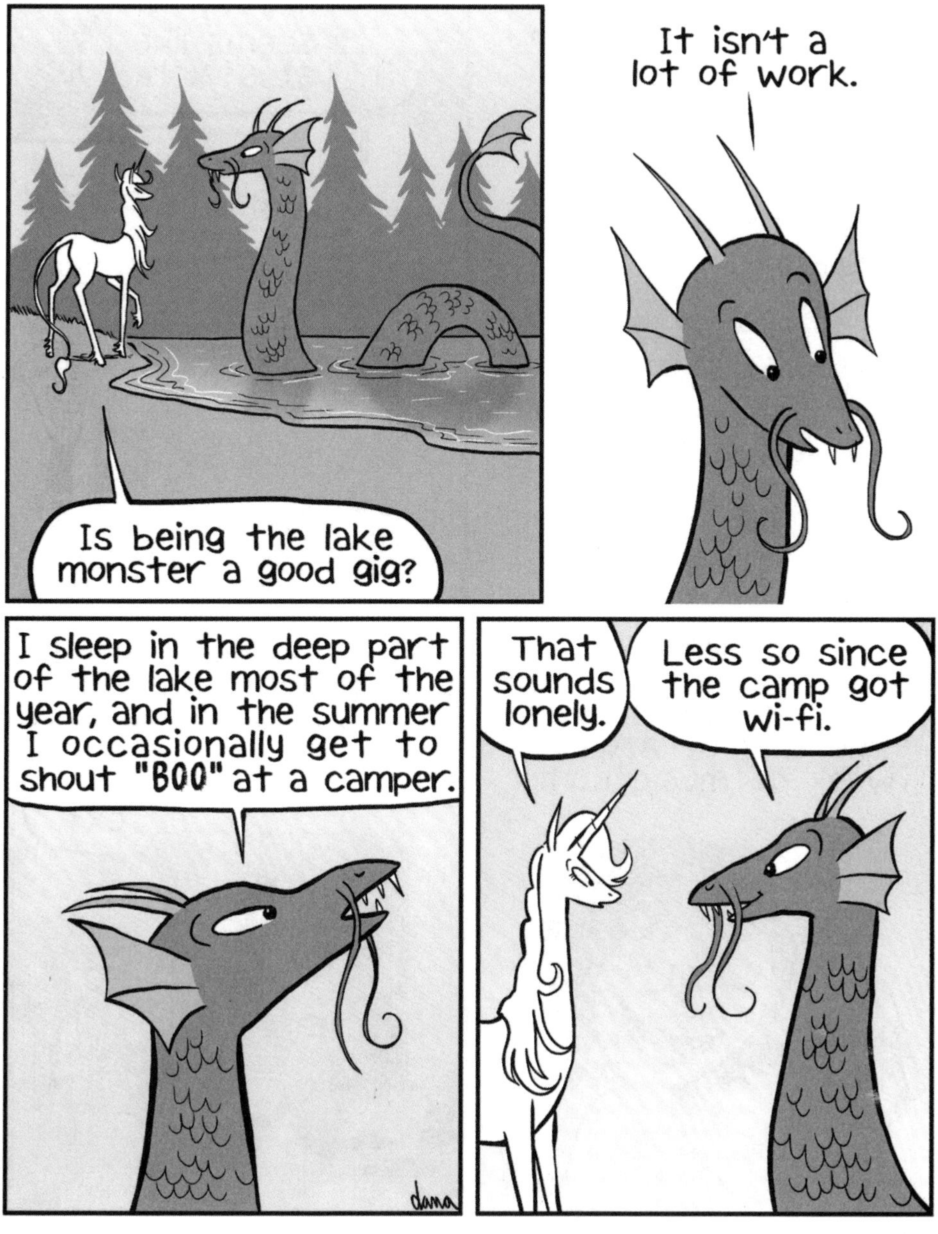
Is being the lake monster a good gig?
It isn't a lot of work.
I sleep in the deep part of the lake most of the year, and in the summer I occasionally get to shout "BOO" at a camper.
dana
That sounds lonely.
Less so since the camp got wi-fi.

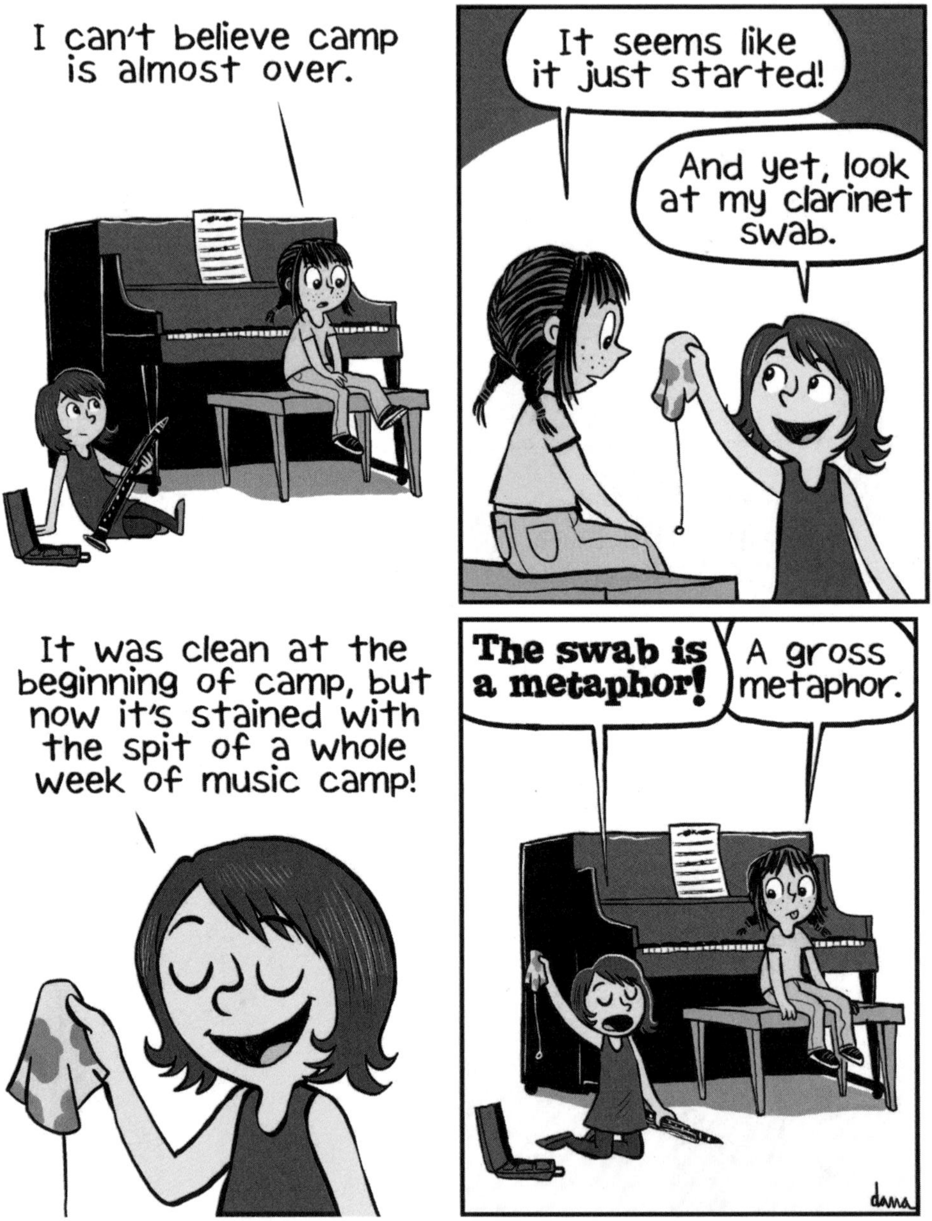
I can't believe camp is almost over.
It seems like it just started!
And yet, look at my clarinet swab.
It was clean at the beginning of camp, but now it's stained with the spit of a whole week of music camp!
The swab is a metaphor!
A gross metaphor.
dana

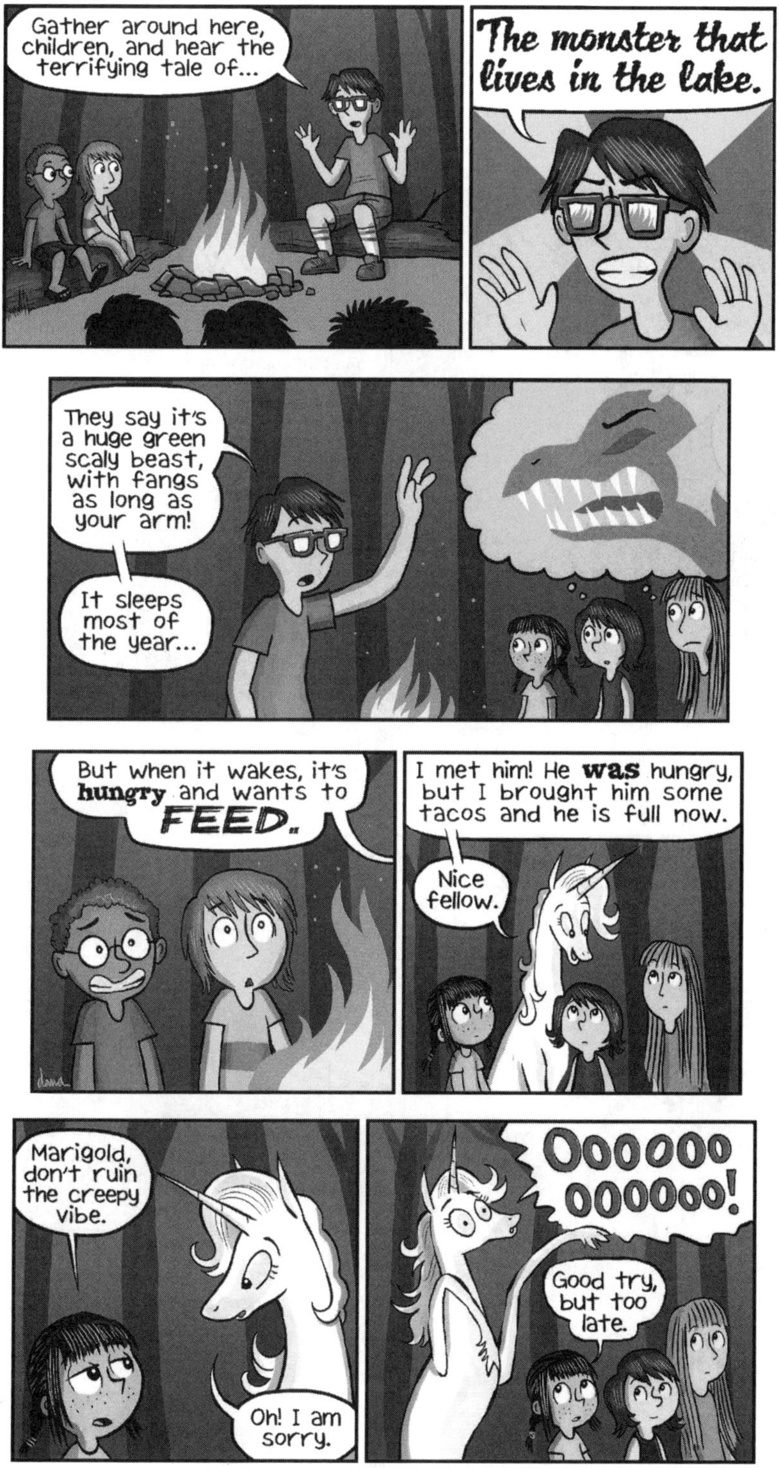
Gather around here, children, and hear the terrifying tale of...
The monster that lives in the lake.
They say it's a huge green scaly beast, with fangs as long as your arm!
It sleeps most of the year...
But when it wakes, it's hungry and wants to FEED.
I met him! He was hungry, but I brought him some tacos and he is full now.
Nice fellow.
Marigold, don't ruin the creepy vibe.
Oh! I am sorry.
OOOOOO OOOOoo!
Good try, but too late.

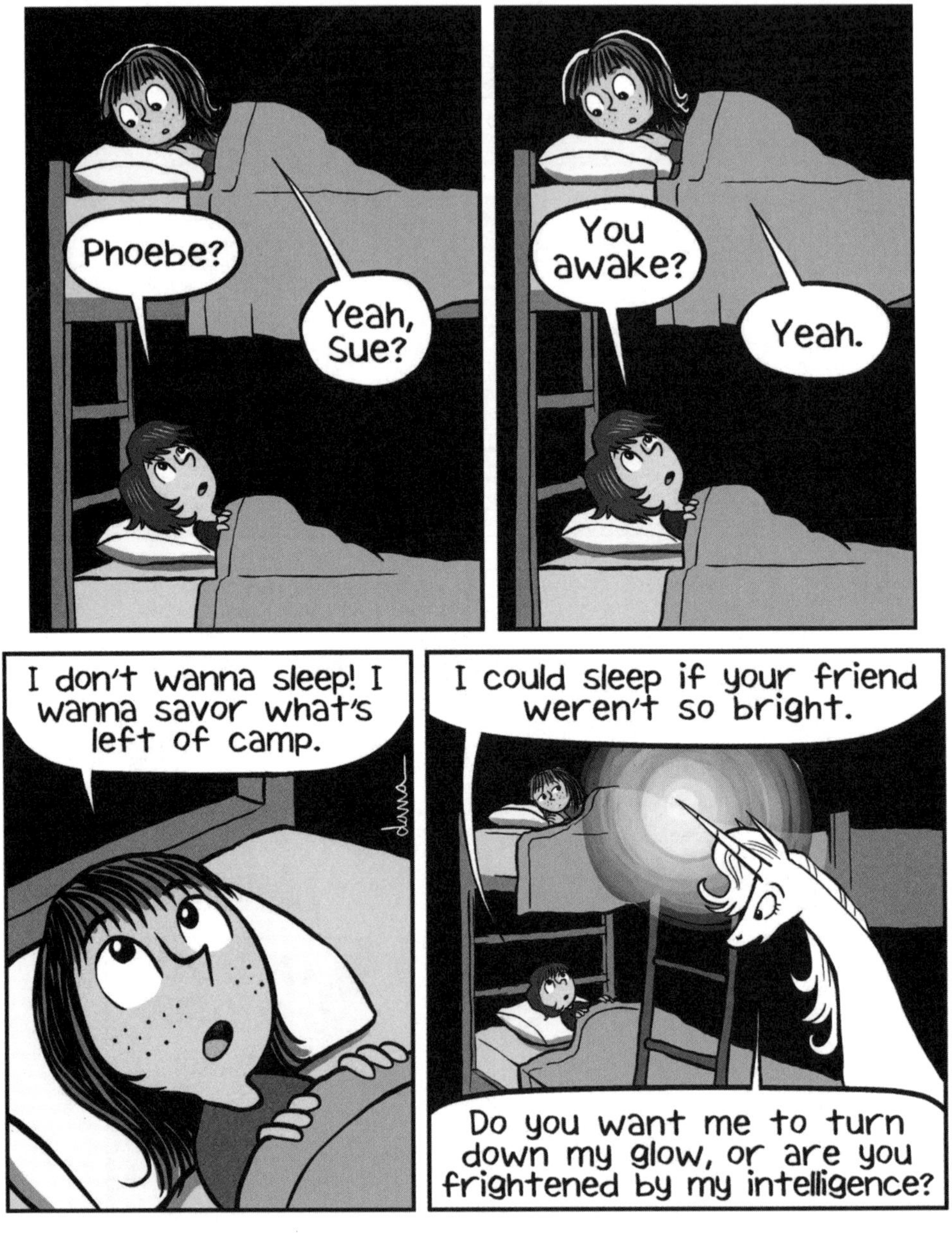
Phoebe?
Yeah, Sue?
You awake?
Yeah.
I don't wanna sleep! I wanna savor what's left of camp.
I could sleep if your friend weren't so bright.
Do you want me to turn down my glow, or are you frightened by my intelligence?

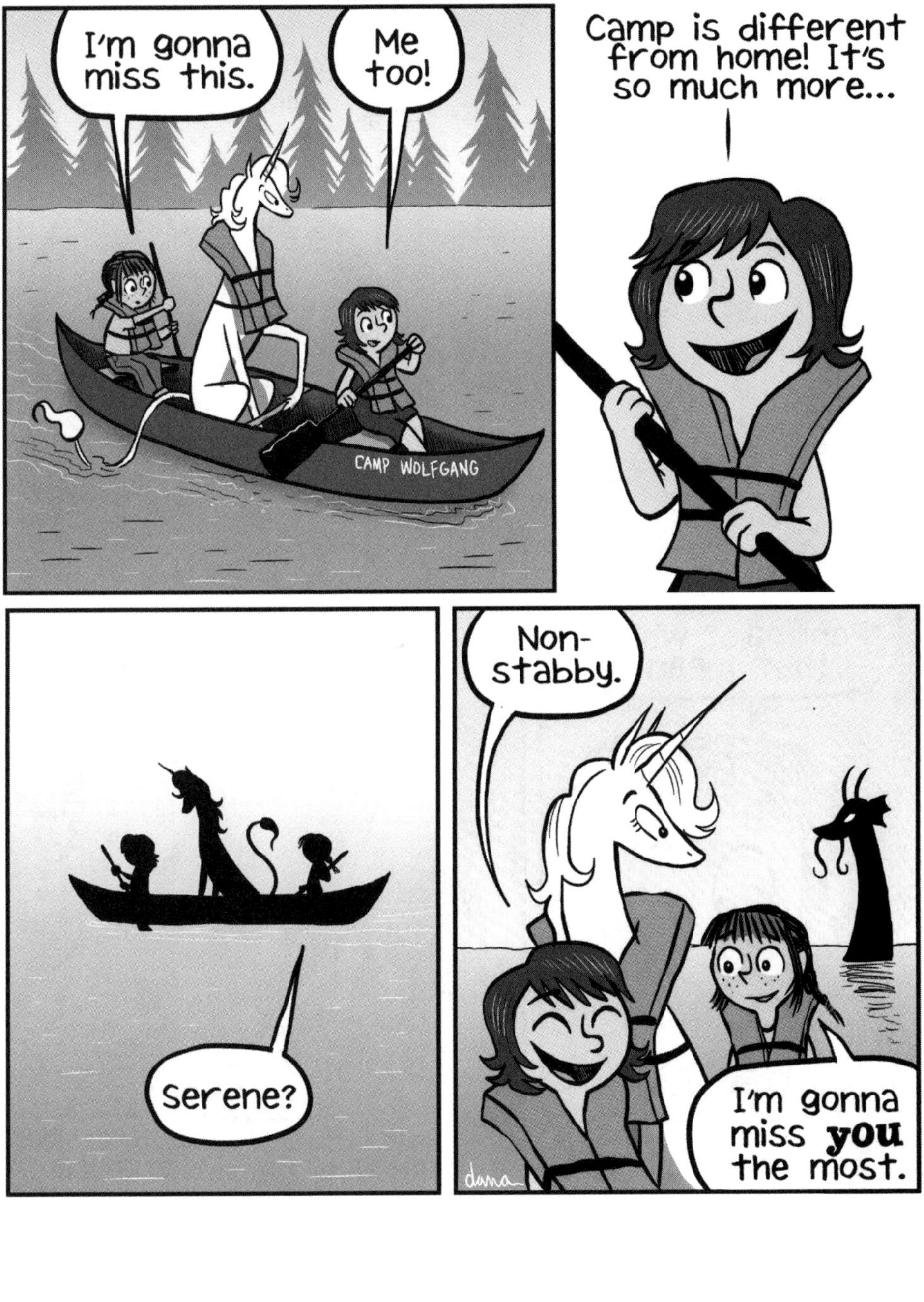
I'm gonna miss this.
Me too!
CAMP WOLFGANG
Camp is different from home! It's so much more...
Serene?
Non-stabby.
I'm gonna miss **you** the most.
dana

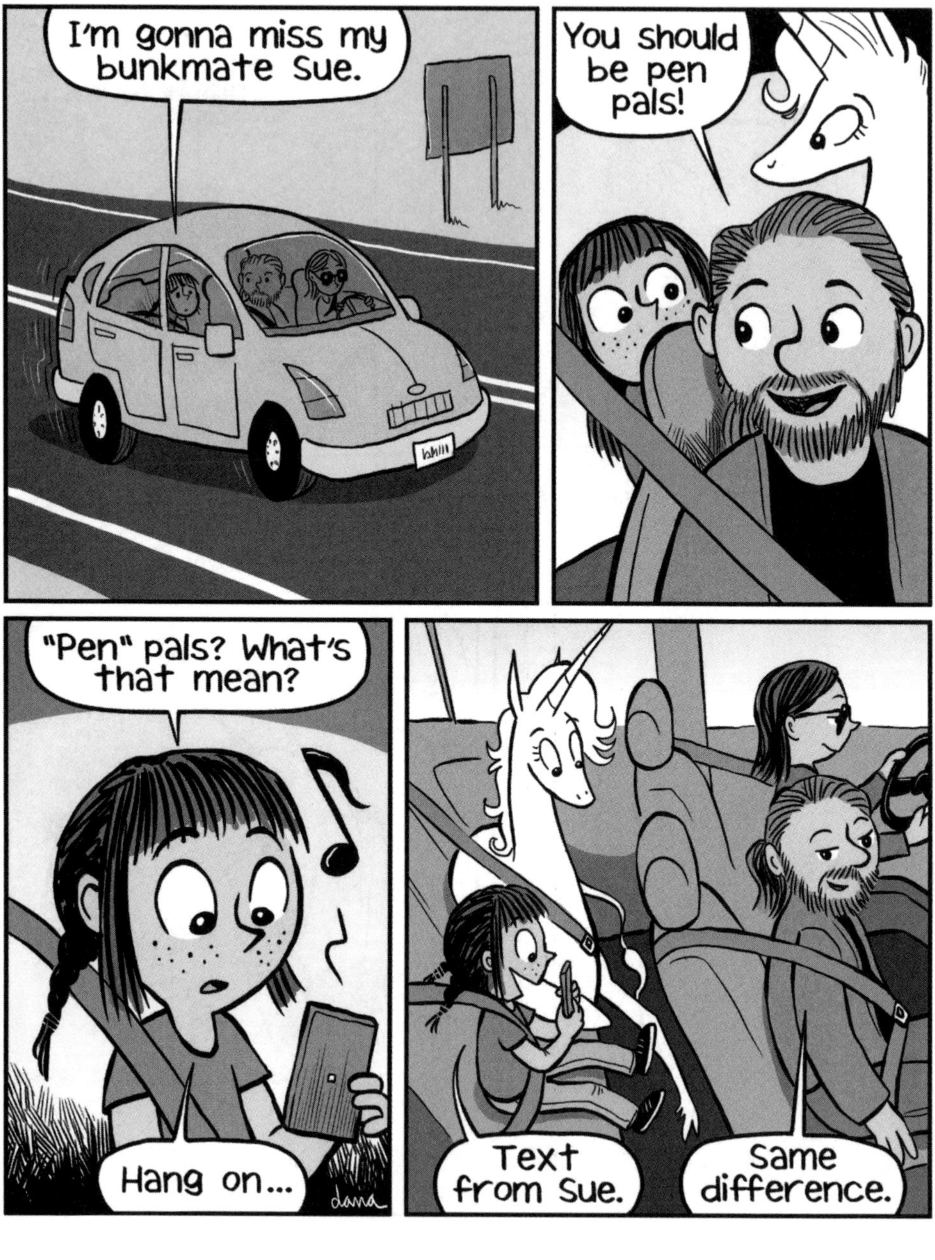
I'm gonna miss my bunkmate Sue.
You should be pen pals!
"Pen" pals? What's that mean?
Hang on...
dana
Text from Sue.
Same difference.

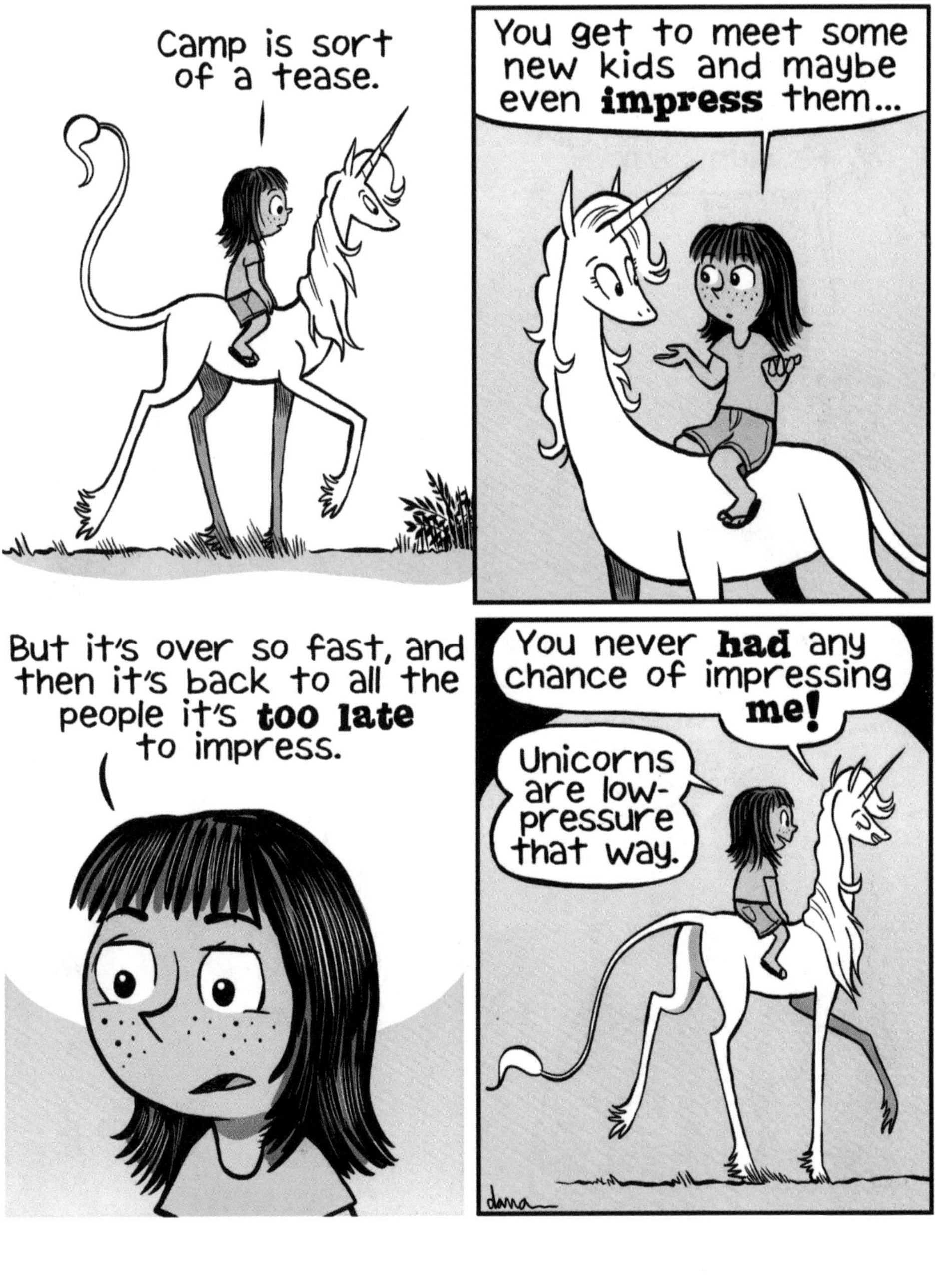
Camp is sort of a tease.
You get to meet some new kids and maybe even **impress** them...
But it's over so fast, and then it's back to all the people it's **too late** to impress.
You never **had** any chance of impressing **me!**
Unicorns are low-pressure that way.
dana

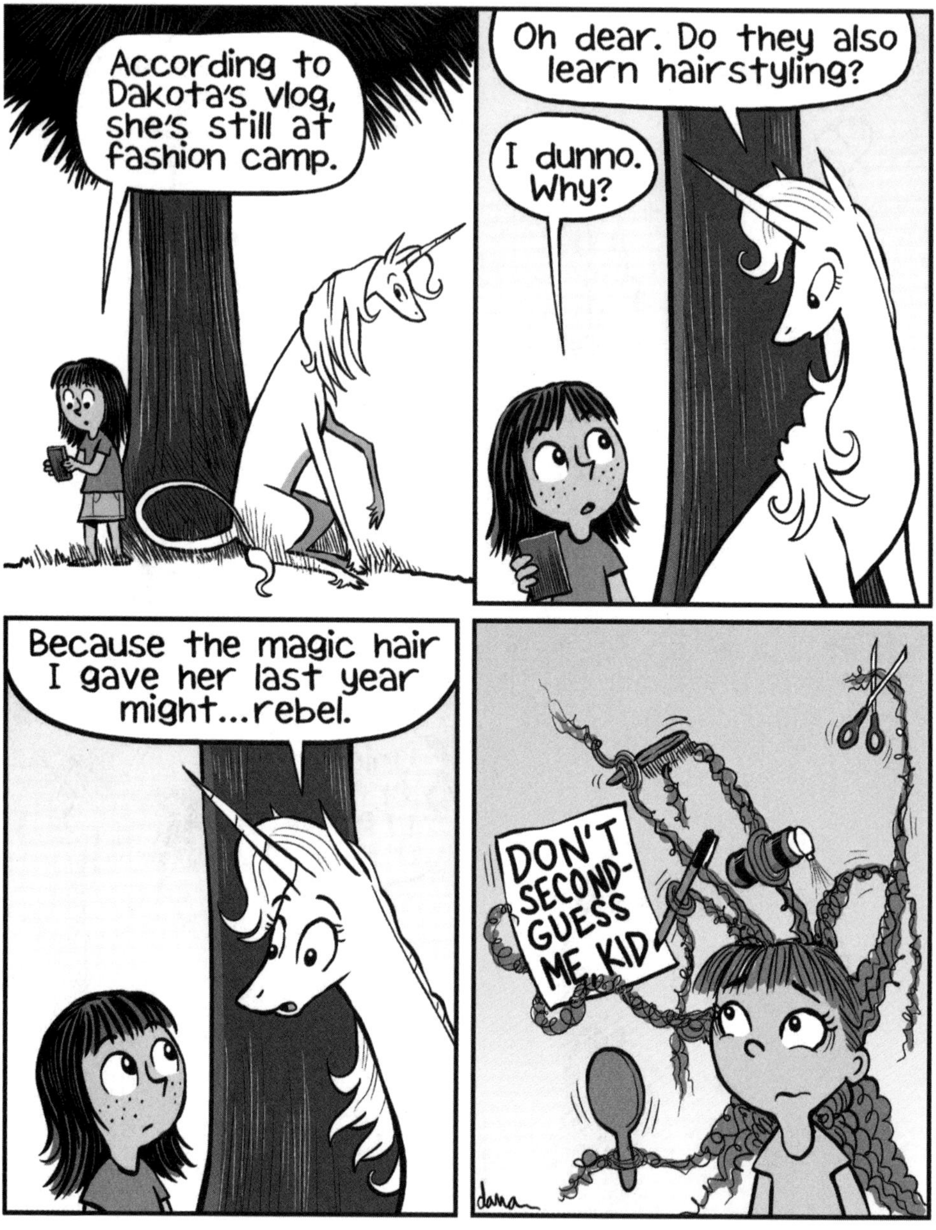
According to Dakota's vlog, she's still at fashion camp.
Oh dear. Do they also learn hairstyling?
I dunno. Why?
Because the magic hair I gave her last year might...rebel.
DON'T SECOND-GUESS ME KID
dana

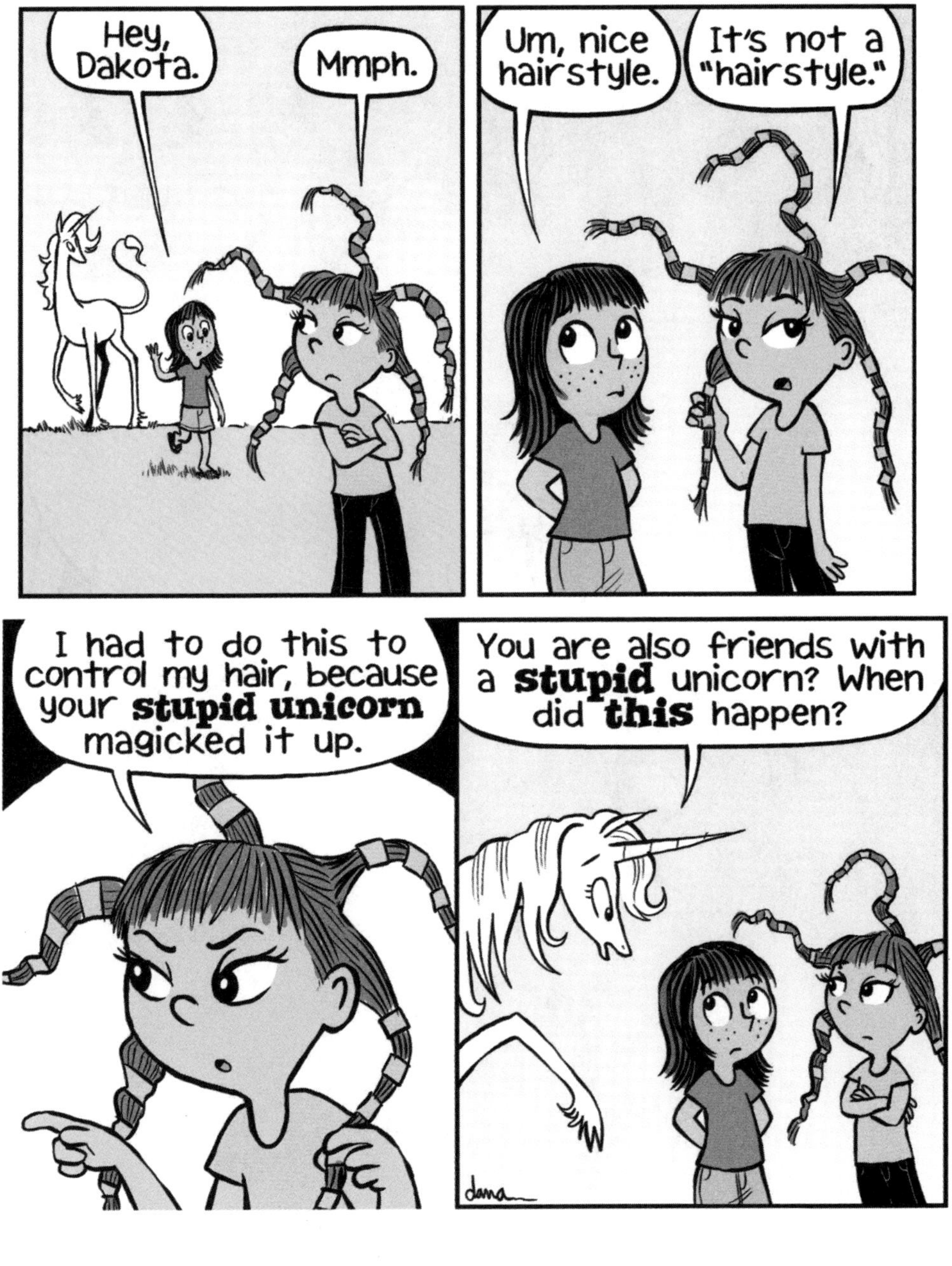
Hey, Dakota.
Mmph.
Um, nice hairstyle.
It's not a "hairstyle."
I had to do this to control my hair, because your **stupid unicorn** magicked it up.
You are also friends with a **stupid** unicorn? When did **this** happen?
dana

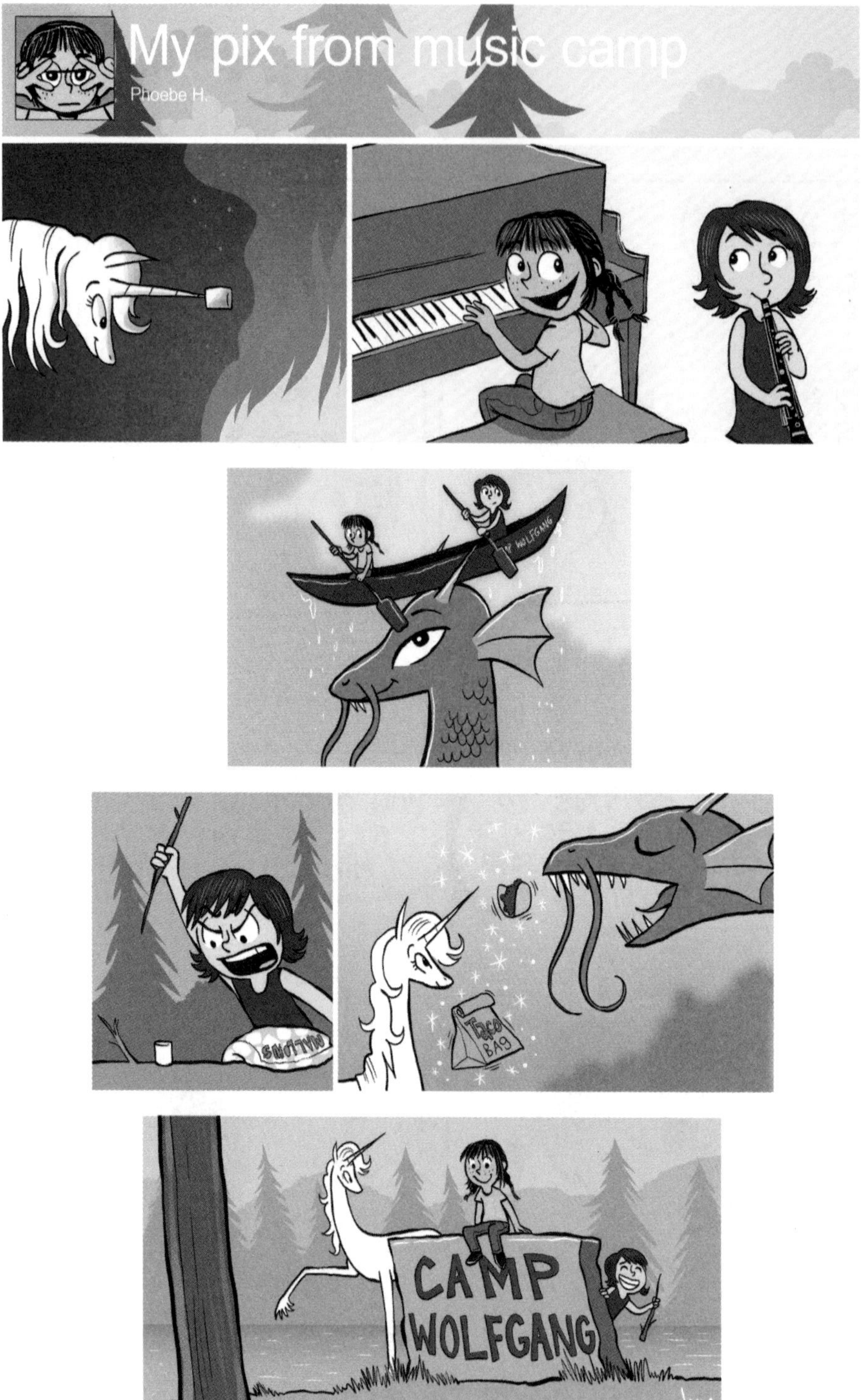
My pix from music camp
Phoebe H.
WOLFGANG
TACO BAG
CAMP WOLFGANG
dana

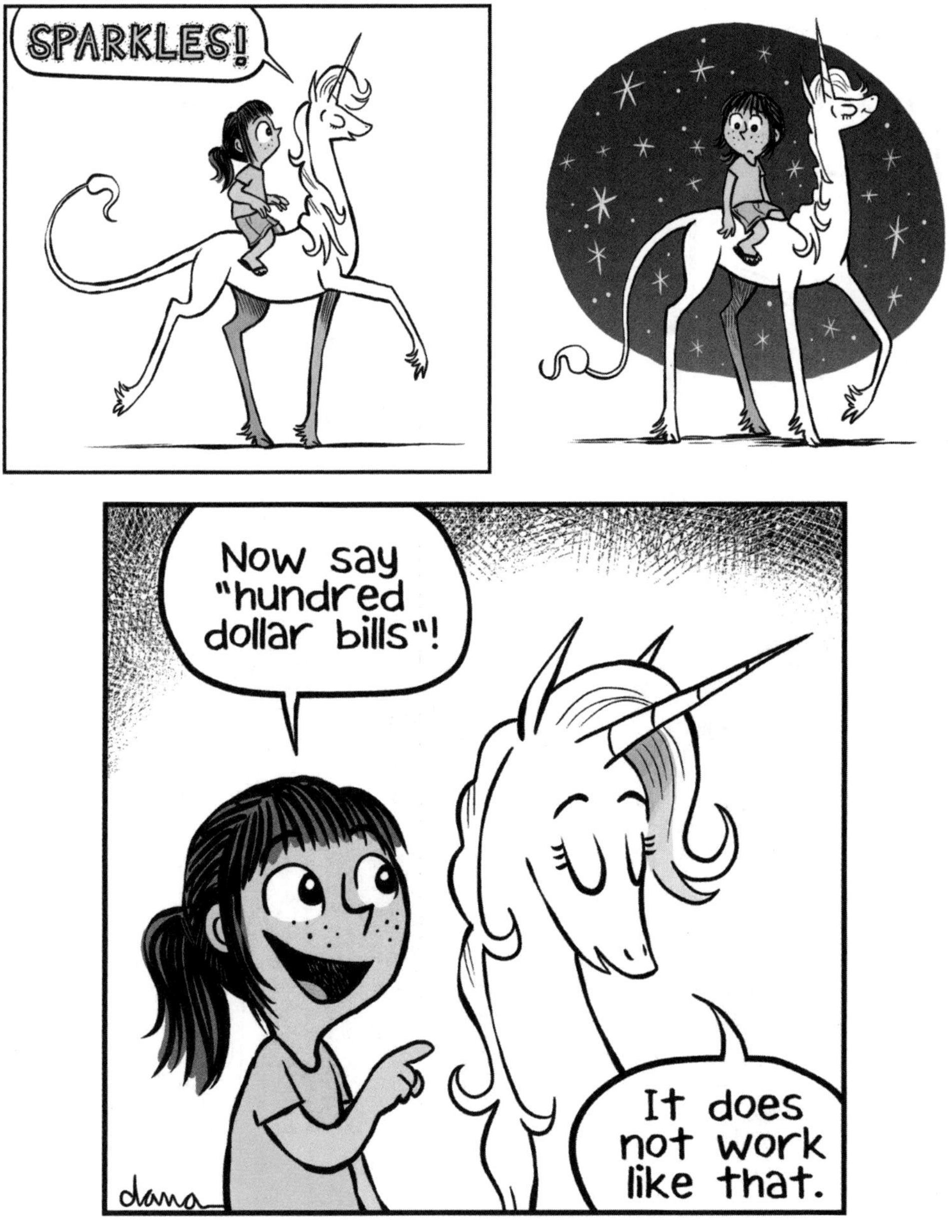
SPARKLES!
Now say "hundred dollar bills"!
It does not work like that.
dana

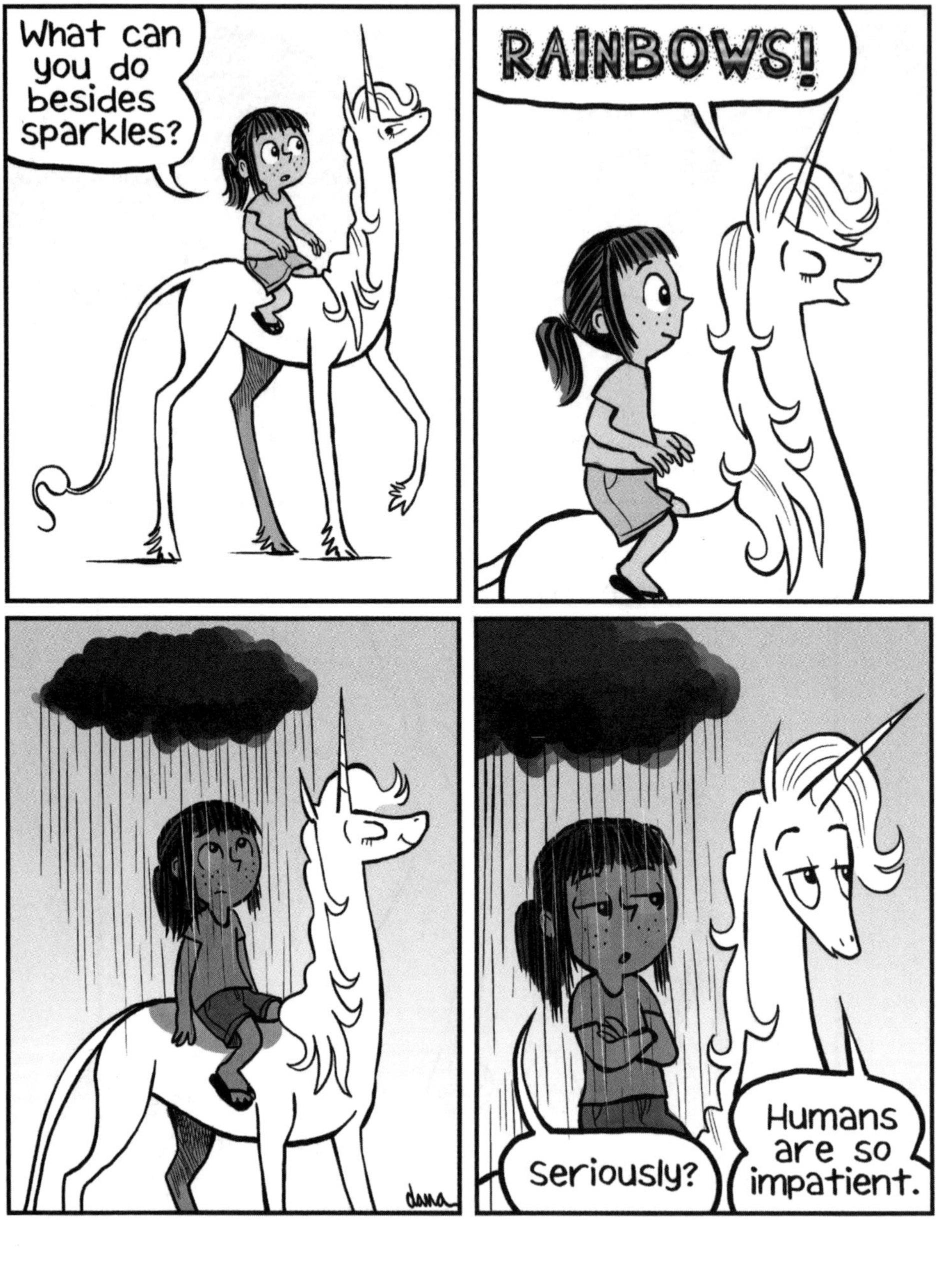
What can you do besides sparkles?
RAINBOWS!
Seriously?
Humans are so impatient.
dana

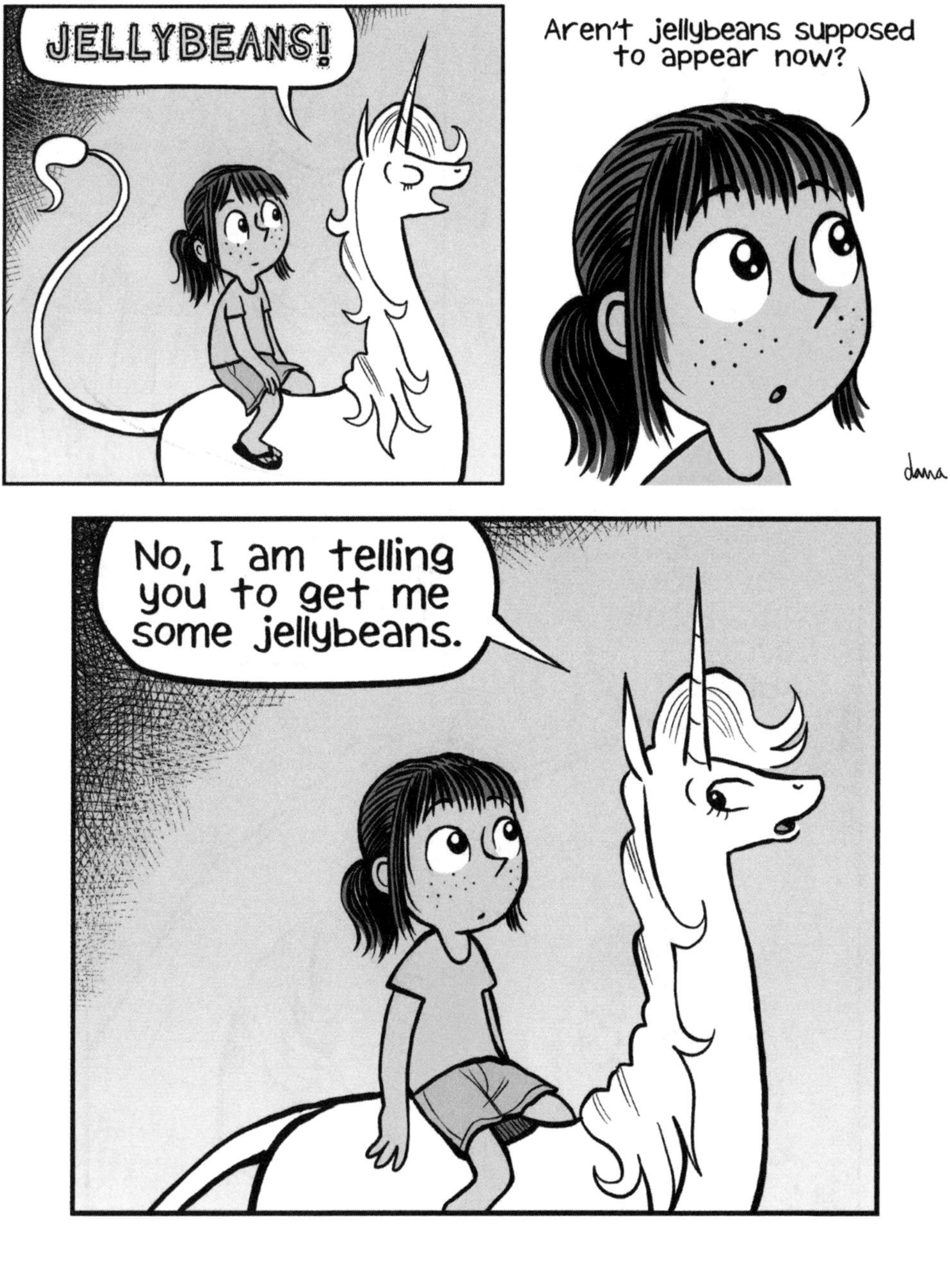
JELLYBEANS!
Aren't jellybeans supposed to appear now?
dana
No, I am telling you to get me some jellybeans.

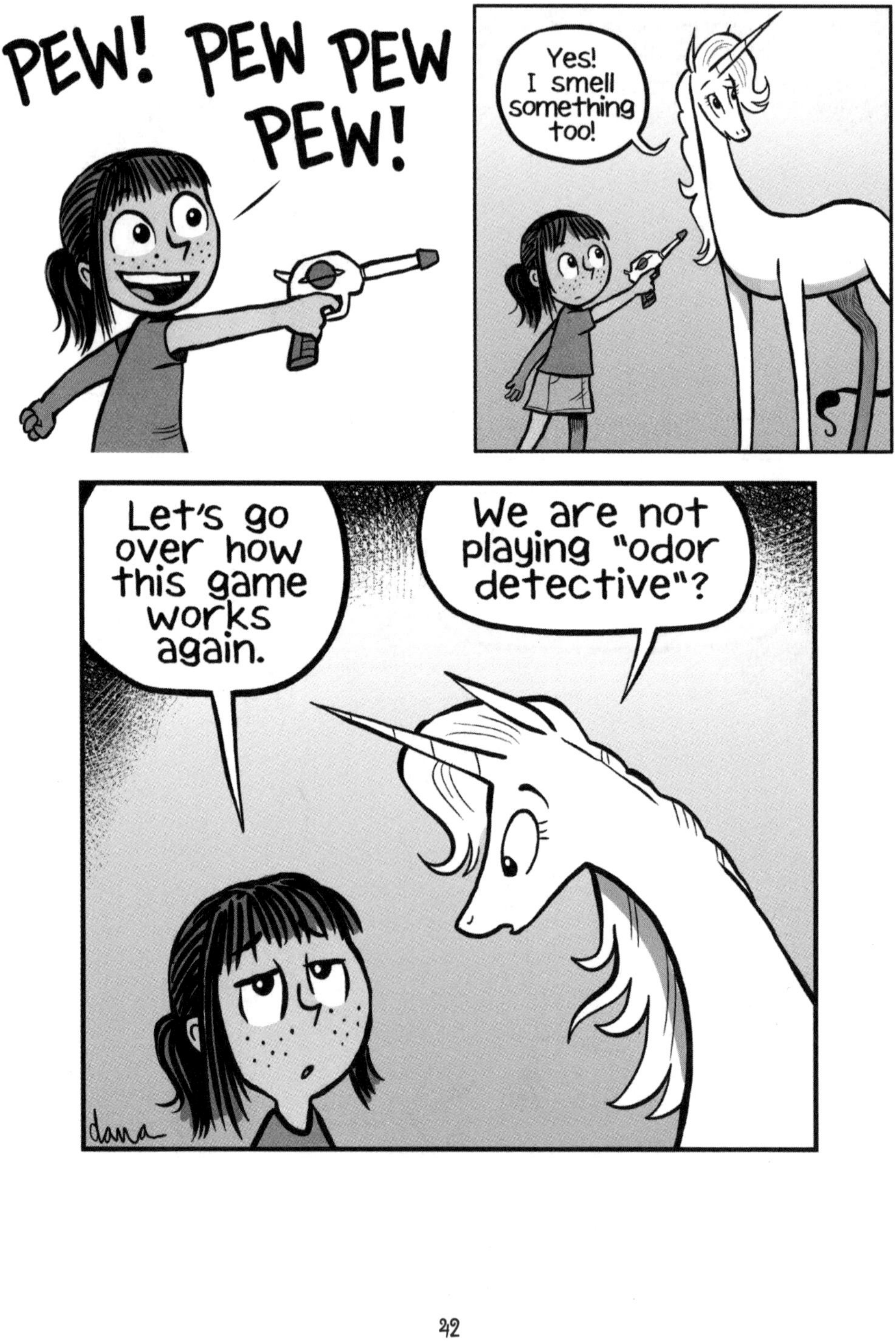
PEW! PEW PEW PEW!
Yes! I smell something too!
Let's go over how this game works again.
We are not playing "odor detective"?
dana

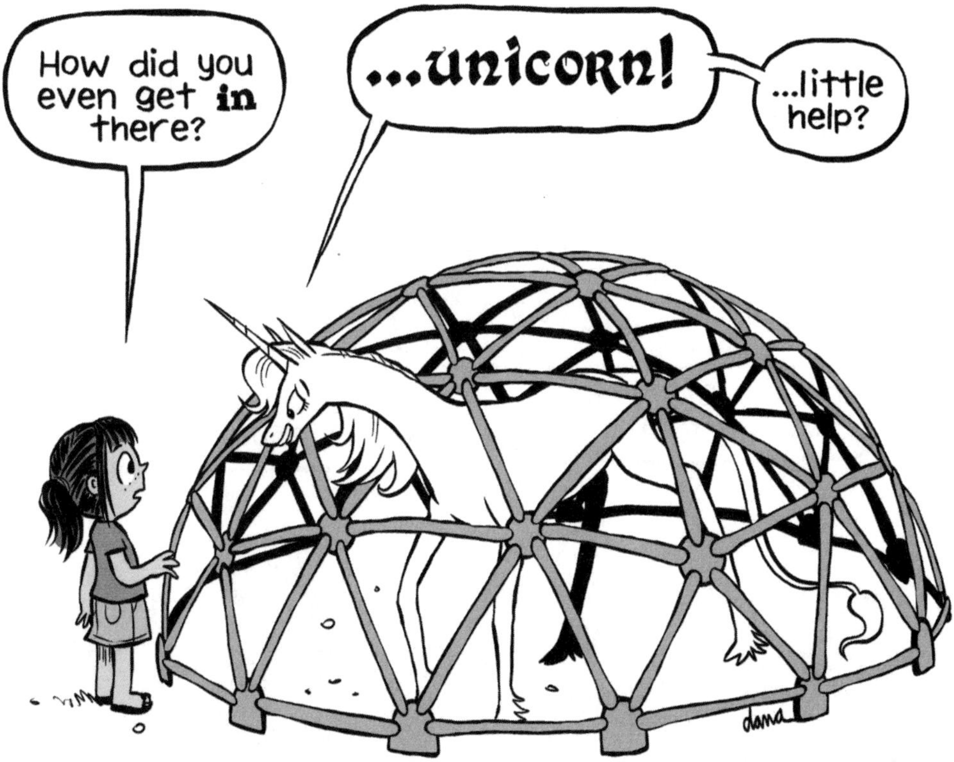
How did you even get **in** there?
...UNICORN!
...little help?
dana

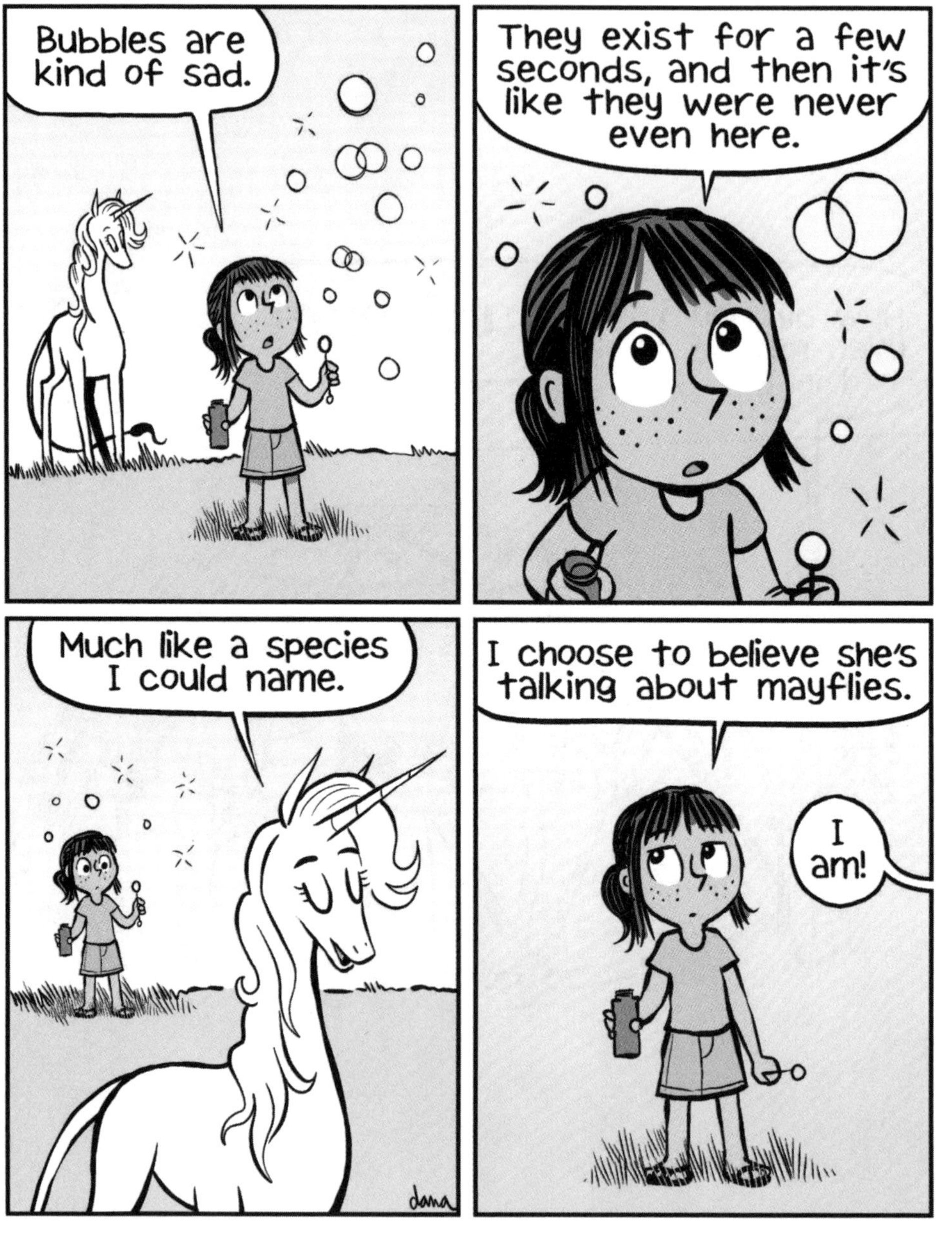
Bubbles are kind of sad.
They exist for a few seconds, and then it's like they were never even here.
Much like a species I could name.
dana
I choose to believe she's talking about mayflies.
I am!

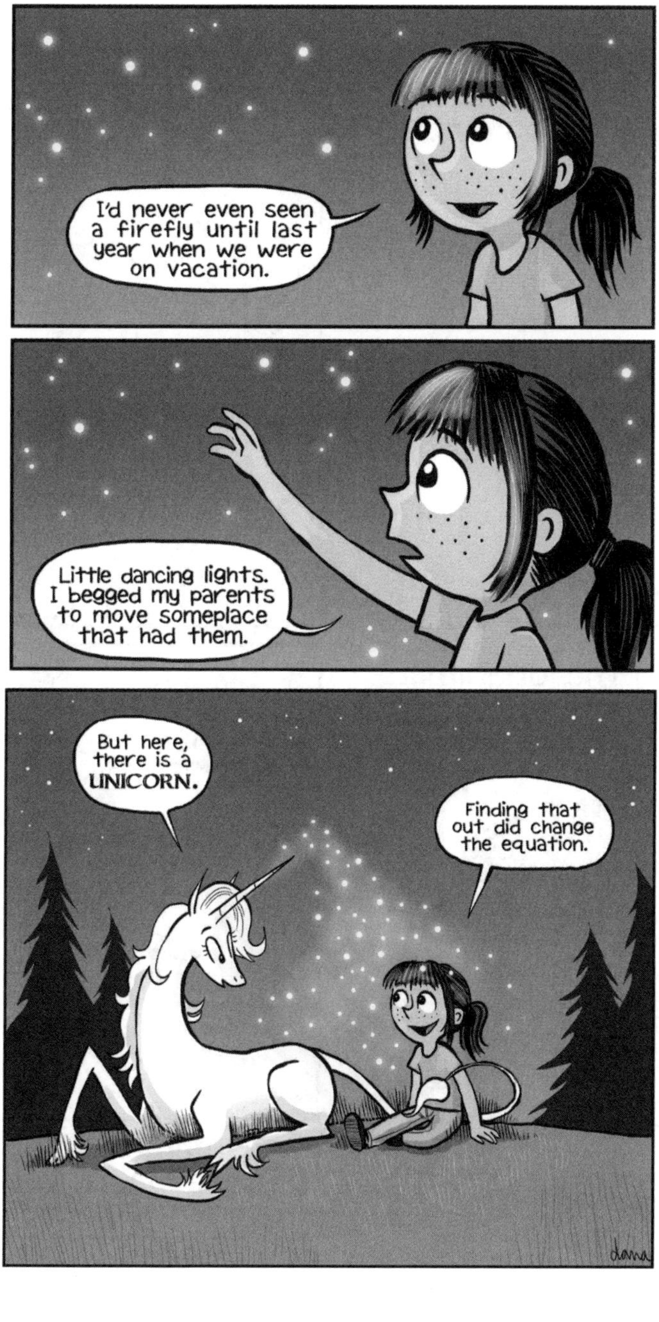
I'd never even seen a firefly until last year when we were on vacation.
Little dancing lights. I begged my parents to move someplace that had them.
But here, there is a UNICORN.
Finding that out did change the equation.
dana

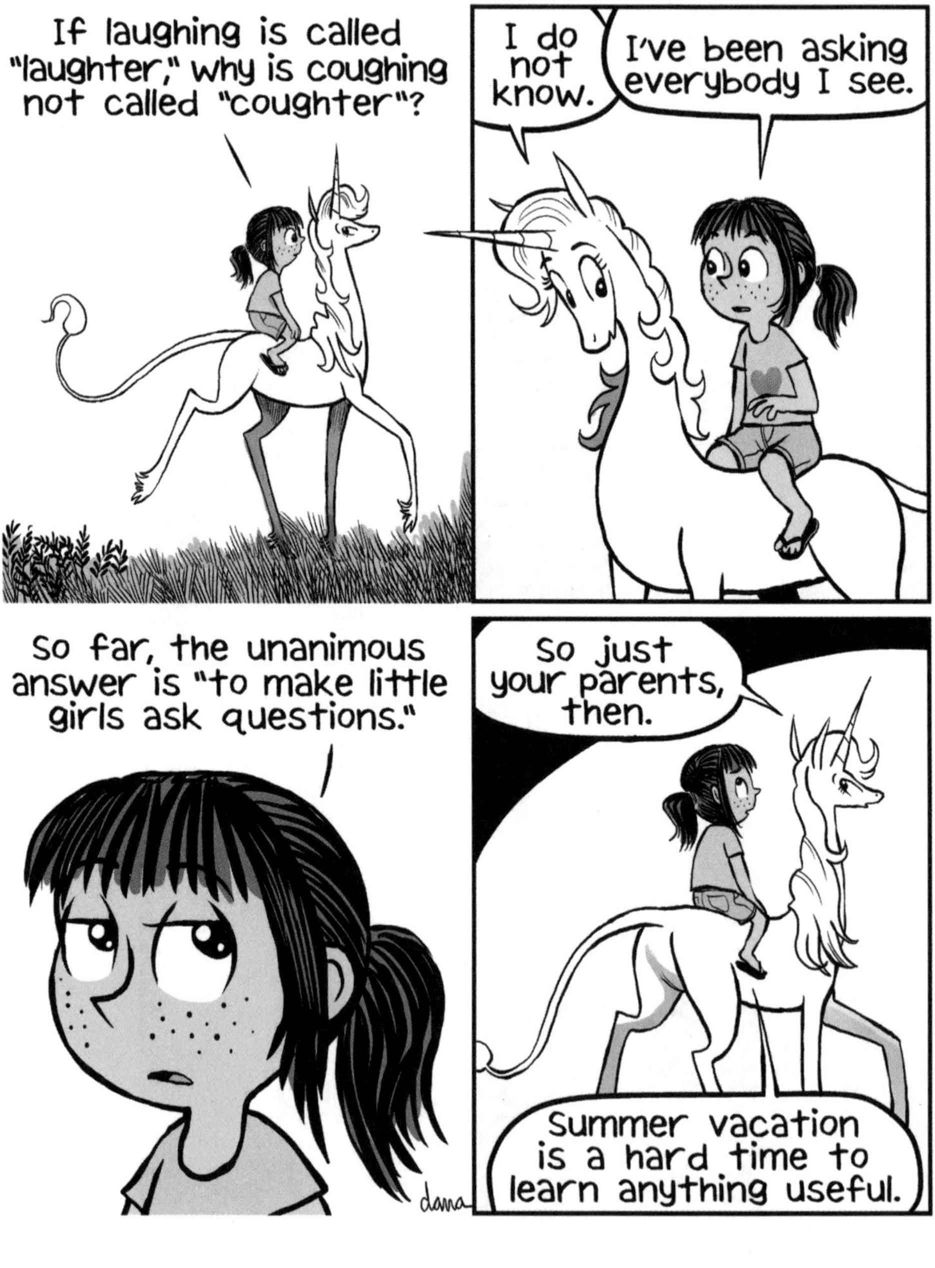
If laughing is called "laughter," why is coughing not called "coughter"?
I do not know.
I've been asking everybody I see.
So far, the unanimous answer is "to make little girls ask questions."
So just your parents, then.
Summer vacation is a hard time to learn anything useful.
dana

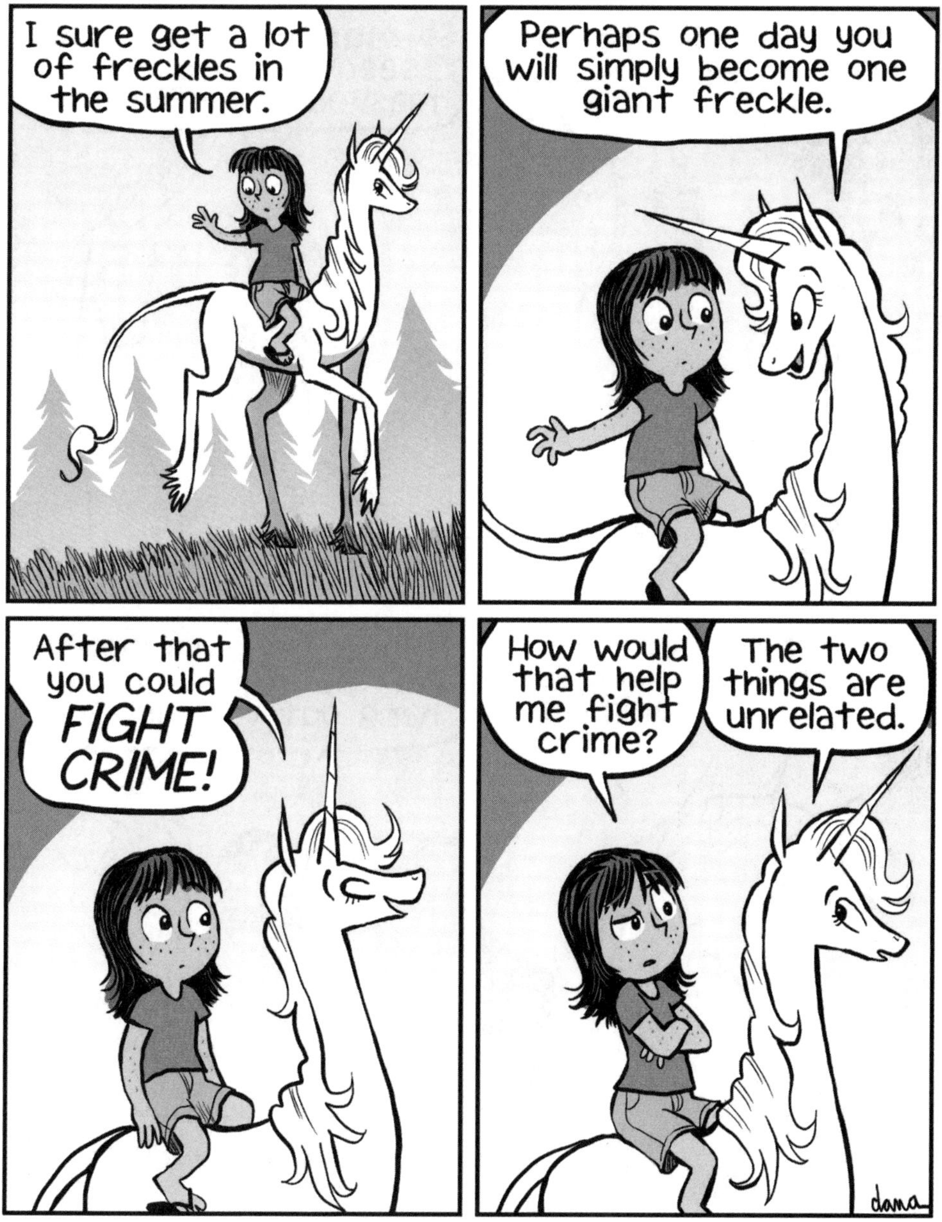
I sure get a lot of freckles in the summer.
Perhaps one day you will simply become one giant freckle.
After that you could *FIGHT CRIME!*
How would that help me fight crime?
The two things are unrelated.
dana

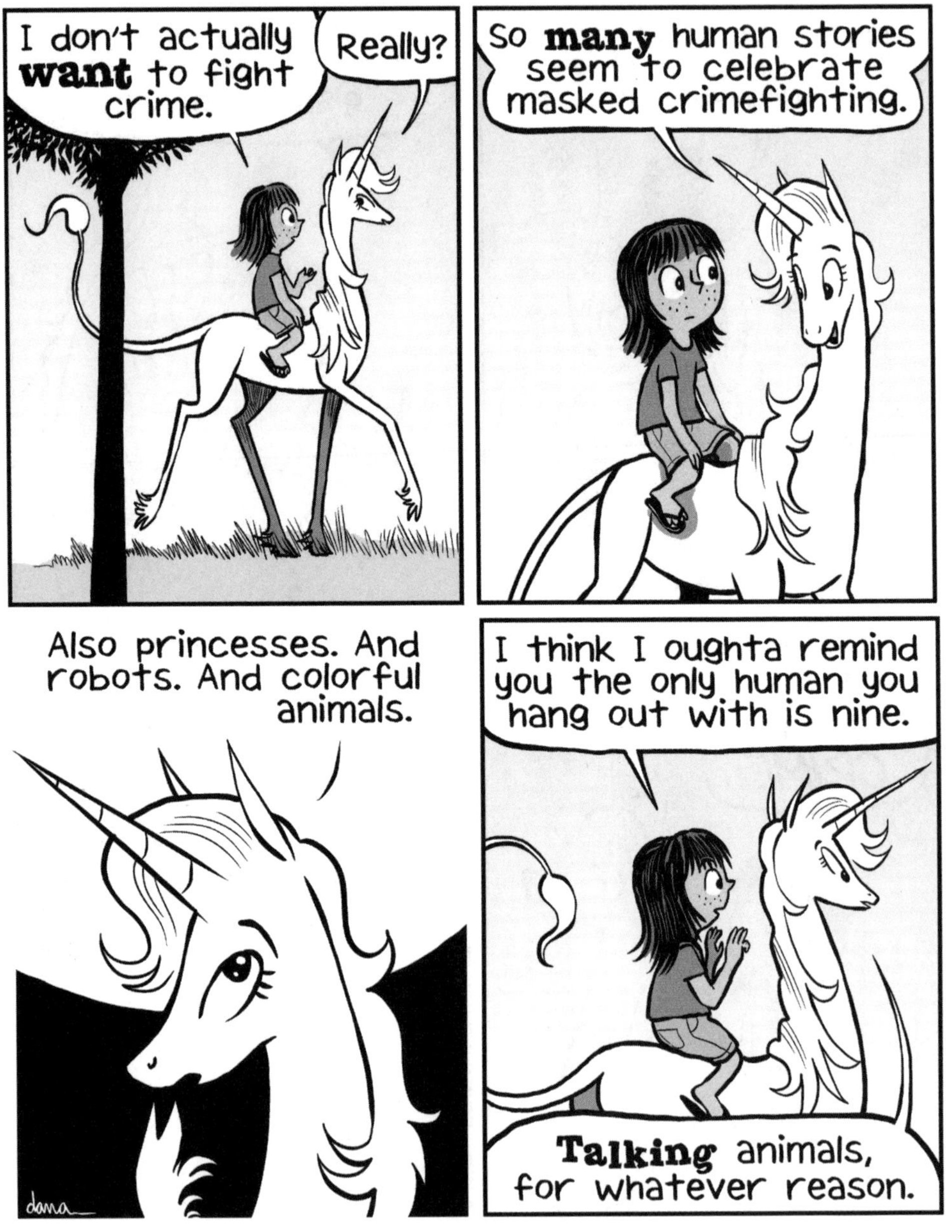
I don't actually **want** to fight crime.
Really?
So **many** human stories seem to celebrate masked crimefighting.
Also princesses. And robots. And colorful animals.
I think I oughta remind you the only human you hang out with is nine.
Talking animals, for whatever reason.
dana

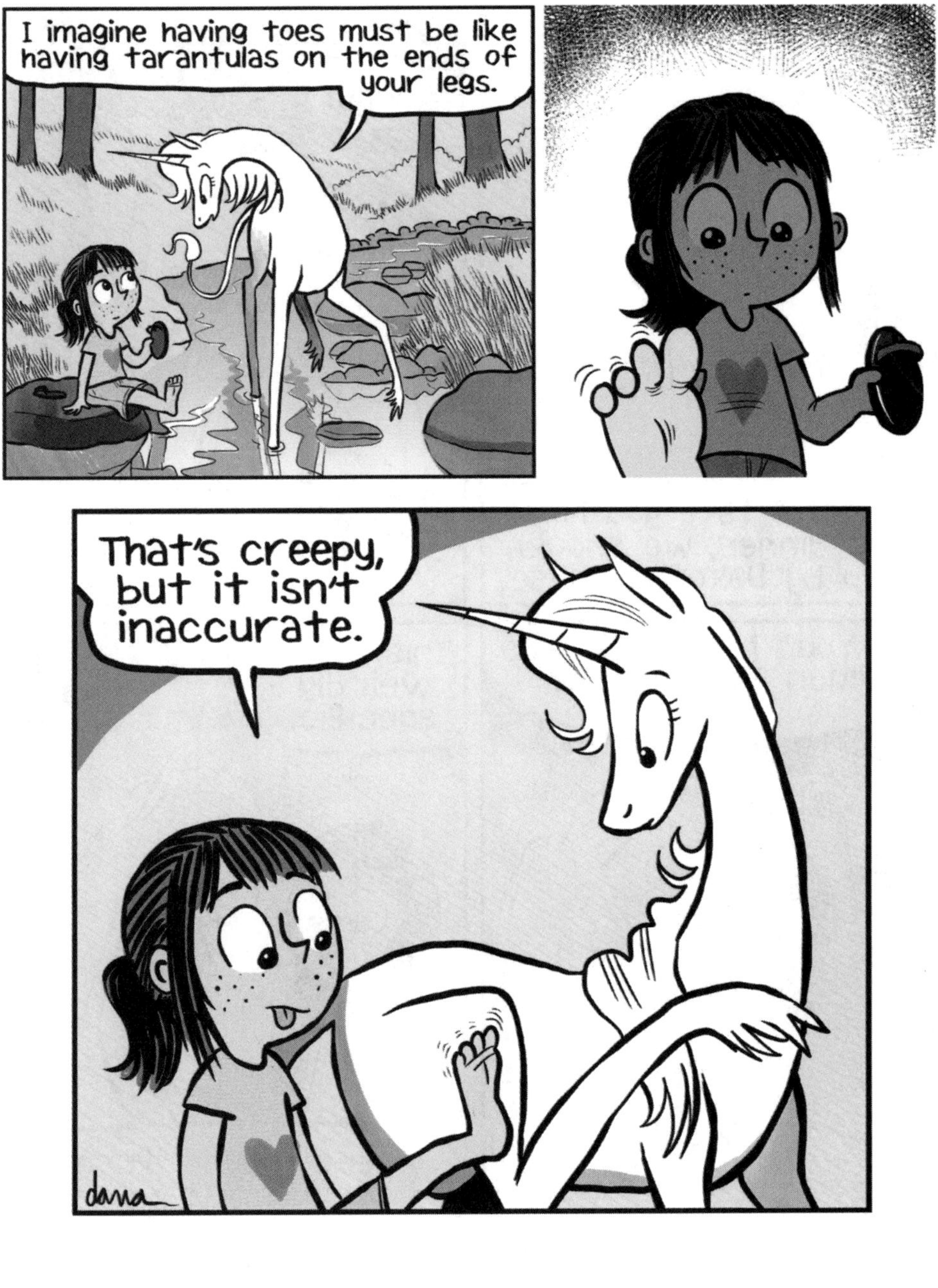
I imagine having toes must be like having tarantulas on the ends of your legs.
That's creepy, but it isn't inaccurate.
dana

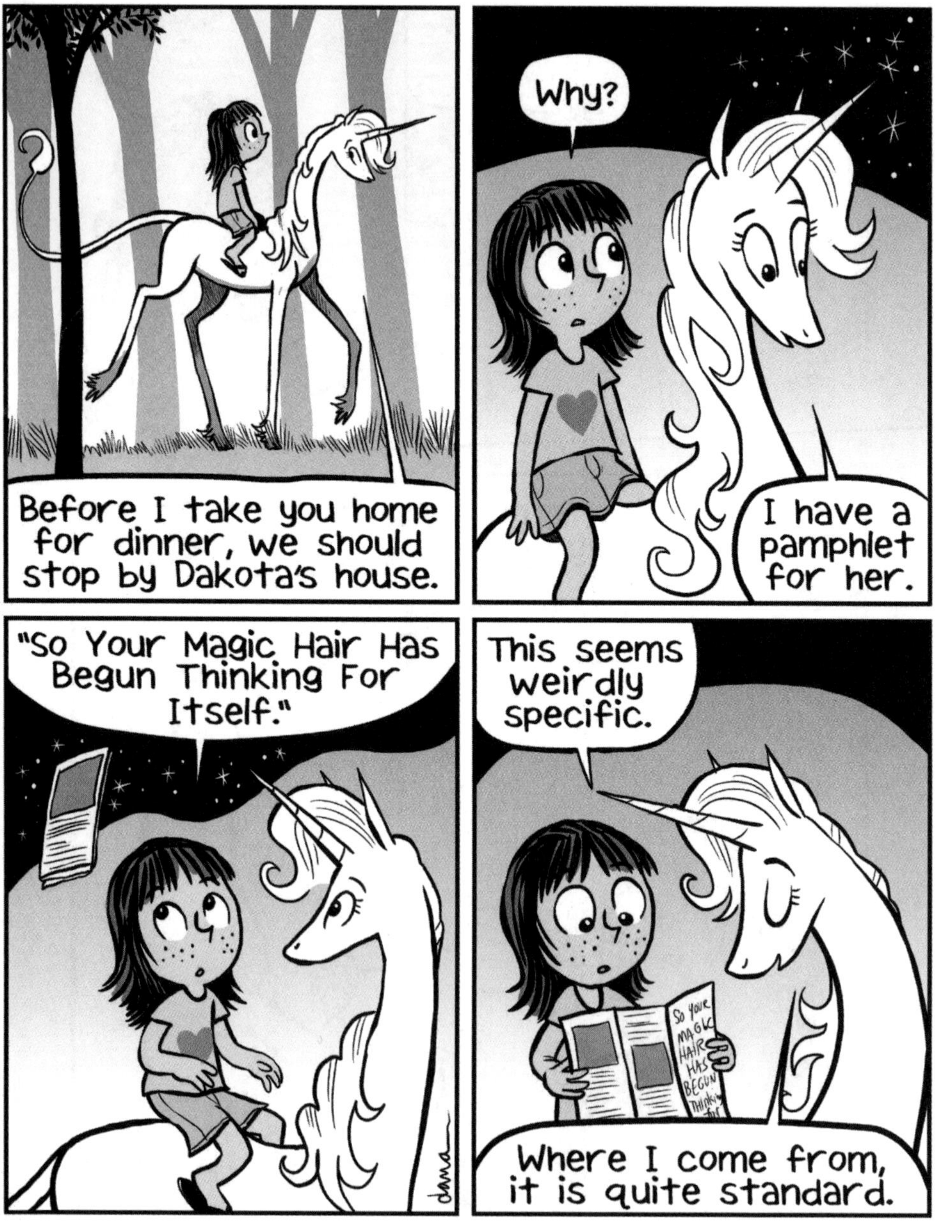

Before I take you home for dinner, we should stop by Dakota's house.
Why?
I have a pamphlet for her.
"So Your Magic Hair Has Begun Thinking For Itself."
This seems weirdly specific.
Where I come from, it is quite standard.

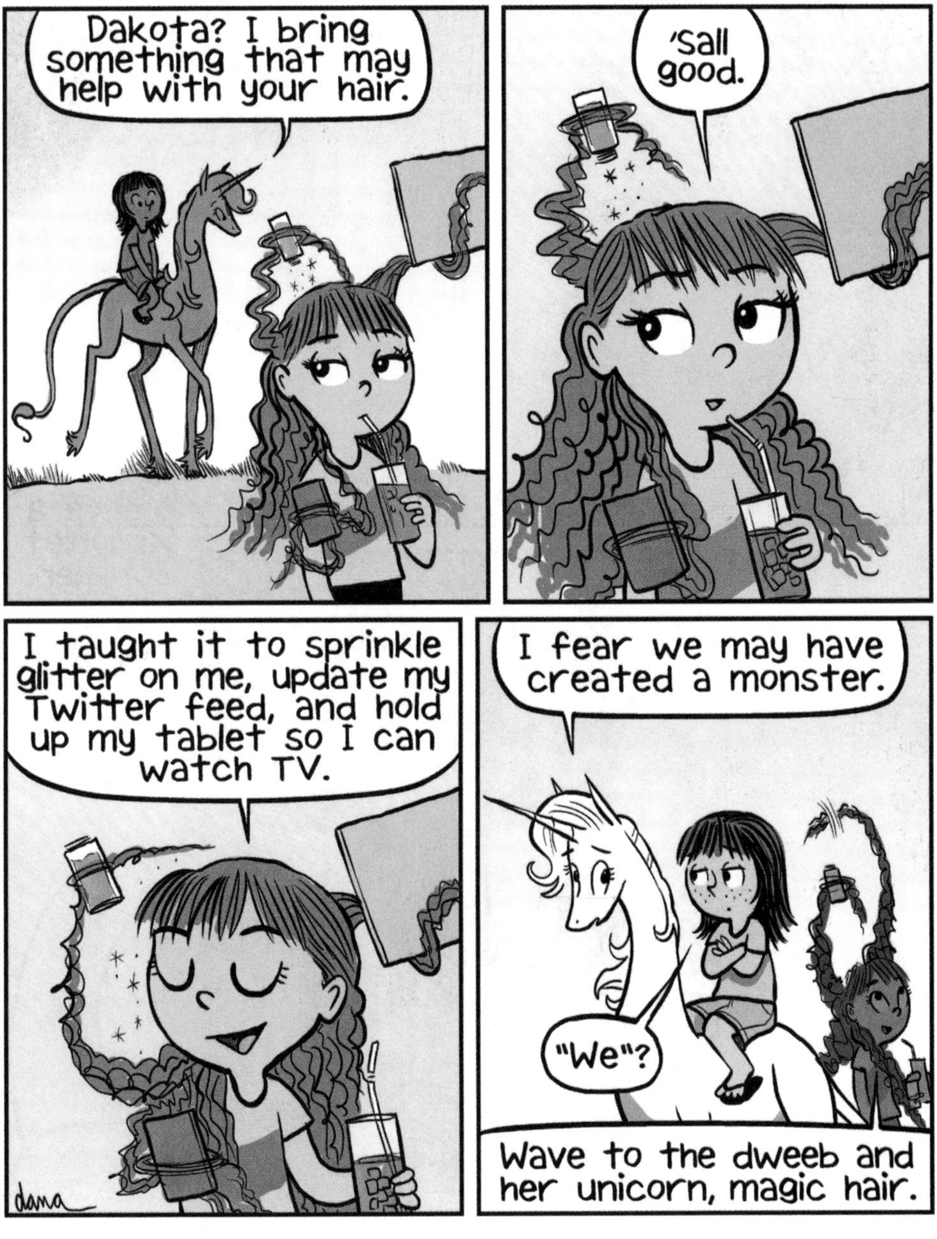
Dakota? I bring something that may help with your hair.
'Sall good.
I taught it to sprinkle glitter on me, update my Twitter feed, and hold up my tablet so I can watch TV.
I fear we may have created a monster.
"We"?
Wave to the dweeb and her unicorn, magic hair.
dana

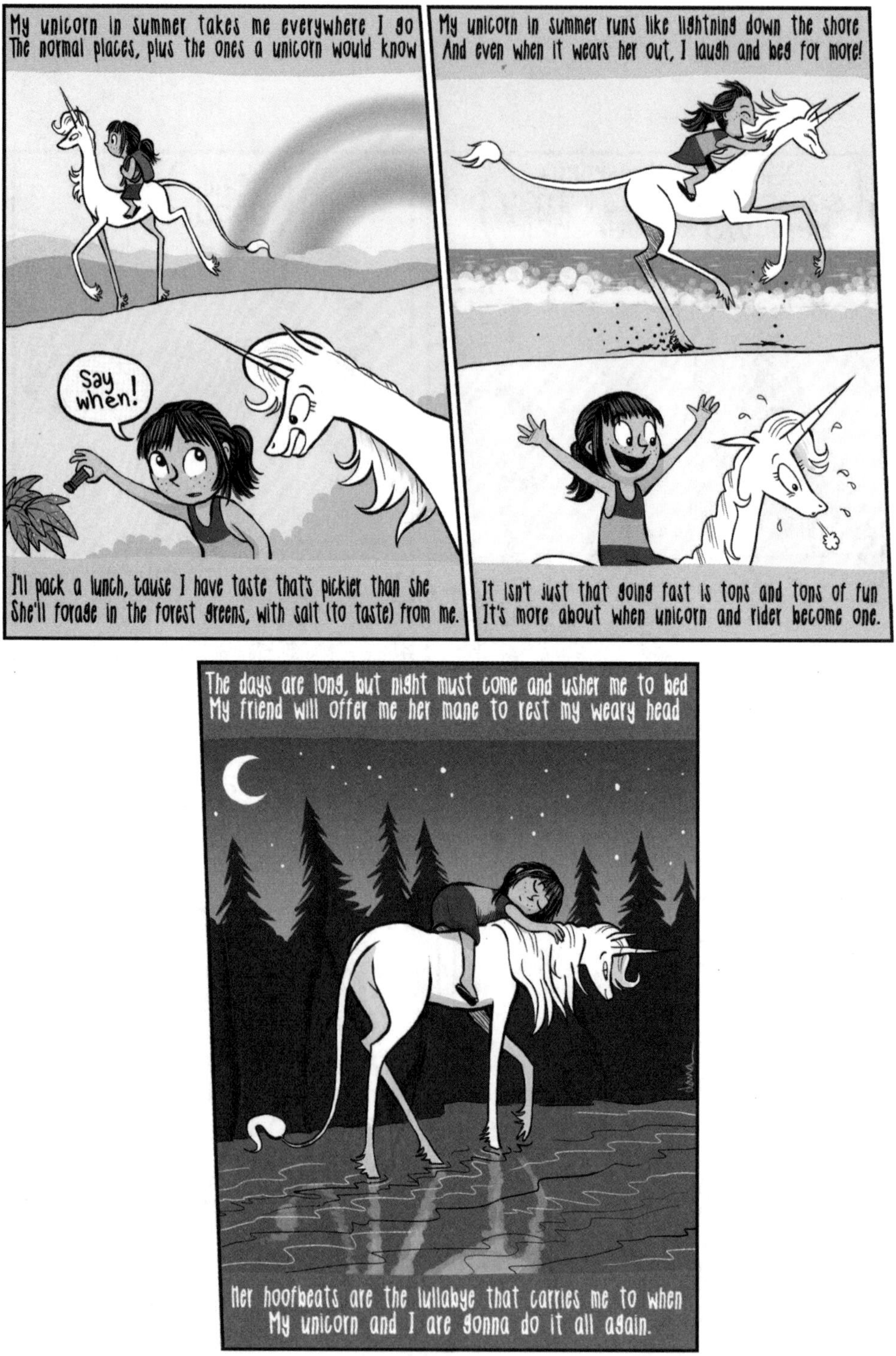
My unicorn in summer takes me everywhere I go
The normal places, plus the ones a unicorn would know
Say when!
I'll pack a lunch, 'cause I have taste that's pickier than she
She'll forage in the forest greens, with salt (to taste) from me.
My unicorn in summer runs like lightning down the shore
And even when it wears her out, I laugh and beg for more!
It isn't just that going fast is tons and tons of fun
It's more about when unicorn and rider become one.
The days are long, but night must come and usher me to bed
My friend will offer me her mane to rest my weary head
Her hoofbeats are the lullabye that carries me to when
My unicorn and I are gonna do it all again.

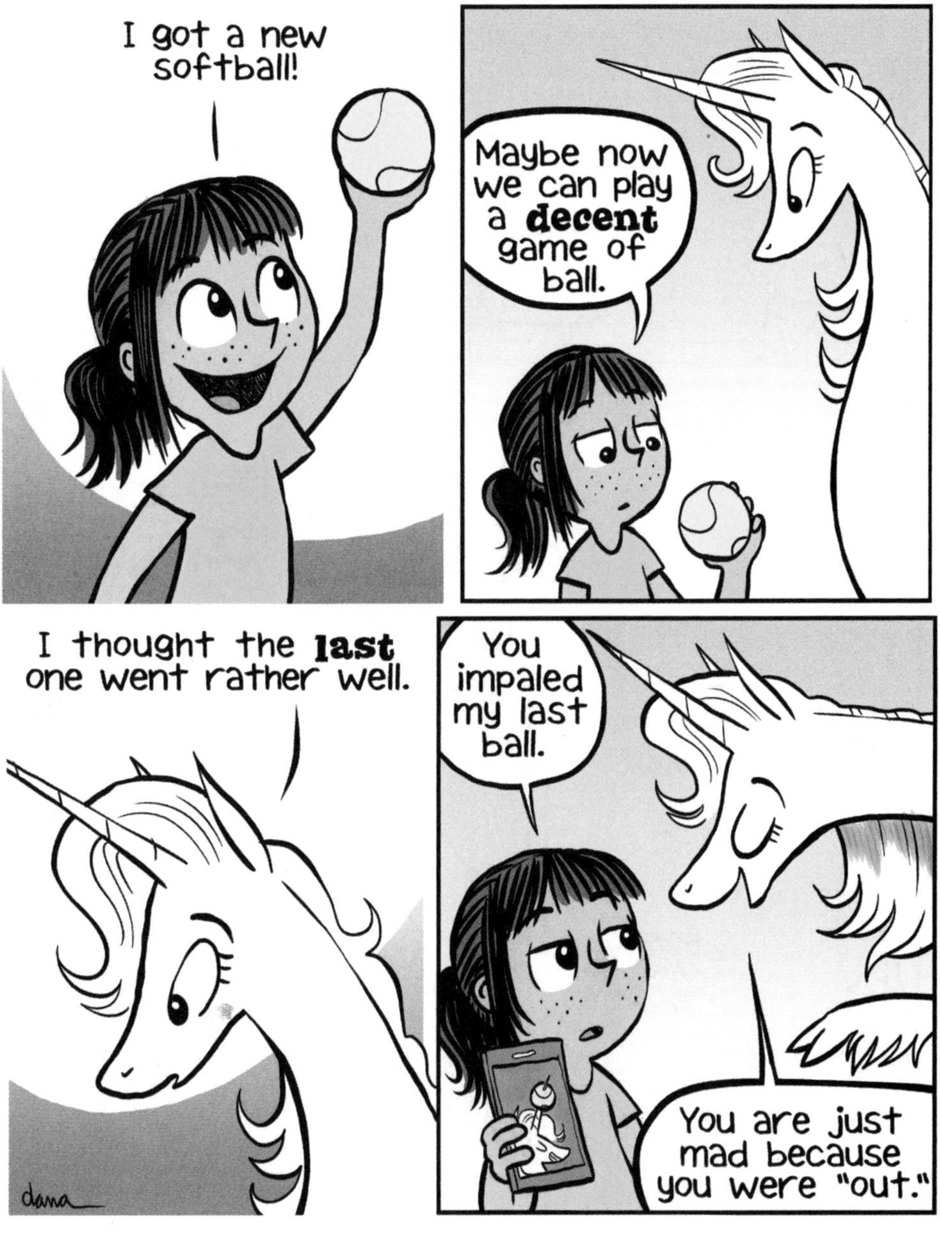
I got a new softball!
Maybe now we can play a **decent** game of ball.
I thought the **last** one went rather well.
You impaled my last ball.
You are just mad because you were "out."
dana

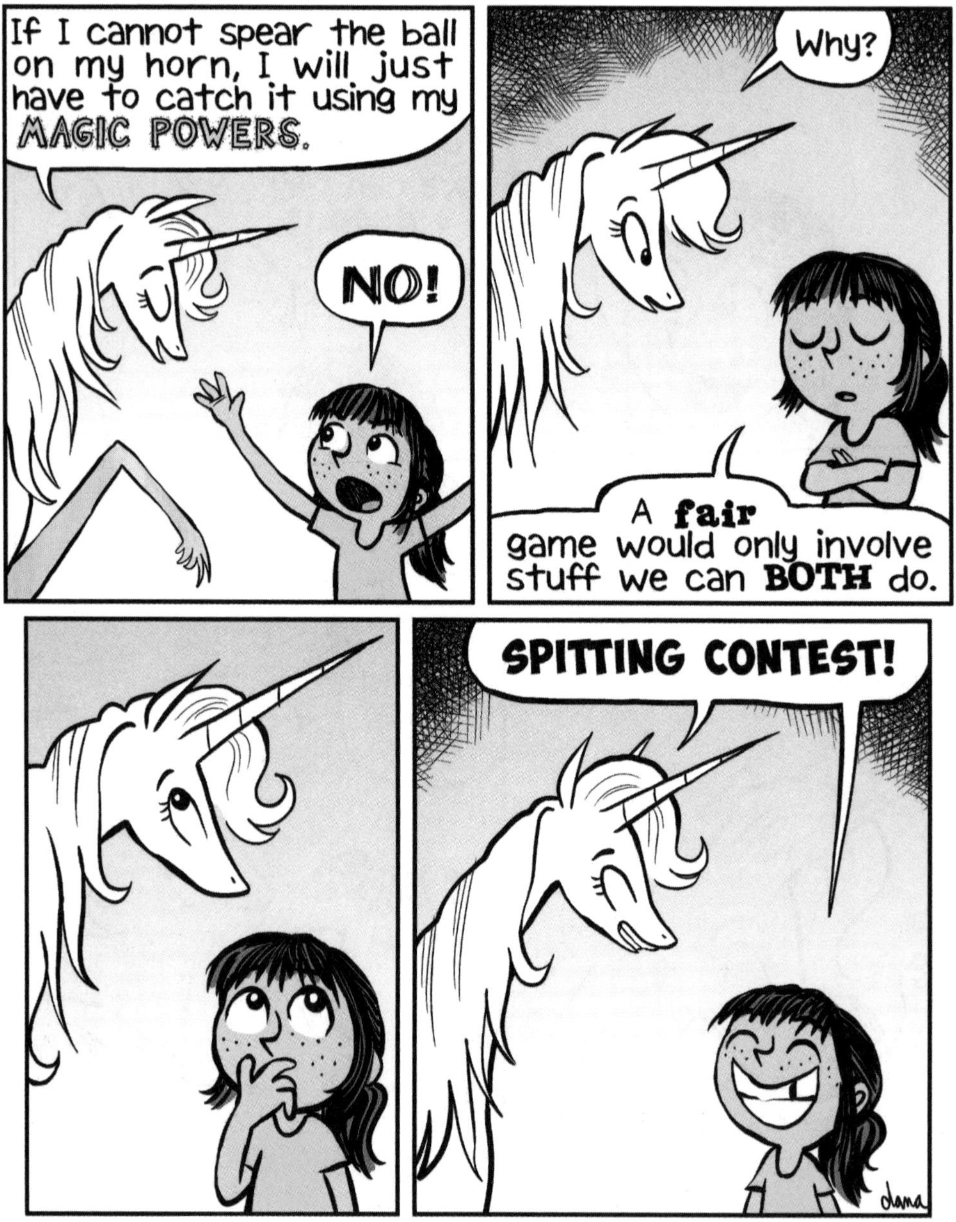
If I cannot spear the ball on my horn, I will just have to catch it using my MAGIC POWERS.
NO!
Why?
A fair game would only involve stuff we can BOTH do.
SPITTING CONTEST!
dana

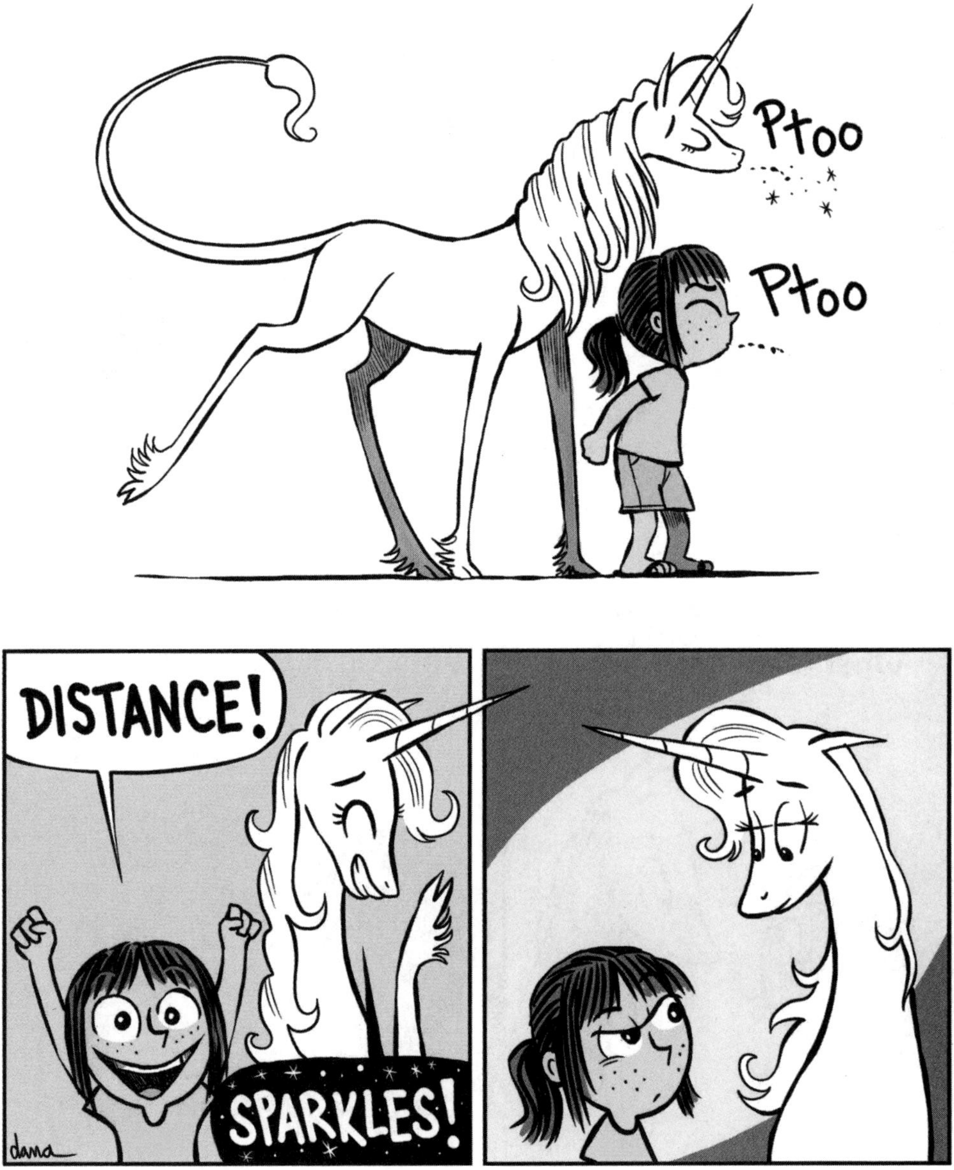
Ptoo
Ptoo
DISTANCE!
SPARKLES!
dana

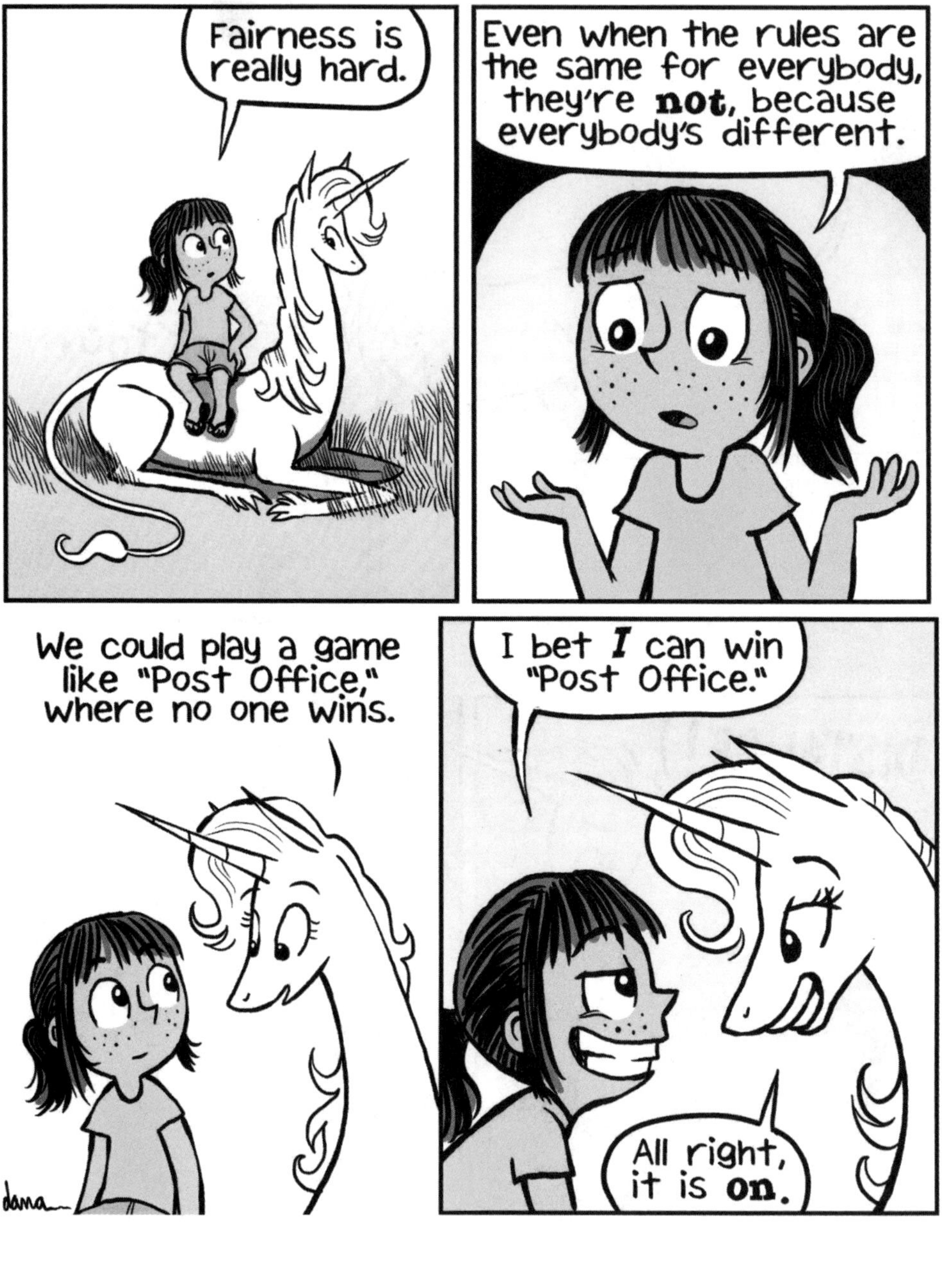
Fairness is really hard.
Even when the rules are the same for everybody, they're **not**, because everybody's different.
We could play a game like "Post Office," where no one wins.
I bet *I* can win "Post Office."
All right, it is **on**.
dana

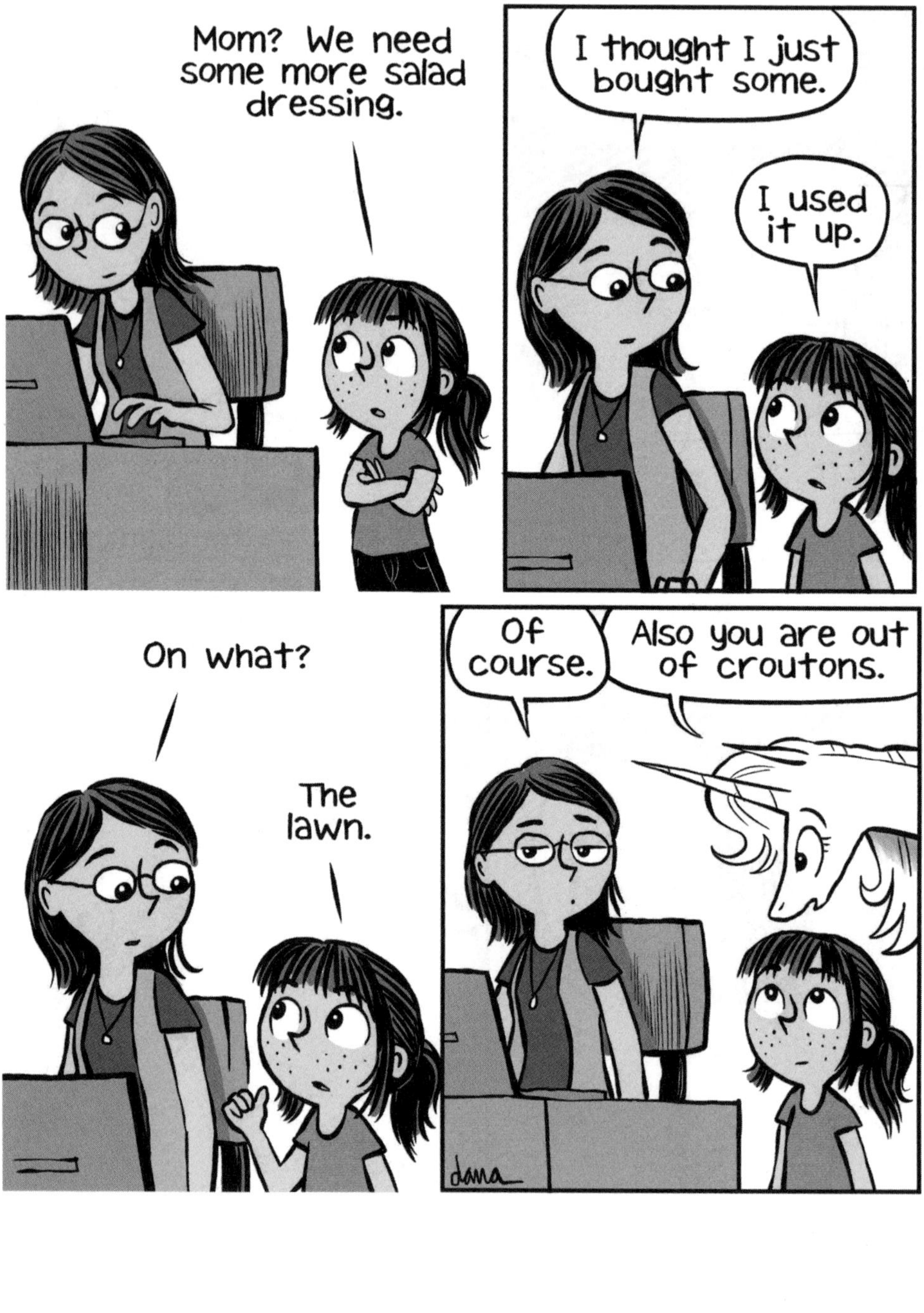
Mom? We need some more salad dressing.
I thought I just bought some.
I used it up.
On what?
The lawn.
Of course.
Also you are out of croutons.
dana

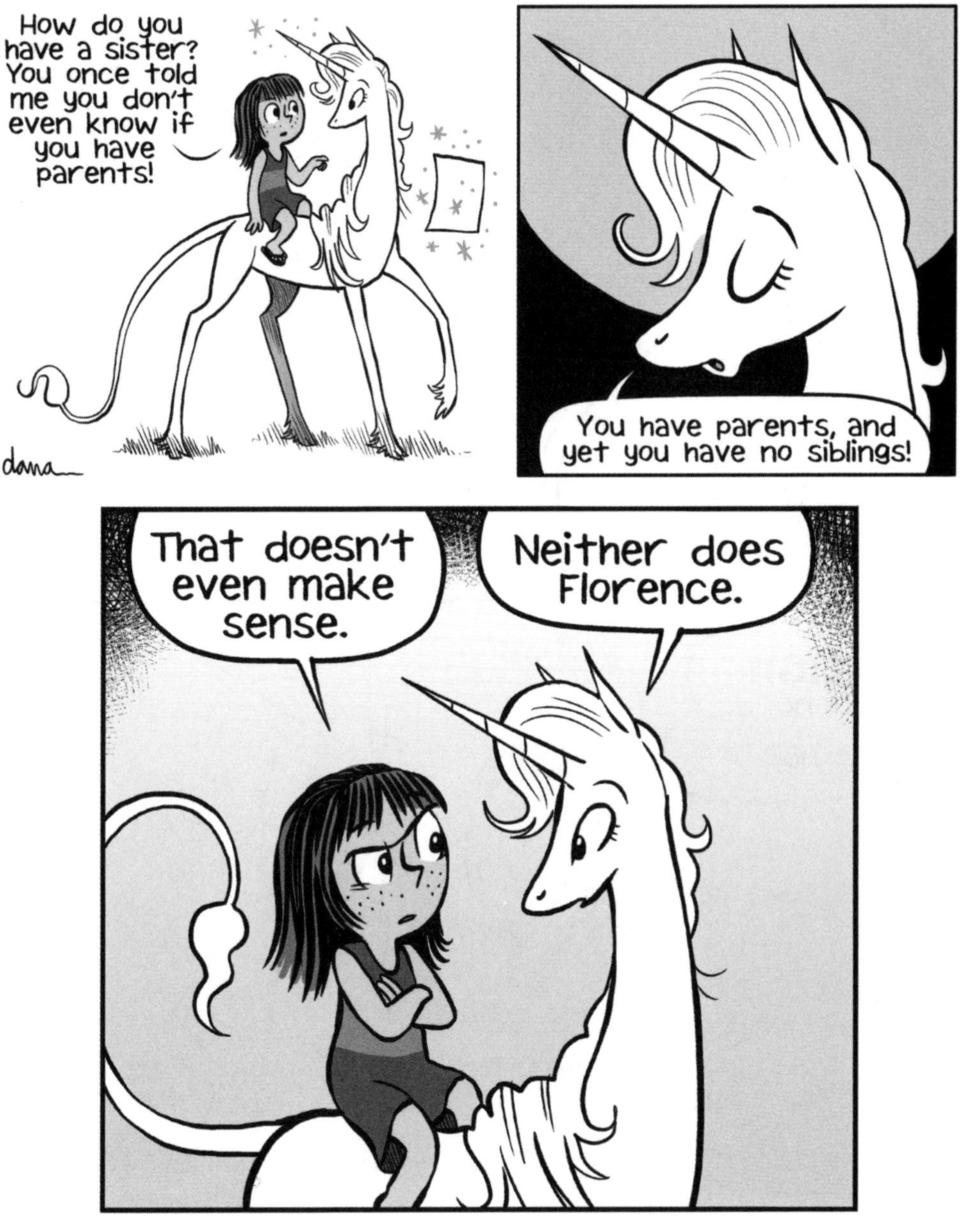
How do you have a sister? You once told me you don't even know if you have parents!
dana
You have parents, and yet you have no siblings!
That doesn't even make sense.
Neither does Florence.

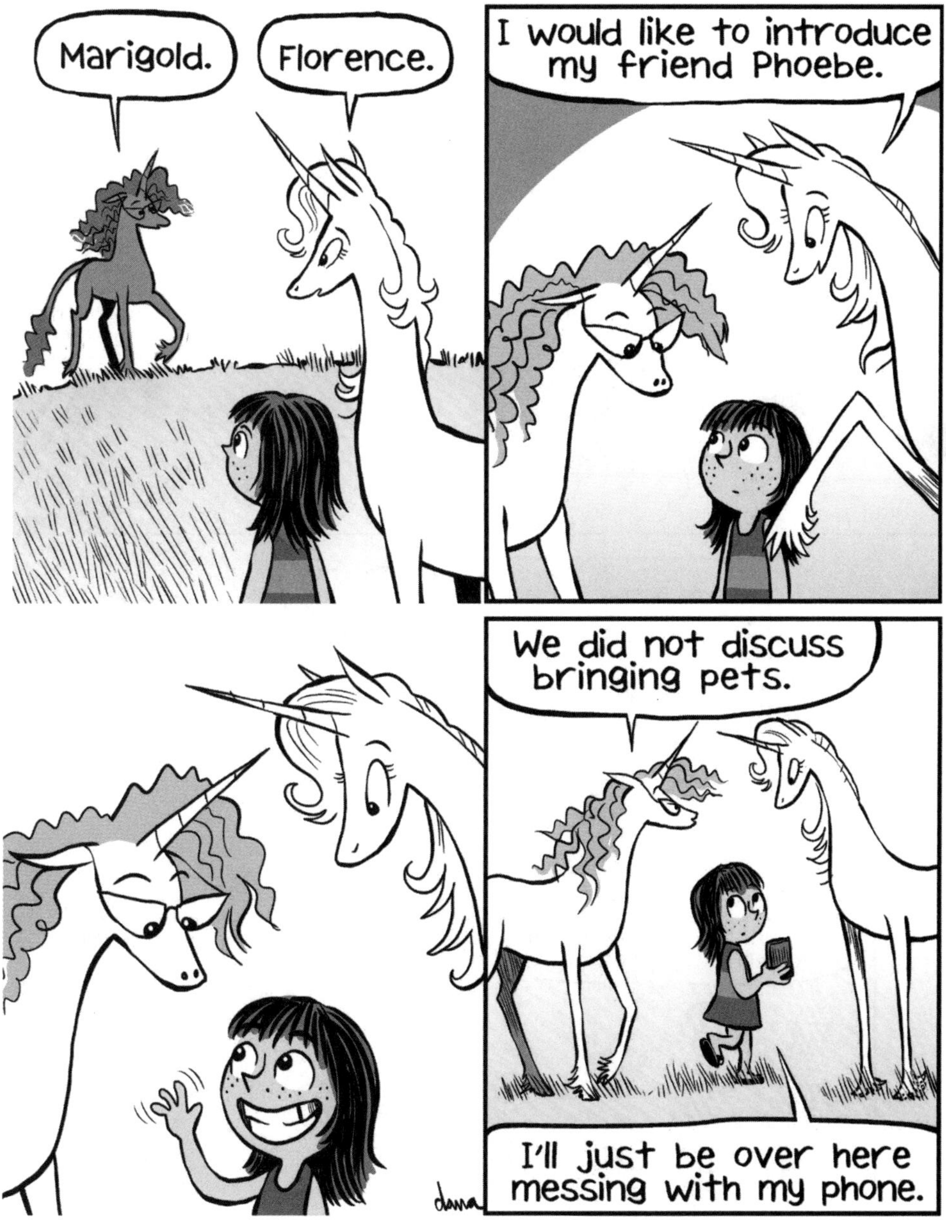
Marigold.
Florence.
I would like to introduce my friend Phoebe.
We did not discuss bringing pets.
I'll just be over here messing with my phone.
dana

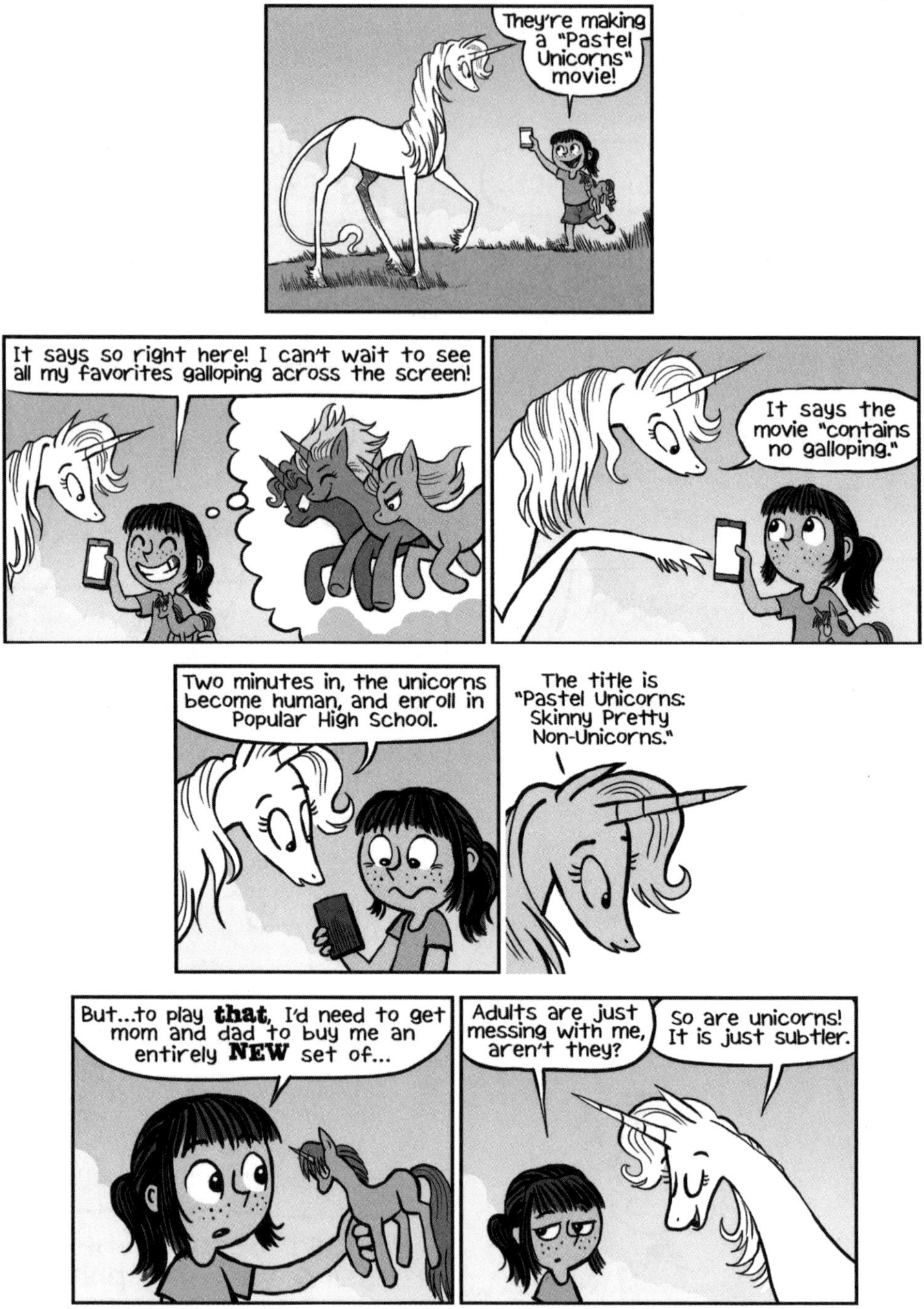
They're making a "Pastel Unicorns" movie!
It says so right here! I can't wait to see all my favorites galloping across the screen!
It says the movie "contains no galloping."
Two minutes in, the unicorns become human, and enroll in Popular High School.
The title is "Pastel Unicorns: Skinny Pretty Non-Unicorns."
But...to play **that**, I'd need to get mom and dad to buy me an entirely **NEW** set of...
Adults are just messing with me, aren't they?
So are unicorns! It is just subtler.

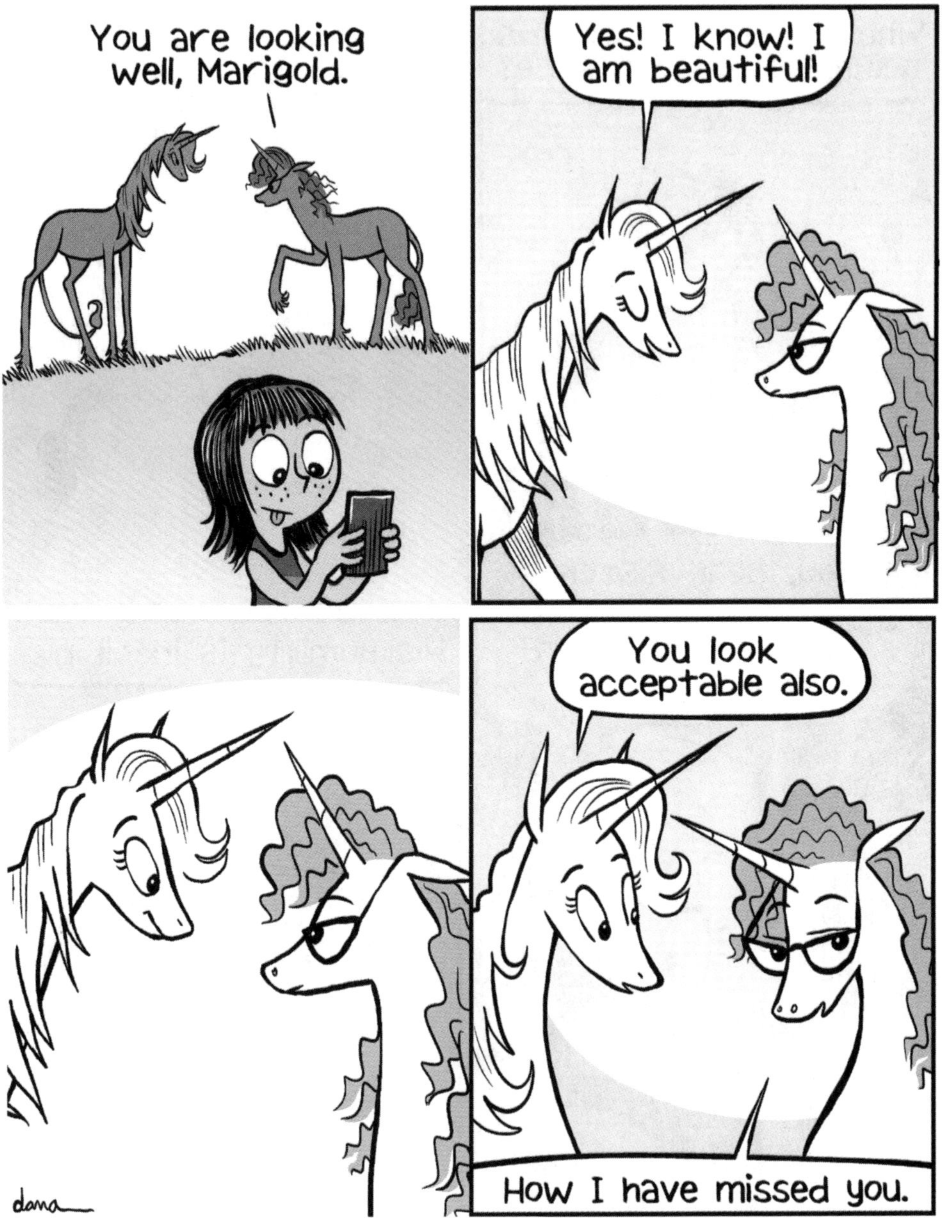
You are looking well, Marigold.
Yes! I know! I am beautiful!
You look acceptable also.
How I have missed you.
dana

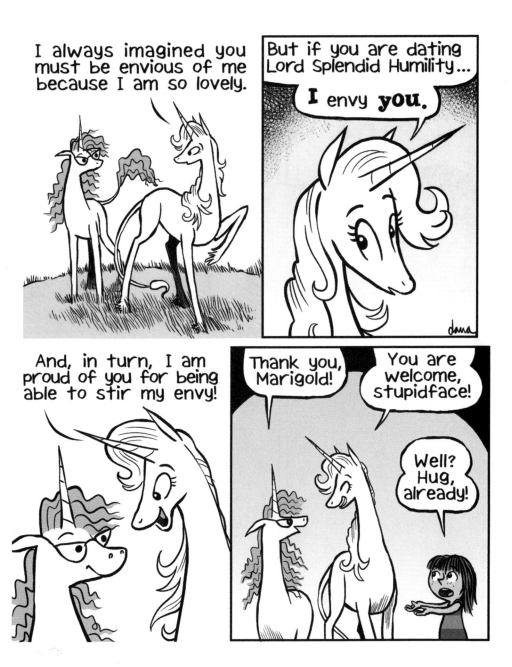

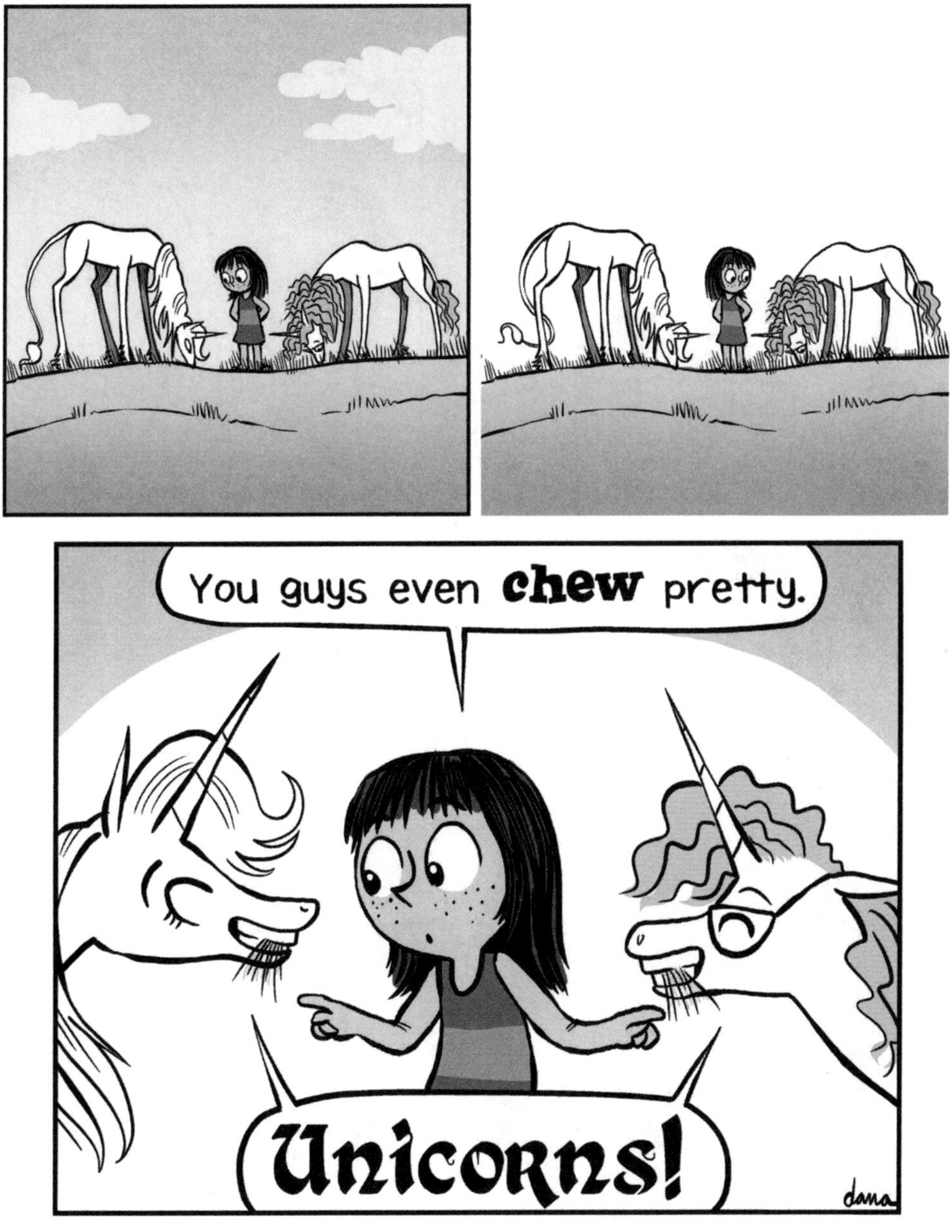
You guys even chew pretty.
Unicorns!
dana

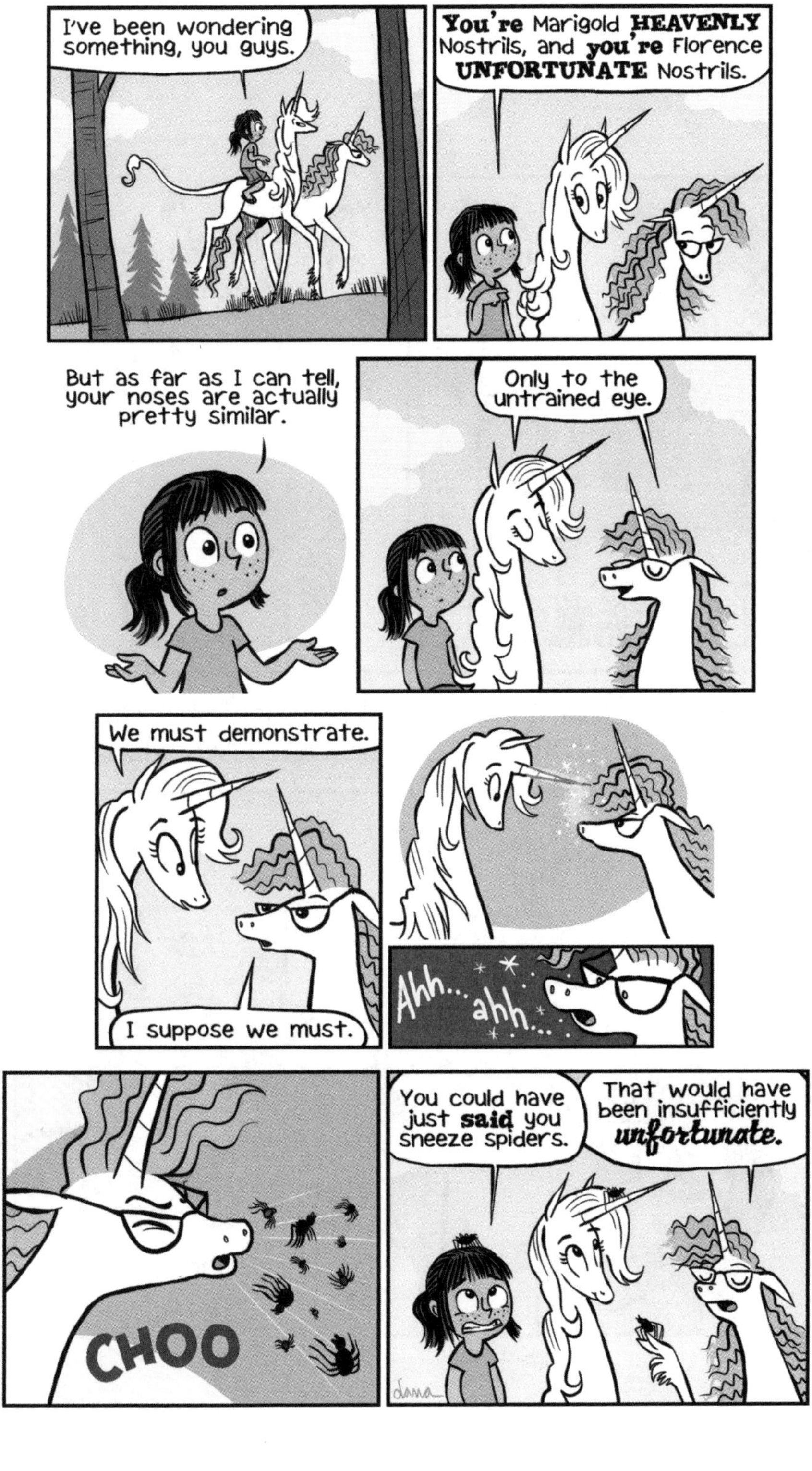
I've been wondering something, you guys.
You're Marigold **HEAVENLY** Nostrils, and **you're** Florence **UNFORTUNATE** Nostrils.
But as far as I can tell, your noses are actually pretty similar.
Only to the untrained eye.
We must demonstrate.
I suppose we must.
Ahh... ahh...
CHOO
You could have just **said** you sneeze spiders.
That would have been insufficiently ***unfortunate.***
dana

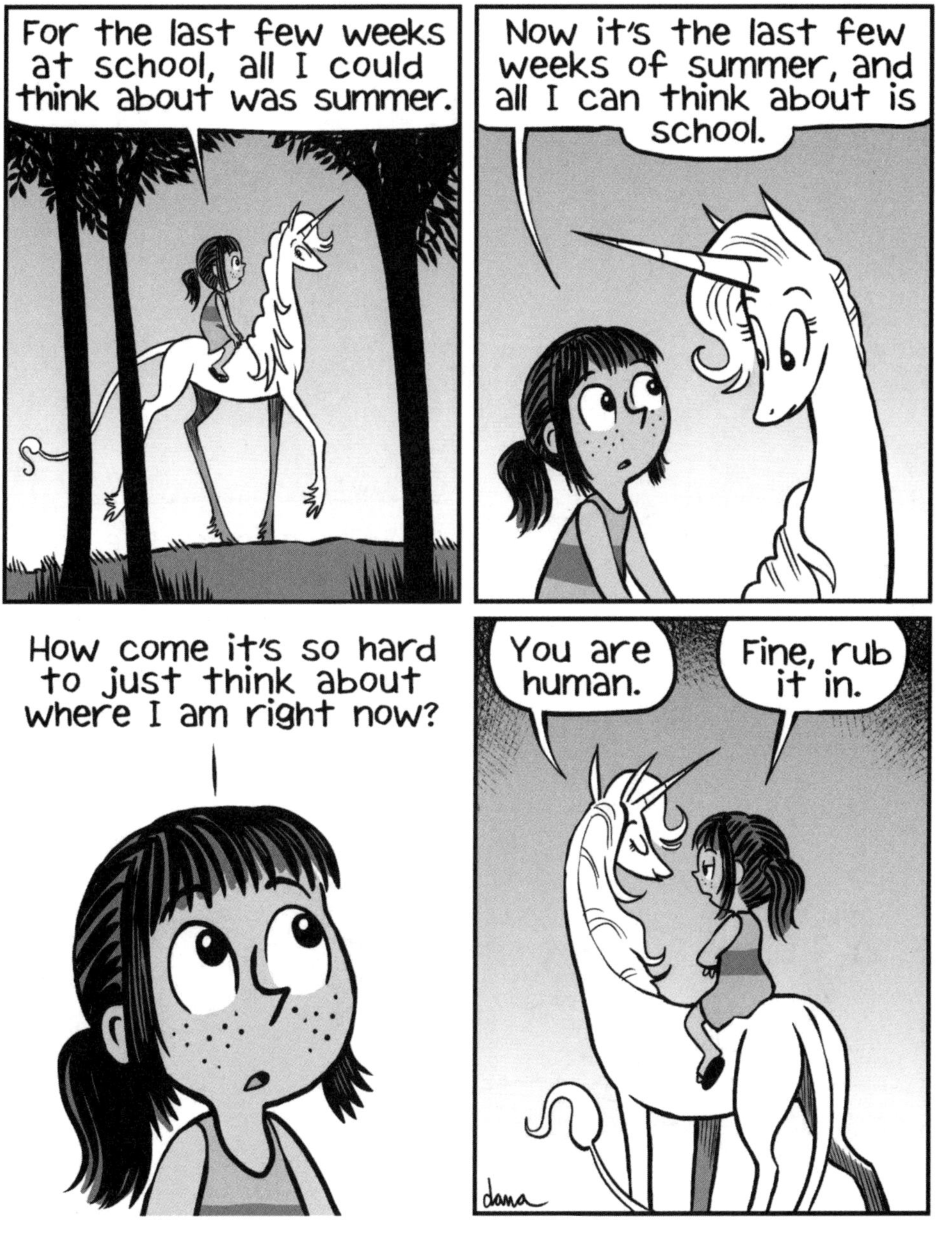
For the last few weeks at school, all I could think about was summer.
Now it's the last few weeks of summer, and all I can think about is school.
How come it's so hard to just think about where I am right now?
You are human.
Fine, rub it in.
dana

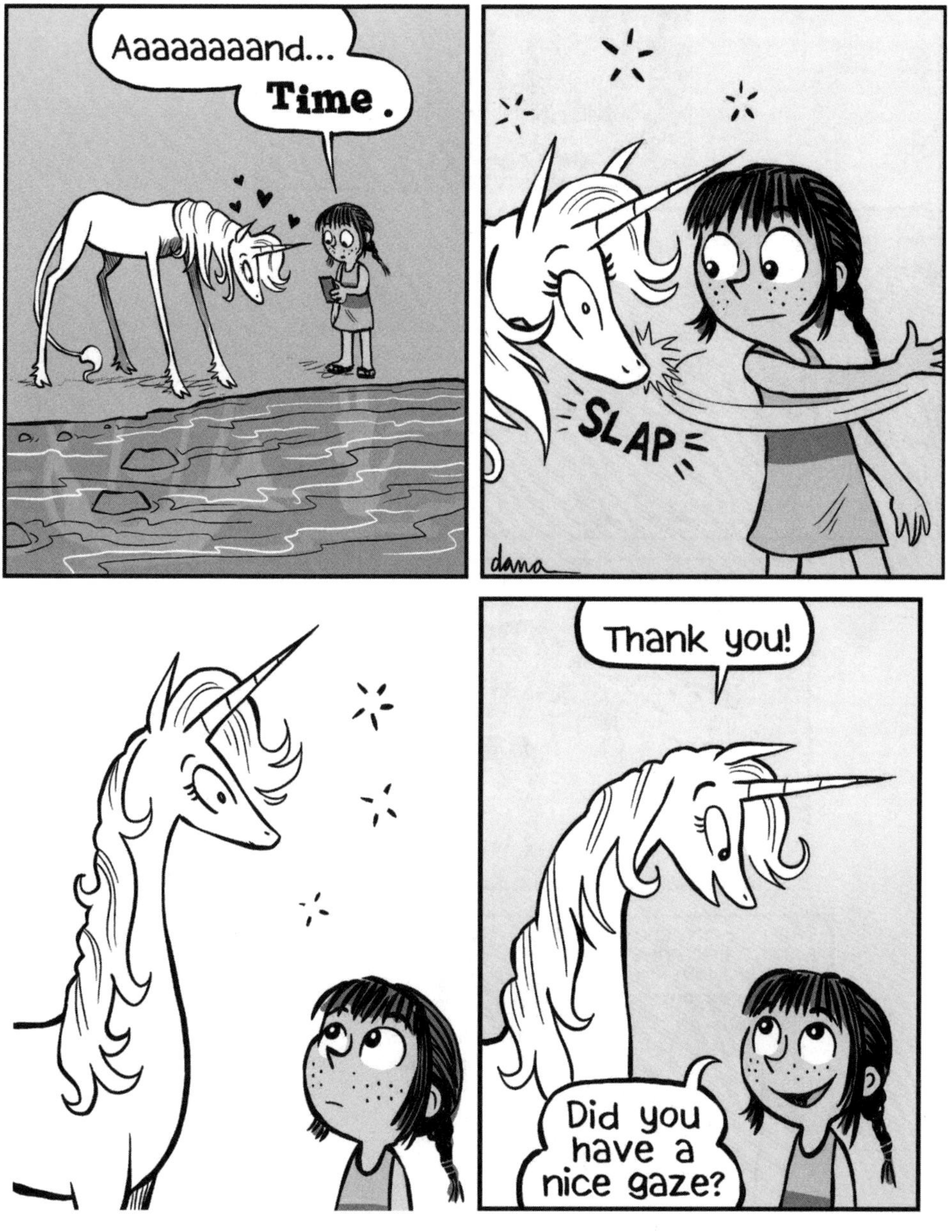
Aaaaaaaaand...
Time.
SLAP
dana
Thank you!
Did you have a nice gaze?

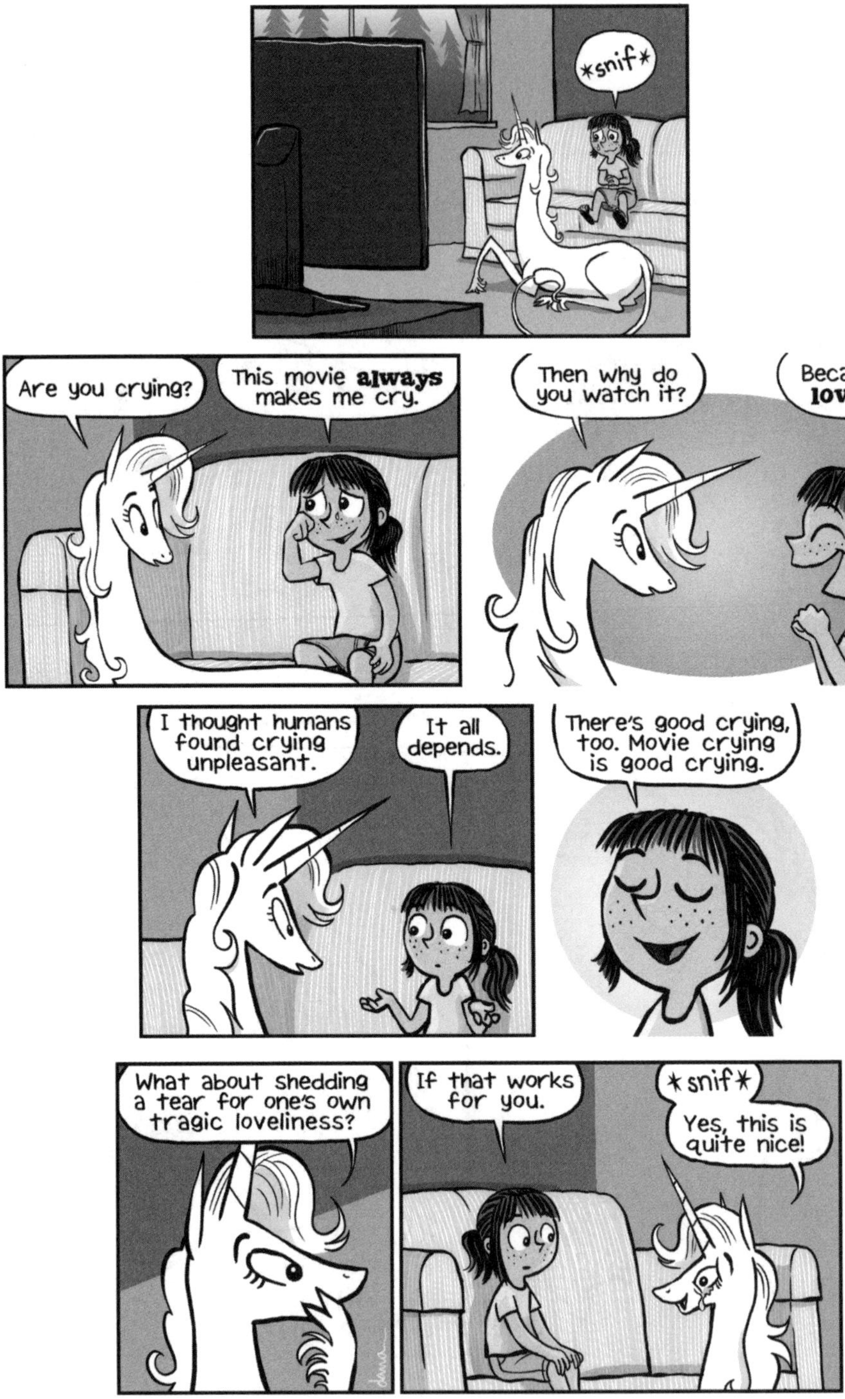
snif
Are you crying?
This movie **always** makes me cry.
Then why do you watch it?
Because I **love** it!
I thought humans found crying unpleasant.
It all depends.
There's good crying, too. Movie crying is good crying.
What about shedding a tear for one's own tragic loveliness?
If that works for you.
snif
Yes, this is quite nice!

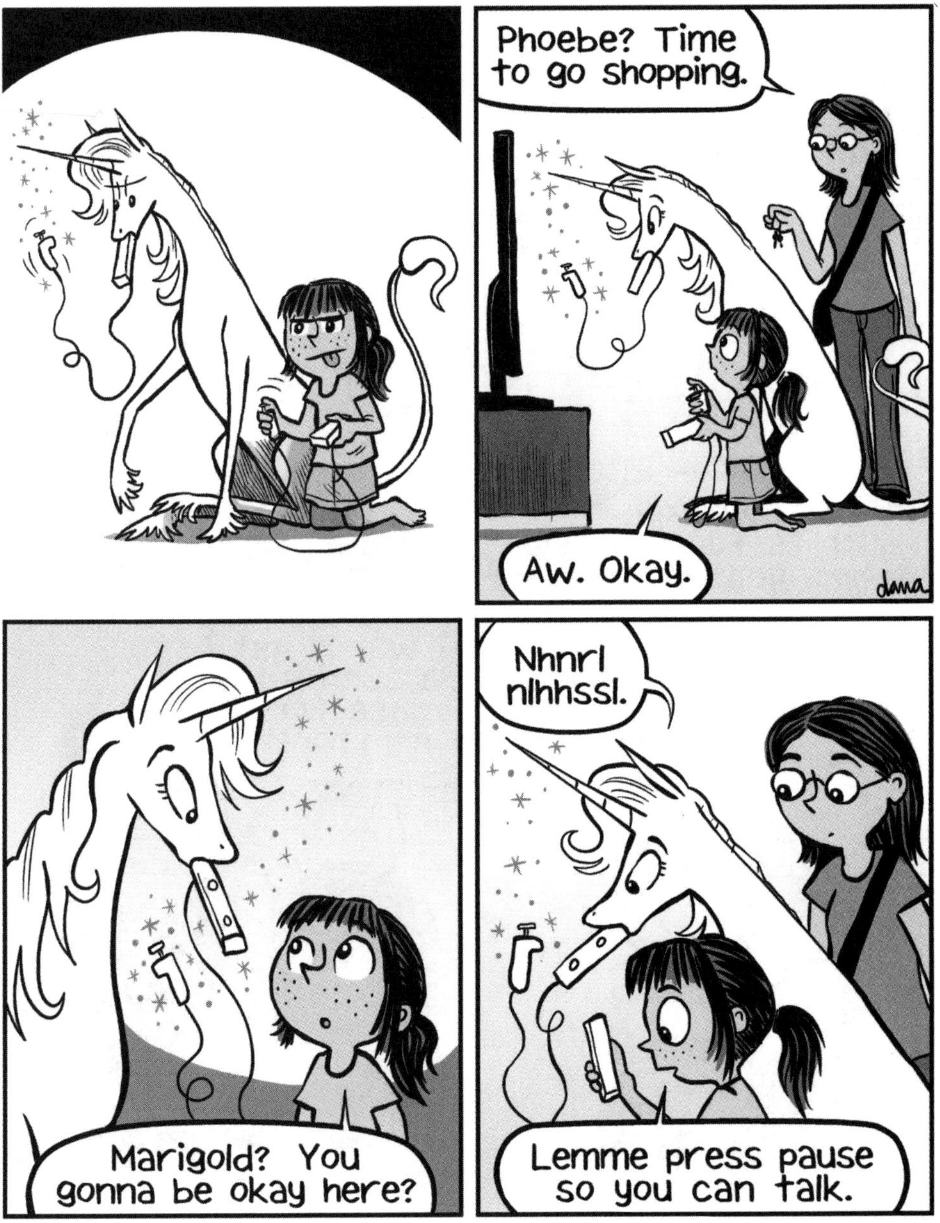
Phoebe? Time to go shopping.
Aw. Okay.
dana
Marigold? You gonna be okay here?
Nhnrl nlhhssl.
Lemme press pause so you can talk.

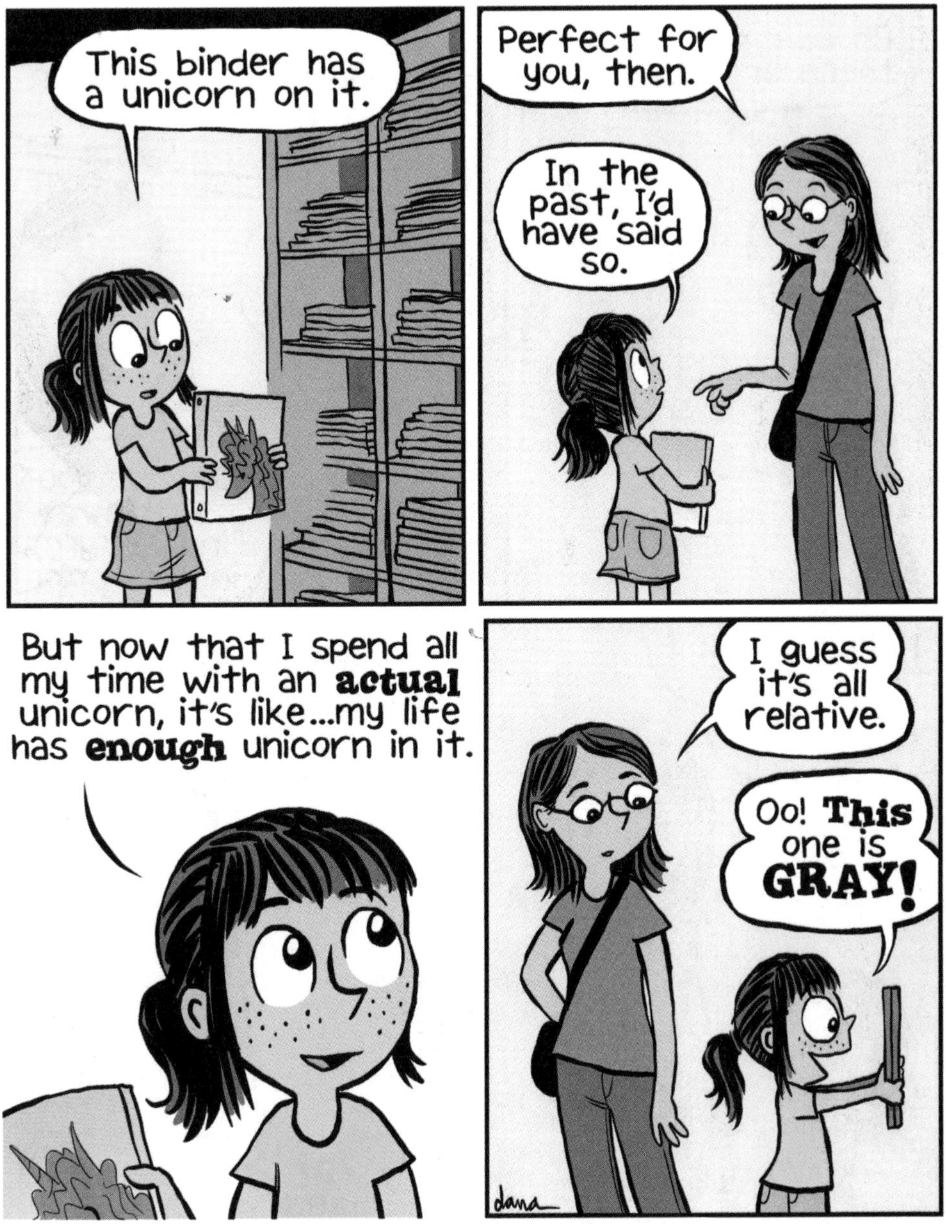
This binder has a unicorn on it.
Perfect for you, then.
In the past, I'd have said so.
But now that I spend all my time with an **actual** unicorn, it's like...my life has **enough** unicorn in it.
I guess it's all relative.
Oo! **This** one is **GRAY!**
dana

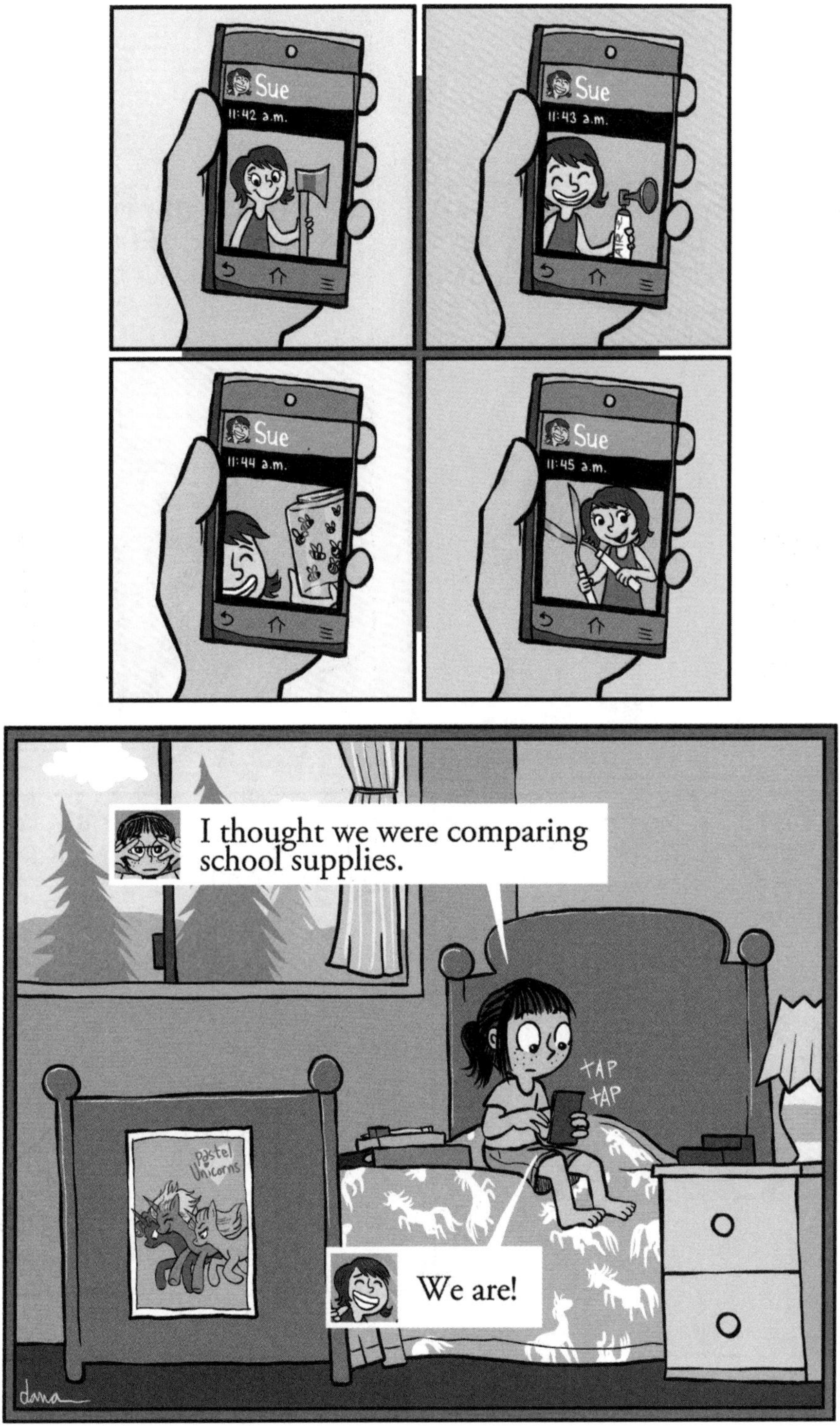
Sue
11:42 a.m.
Sue
11:43 a.m.
AIR
Sue
11:44 a.m.
Sue
11:45 a.m.
I thought we were comparing school supplies.
TAP TAP
Pastel Unicorns
We are!
dana

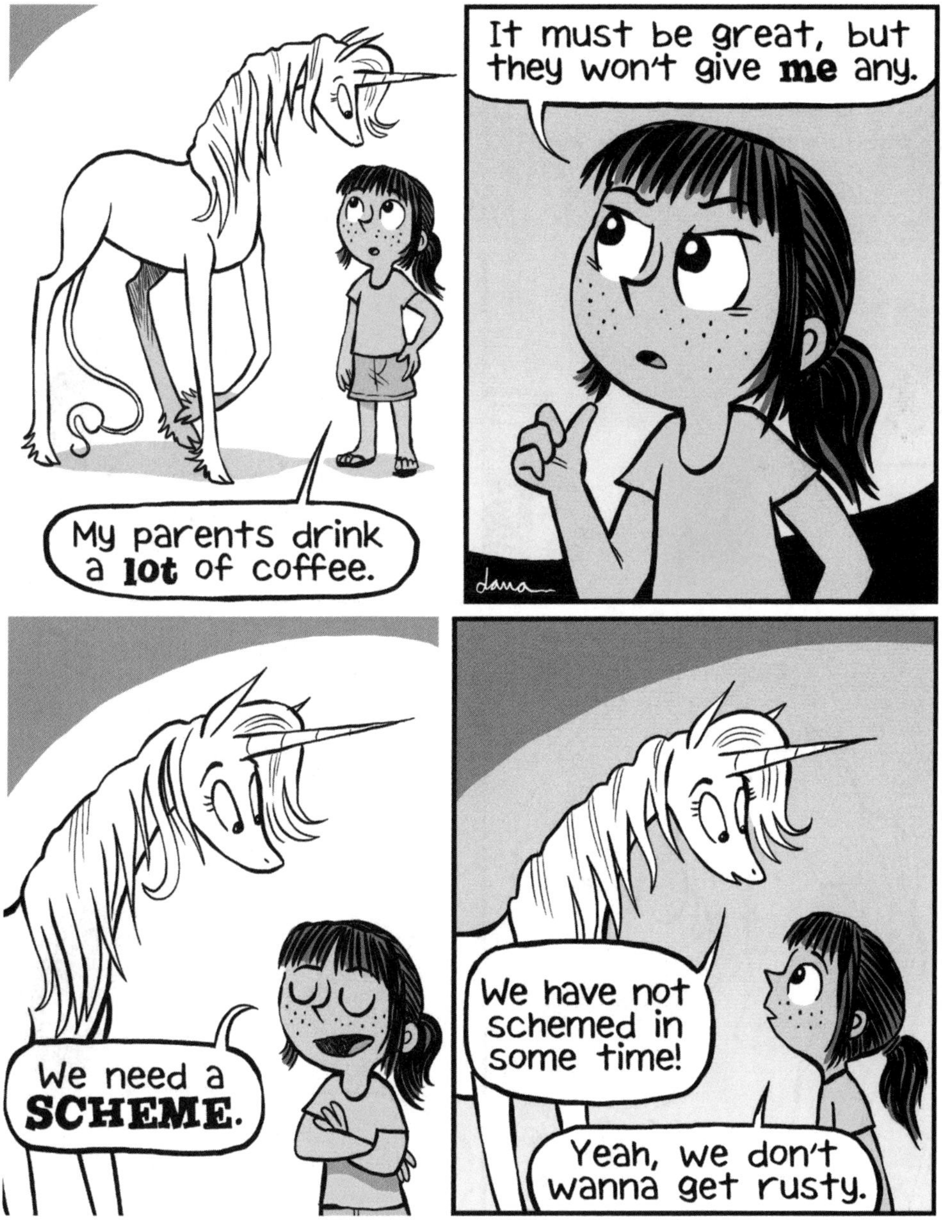
My parents drink a **lot** of coffee.
It must be great, but they won't give **me** any.
We need a **SCHEME**.
We have not schemed in some time!
Yeah, we don't wanna get rusty.
dana

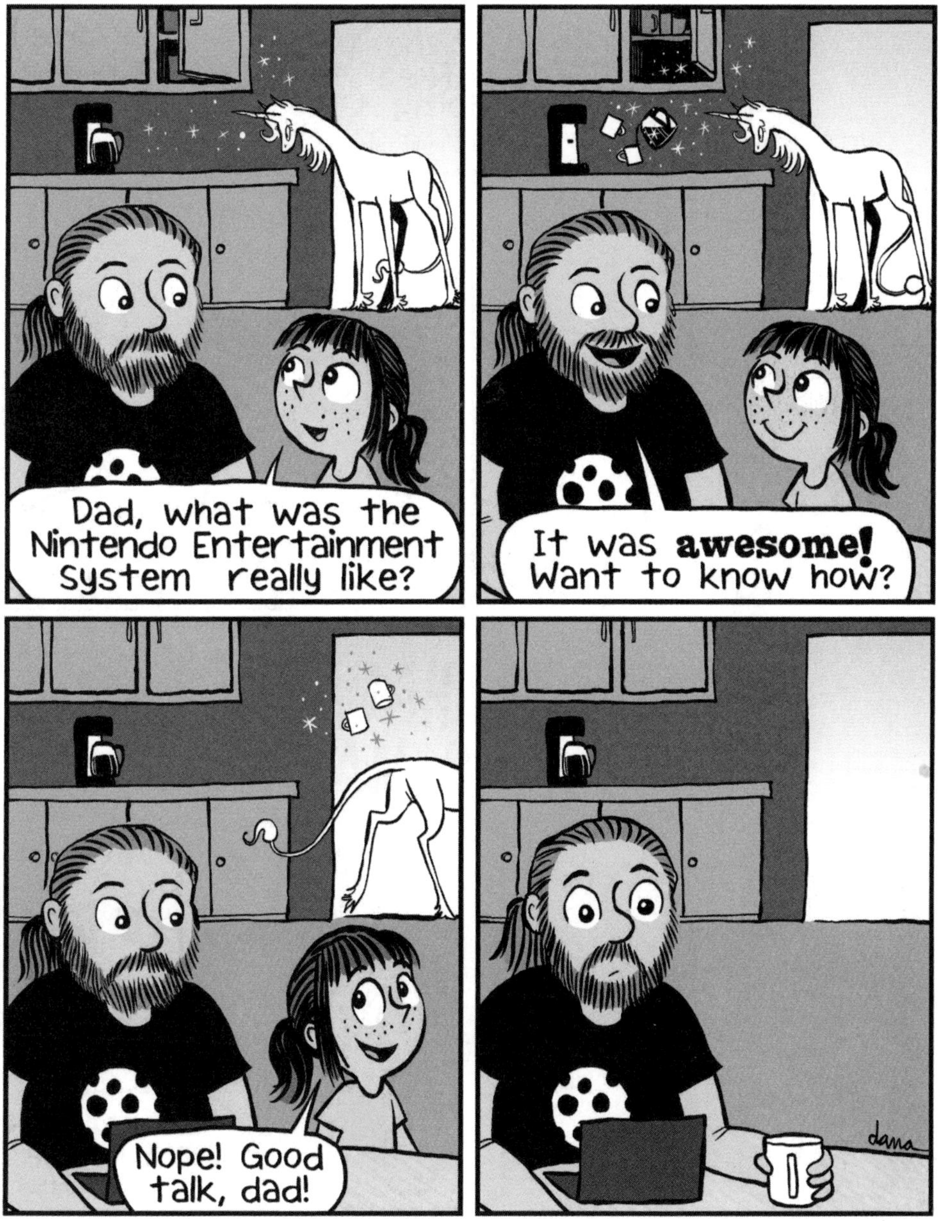
Dad, what was the Nintendo Entertainment System really like?
It was **awesome!** Want to know how?
Nope! Good talk, dad!
dana

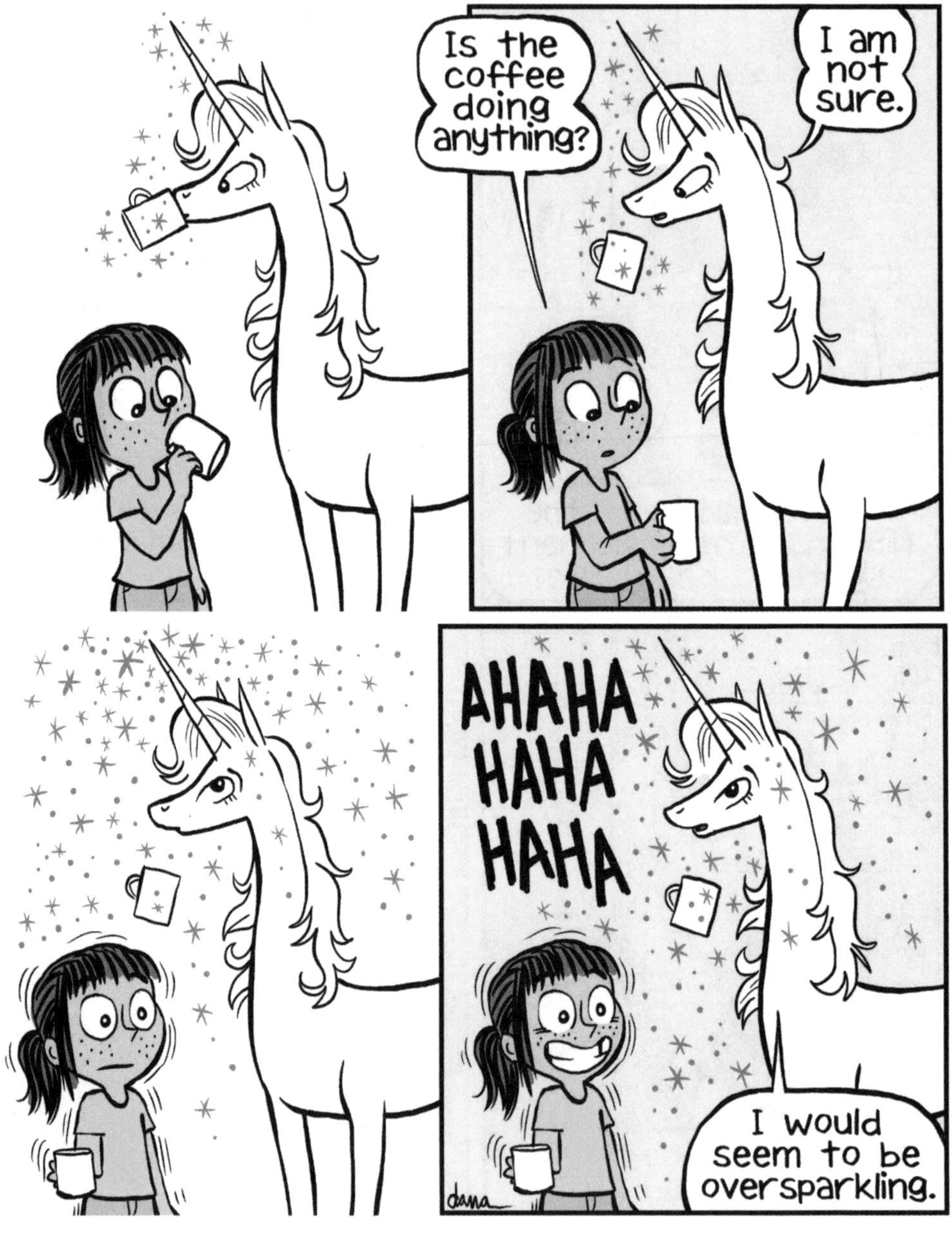
Is the coffee doing anything?
I am not sure.
AHAHA HAHA HAHA
I would seem to be oversparkling.
dana

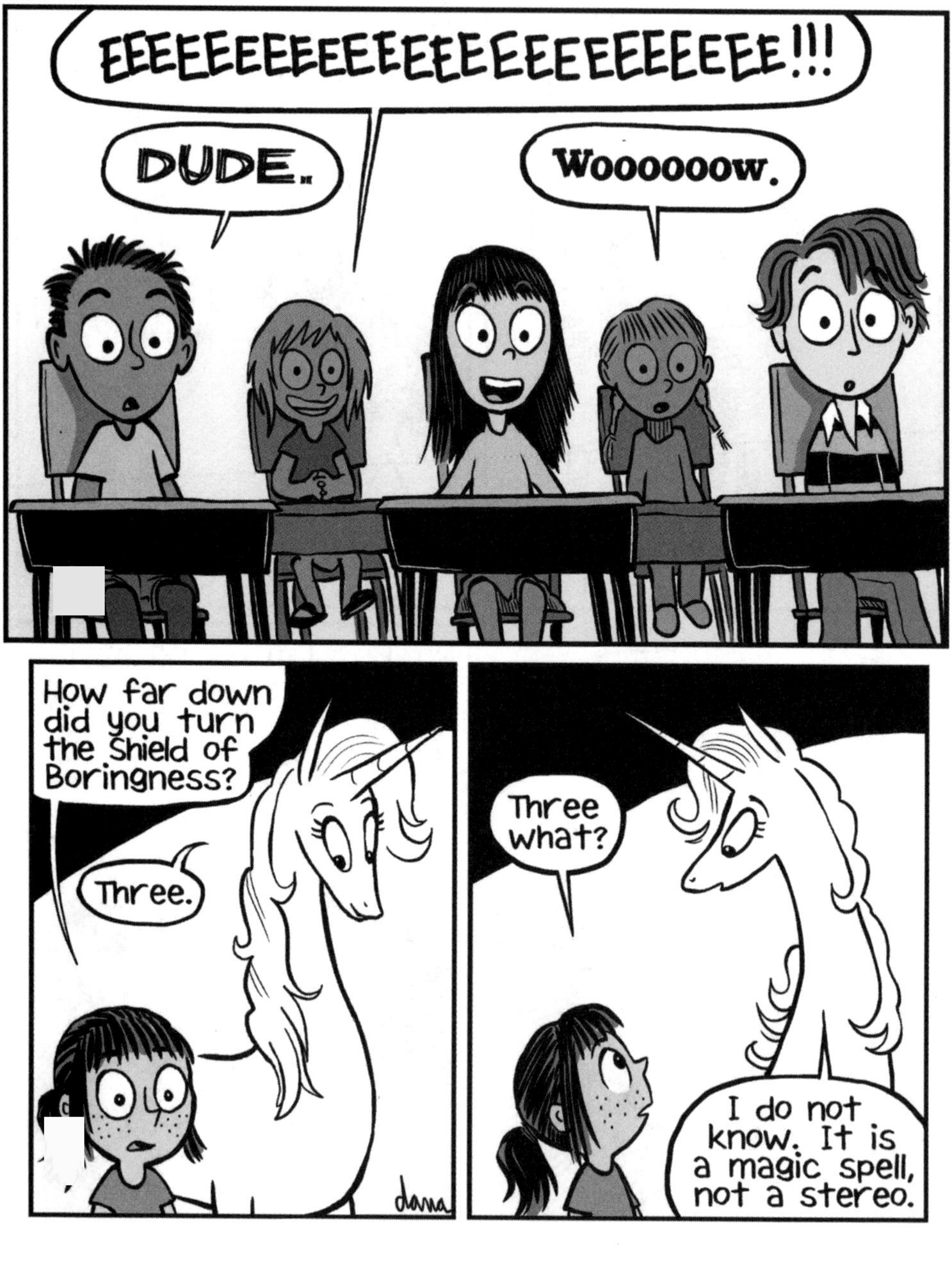
EEEEEEEEEEEEEEEEEEEEEEEEE!!!
DUDE.
Woooooow.
How far down did you turn the Shield of Boringness?
Three.
Three what?
I do not know. It is a magic spell, not a stereo.
dana

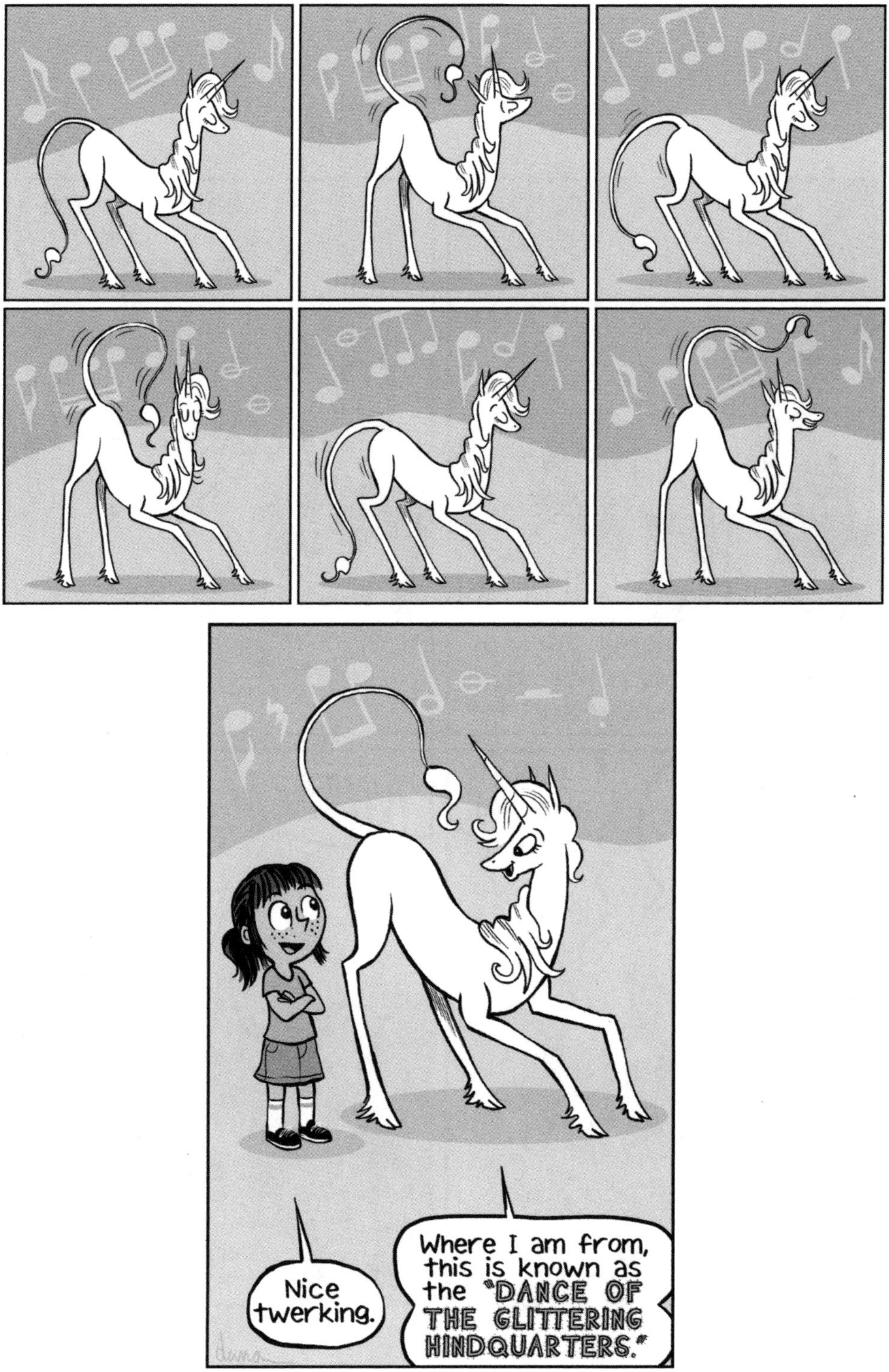
Nice twerking.
Where I am from, this is known as the "DANCE OF THE GLITTERING HINDQUARTERS."

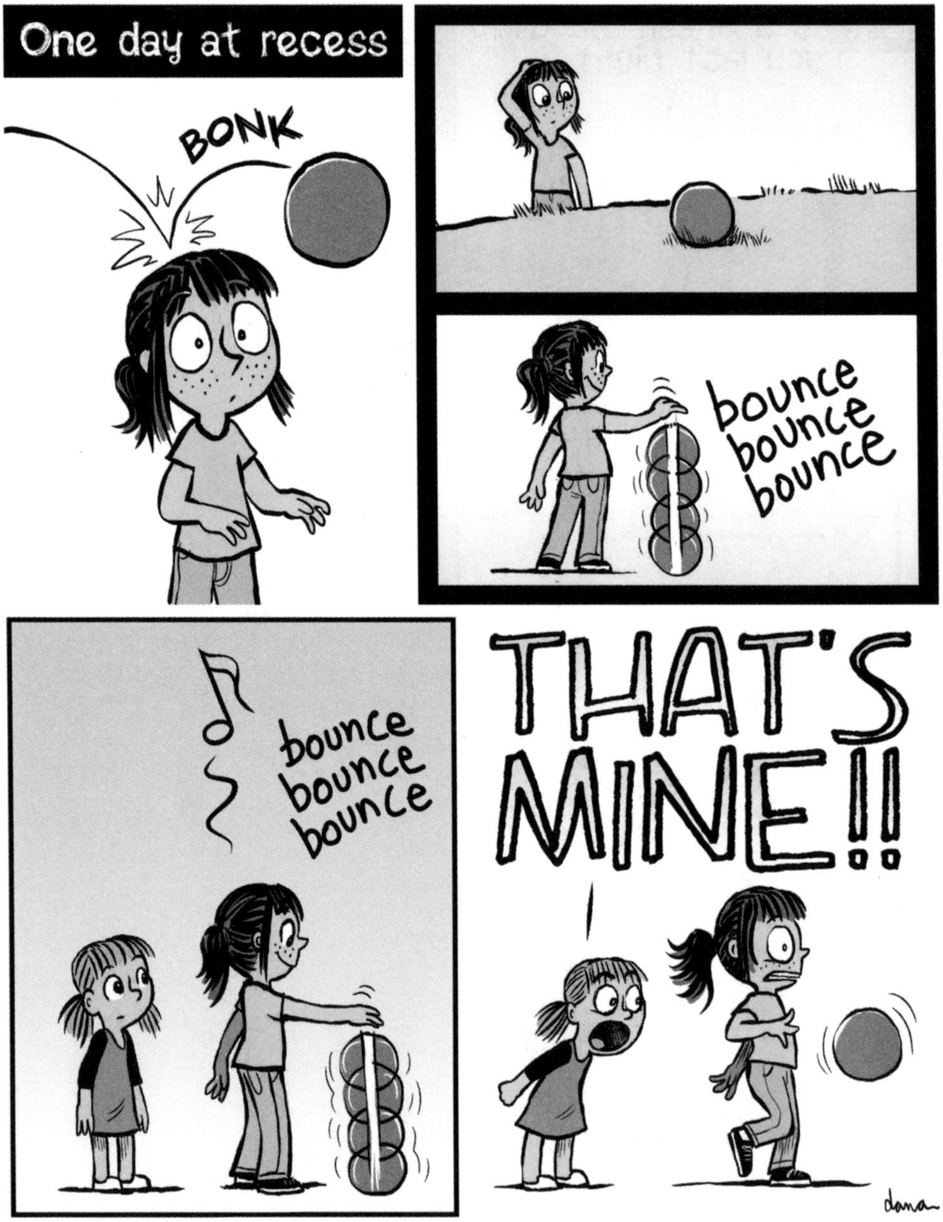
One day at recess
BONK
bounce
bounce
bounce
bounce
bounce
bounce
THAT'S MINE!!
dana

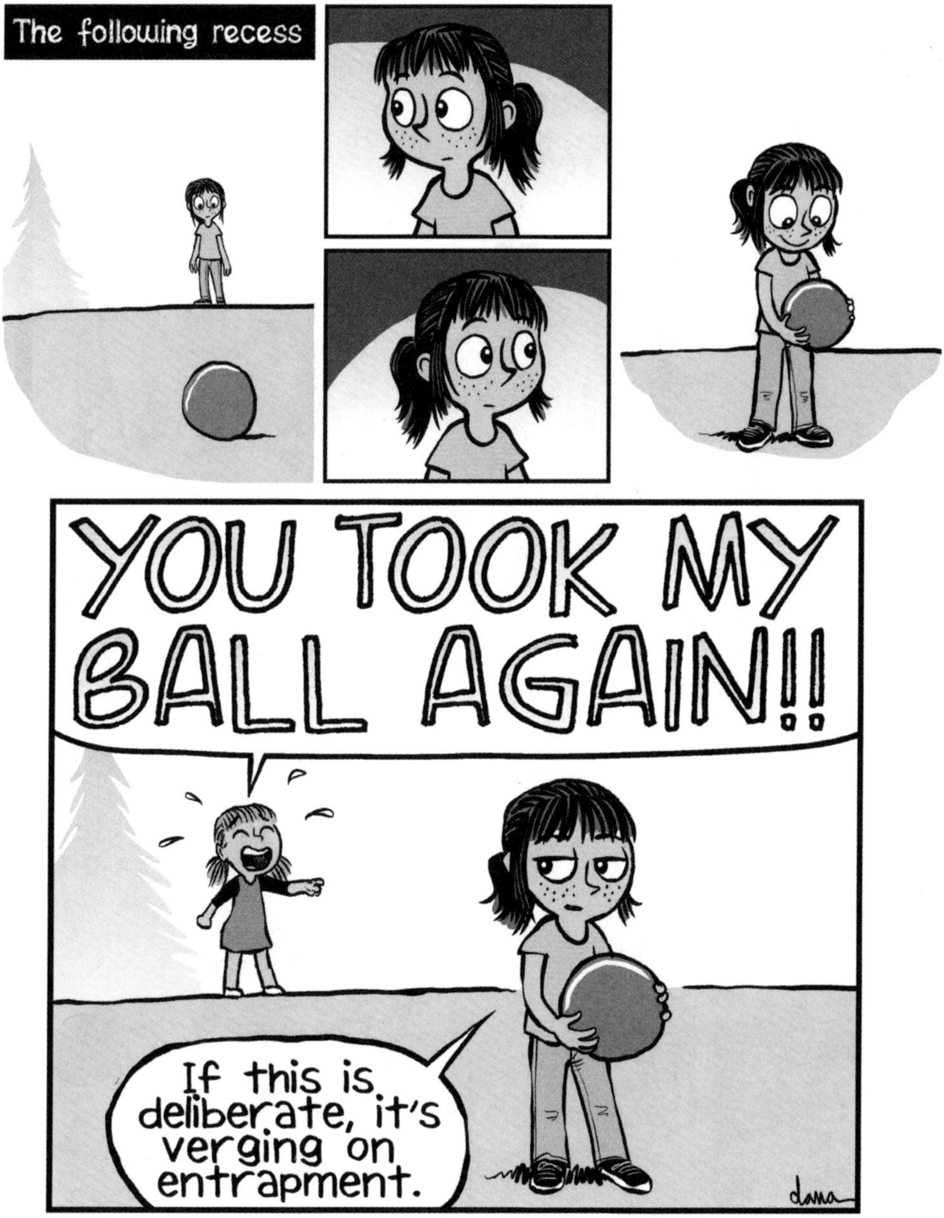
The following recess
YOU TOOK MY BALL AGAIN!!
If this is deliberate, it's verging on entrapment.
dana

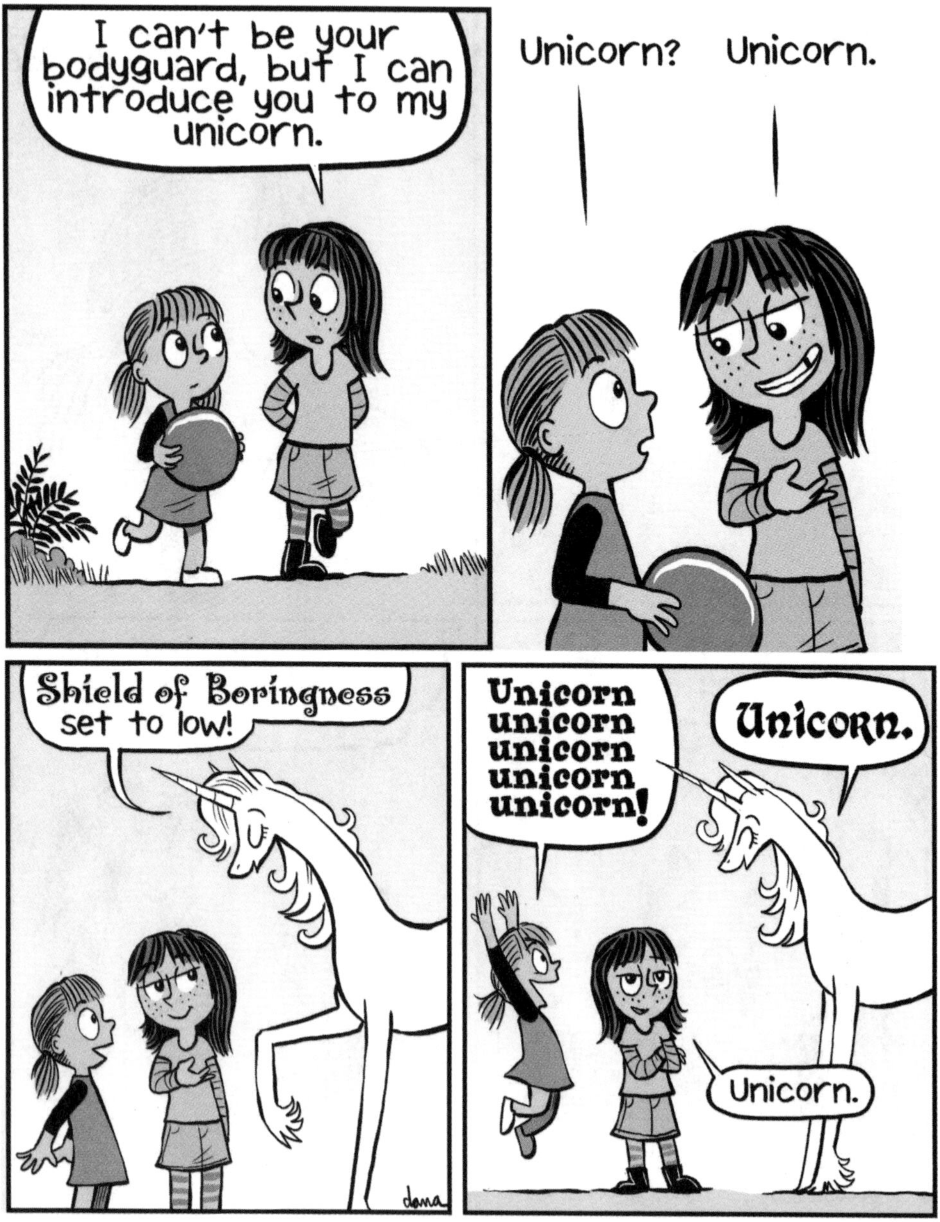
I can't be your bodyguard, but I can introduce you to my unicorn.
Unicorn?
Unicorn.
Shield of Boringness set to low!
dana
Unicorn unicorn unicorn unicorn unicorn!
Unicorn.
Unicorn.

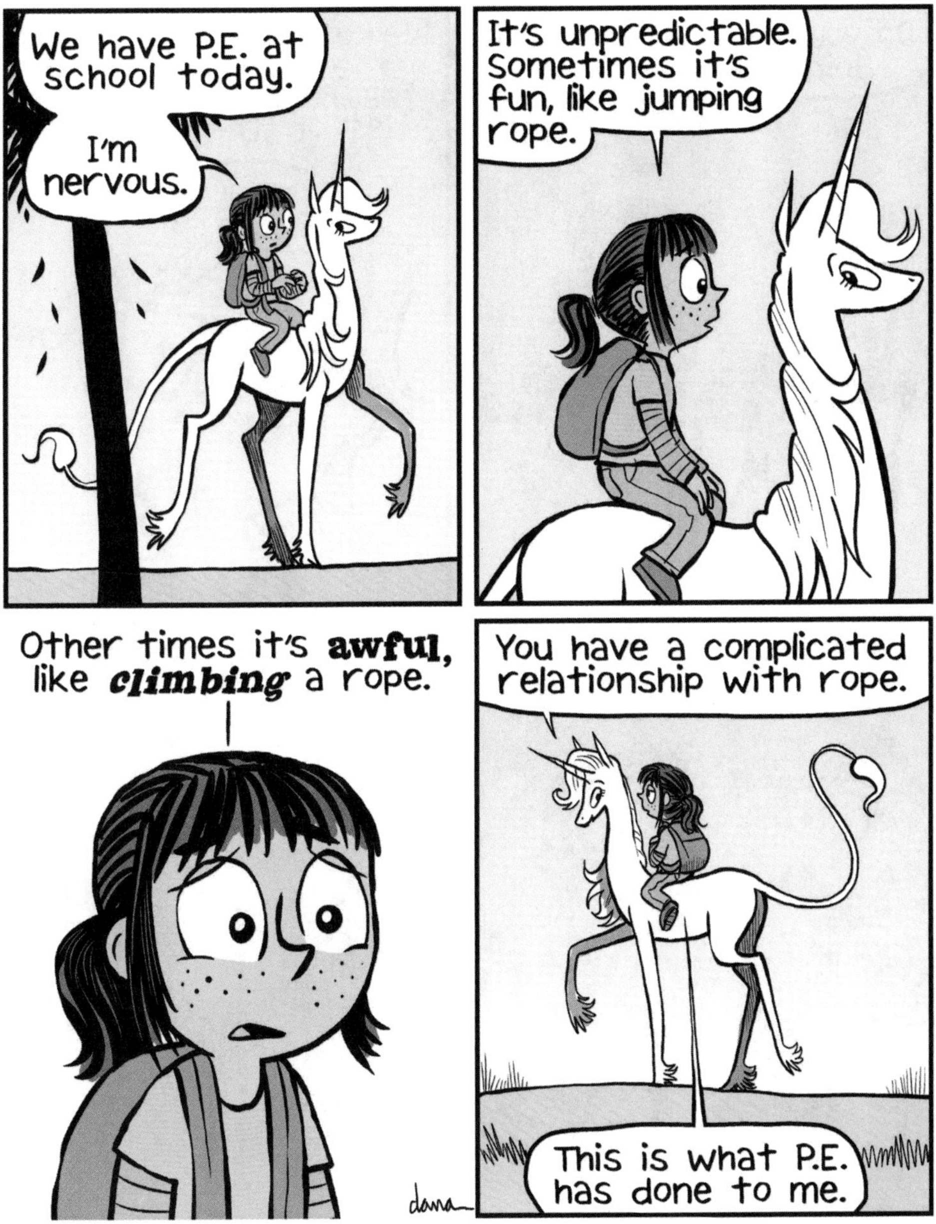
We have P.E. at school today.
I'm nervous.
It's unpredictable. Sometimes it's fun, like jumping rope.
Other times it's **awful**, like ***climbing*** a rope.
You have a complicated relationship with rope.
This is what P.E. has done to me.
dana

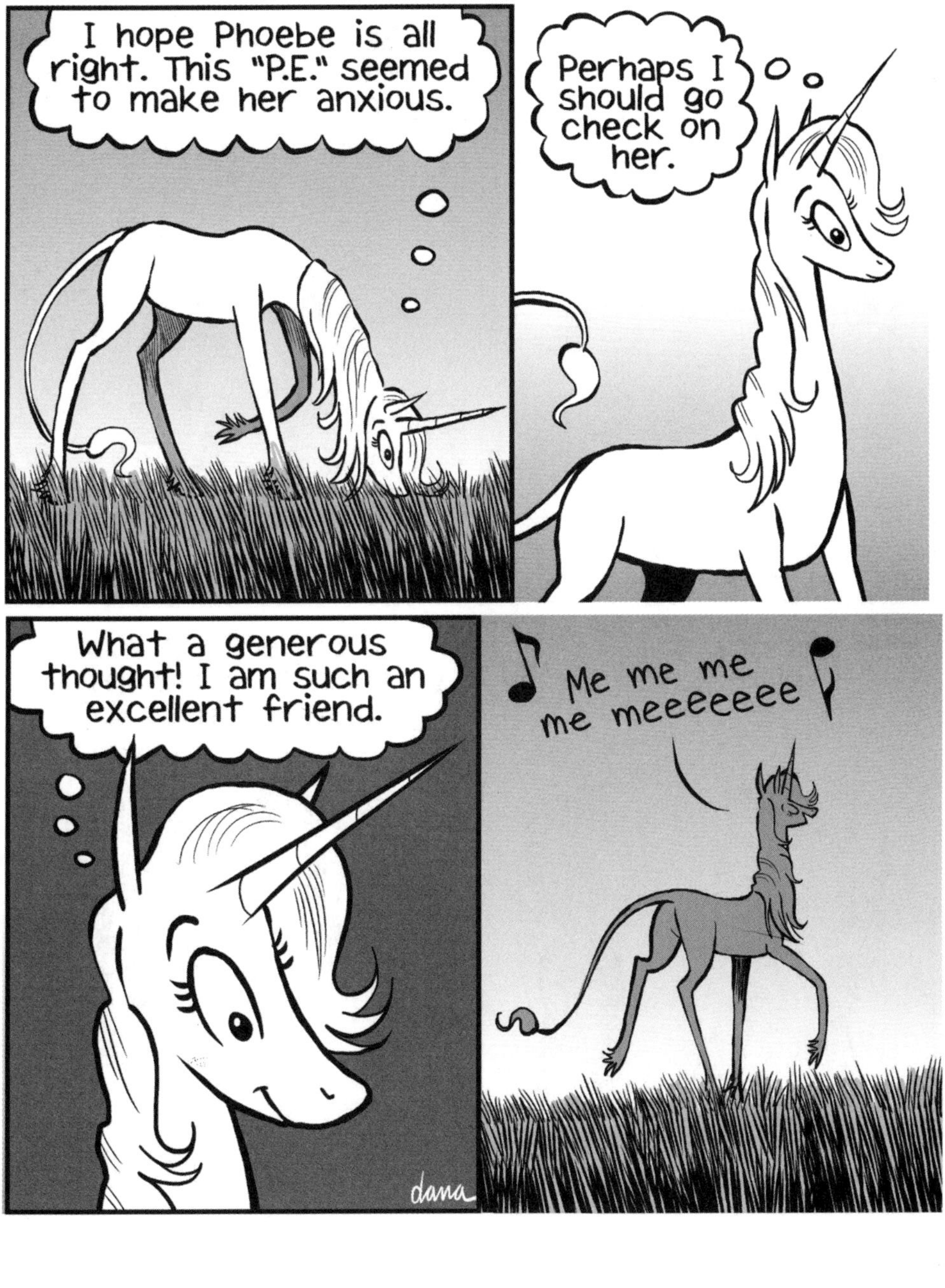
I hope Phoebe is all right. This "P.E." seemed to make her anxious.
Perhaps I should go check on her.
What a generous thought! I am such an excellent friend.
Me me me me meeeeeee
dana

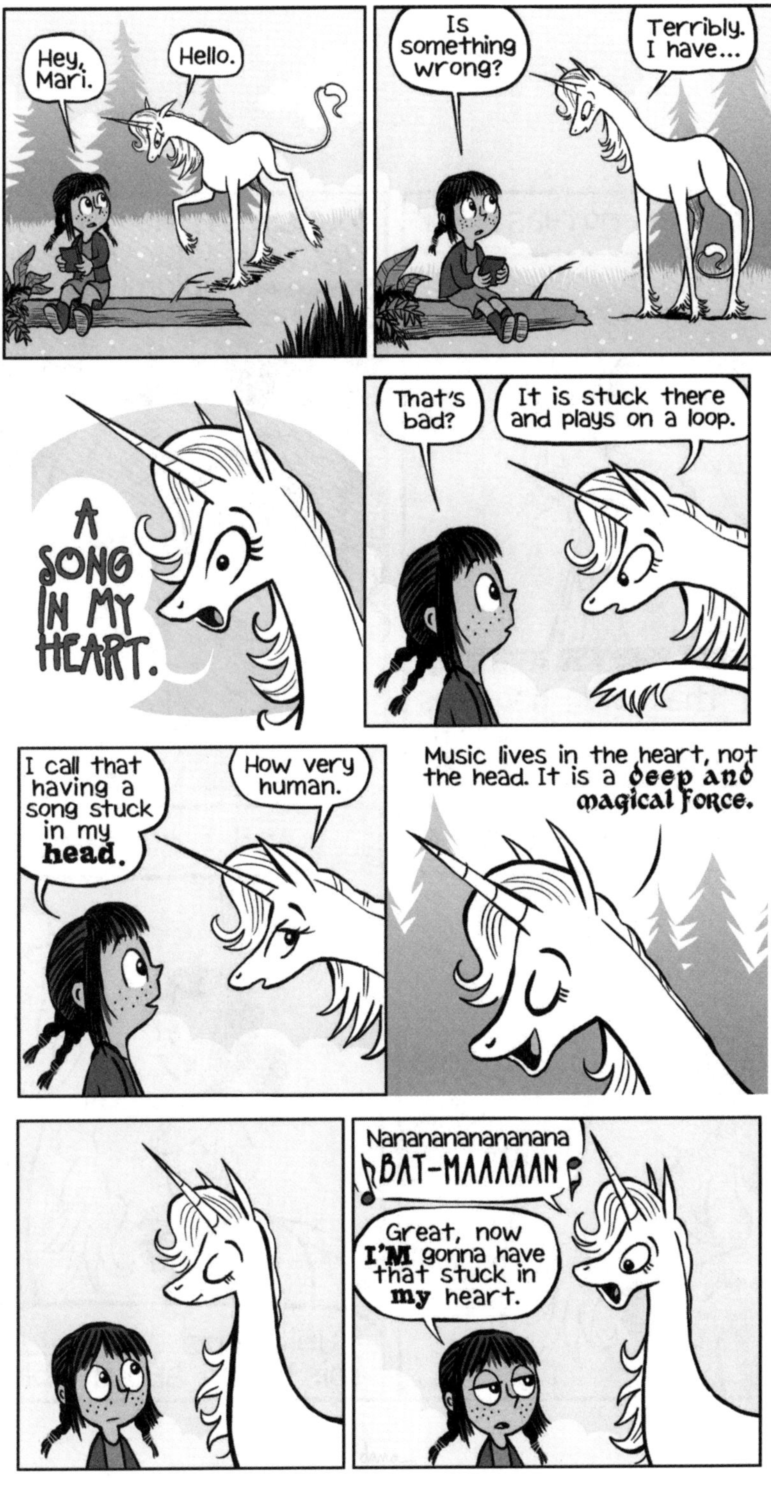
Hey, Mari.
Hello.
Is something wrong?
Terribly. I have...
A SONG IN MY HEART.
That's bad?
It is stuck there and plays on a loop.
I call that having a song stuck in my **head**.
How very human.
Music lives in the heart, not the head. It is a **deep and magical force.**
Nanananananananana BAT-MAAAAAN
Great, now **I'M** gonna have that stuck in **my** heart.

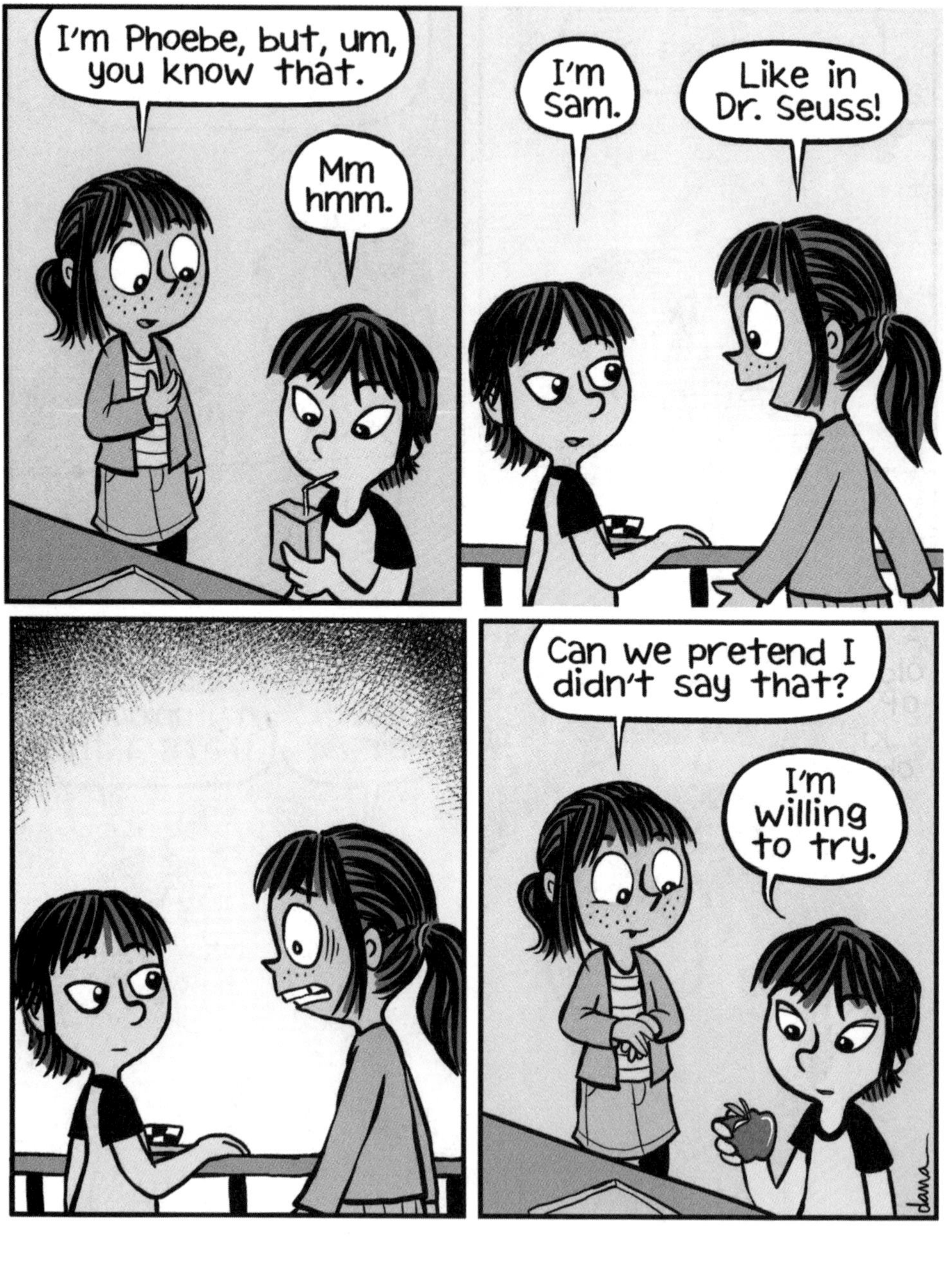
I'm Phoebe, but, um, you know that.
Mm hmm.
I'm Sam.
Like in Dr. Seuss!
Can we pretend I didn't say that?
I'm willing to try.
dana

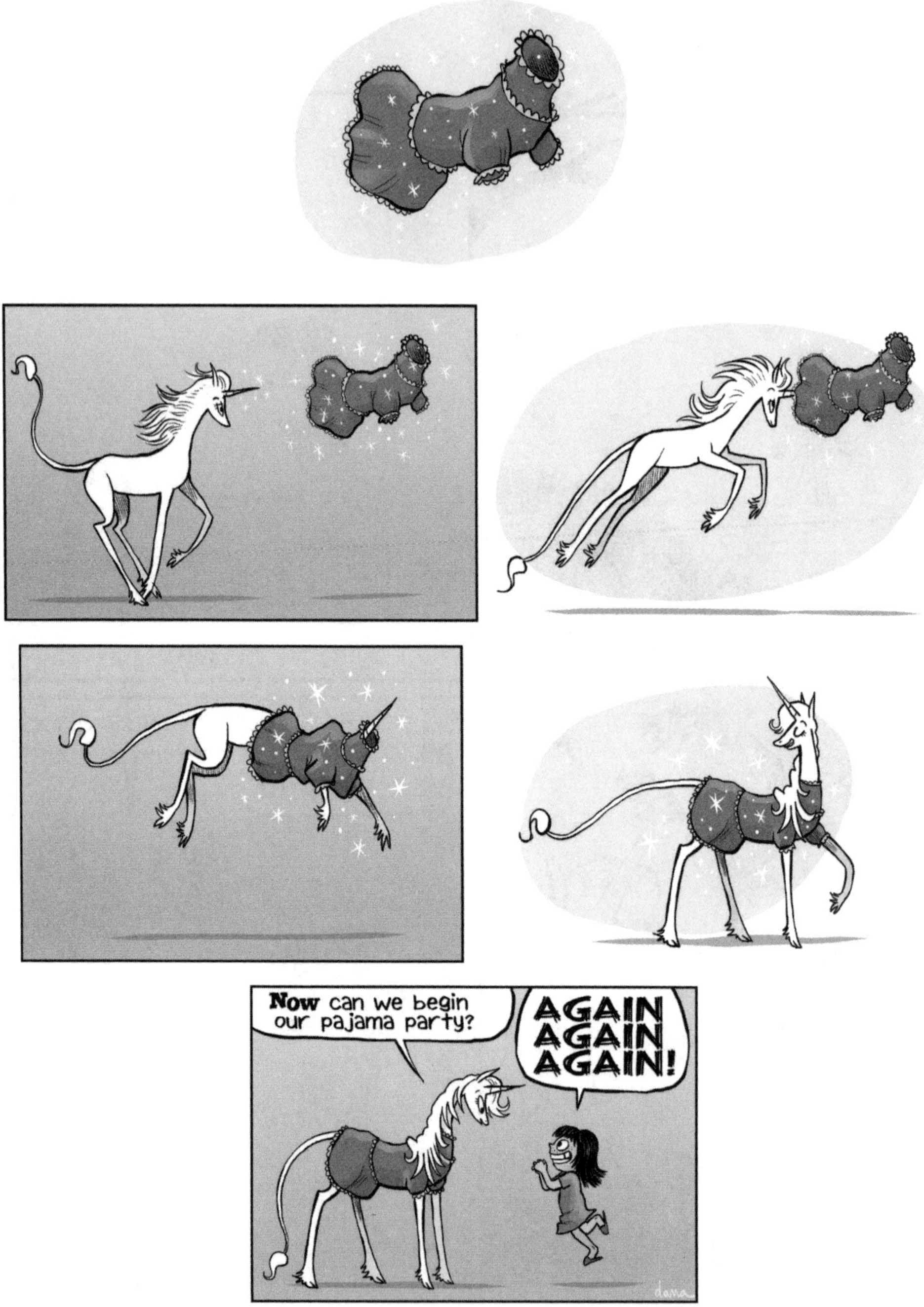
Now can we begin our pajama party?
AGAIN AGAIN AGAIN!

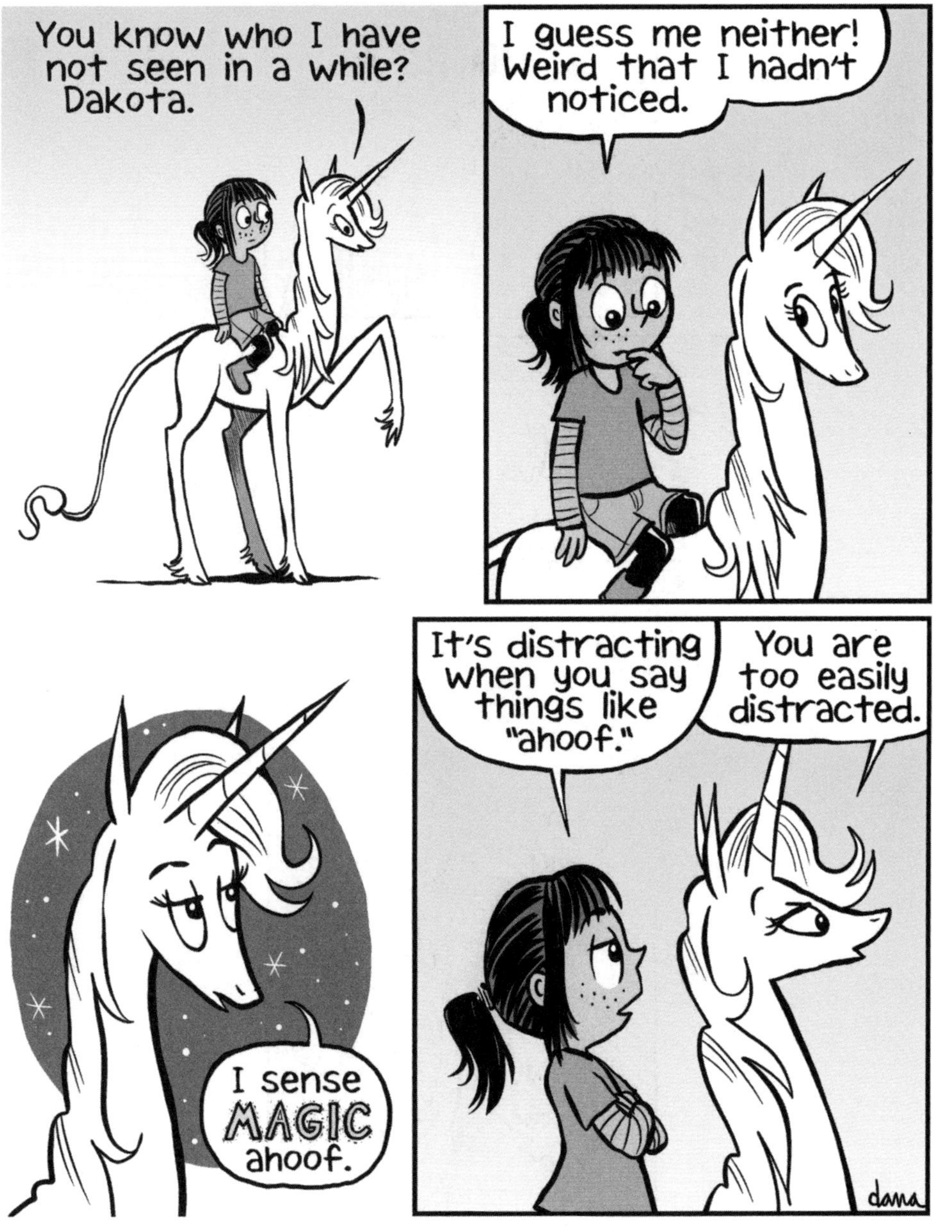
You know who I have not seen in a while? Dakota.
I guess me neither! Weird that I hadn't noticed.
I sense MAGIC ahoof.
It's distracting when you say things like "ahoof."
You are too easily distracted.
dana

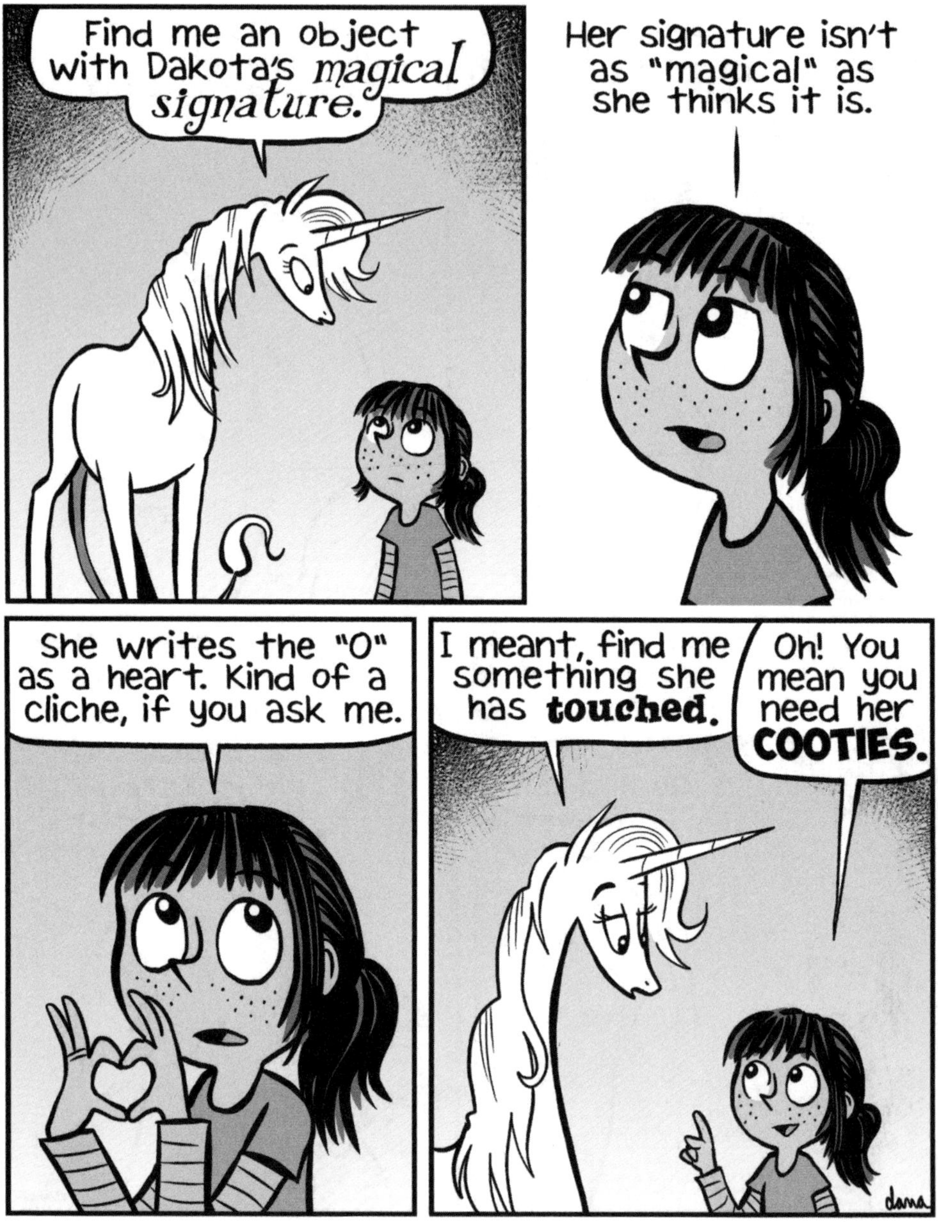
Find me an object with Dakota's *magical signature.*
Her signature isn't as "magical" as she thinks it is.
She writes the "O" as a heart. Kind of a cliche, if you ask me.
I meant, find me something she has **touched.**
Oh! You mean you need her **COOTIES.**
dana

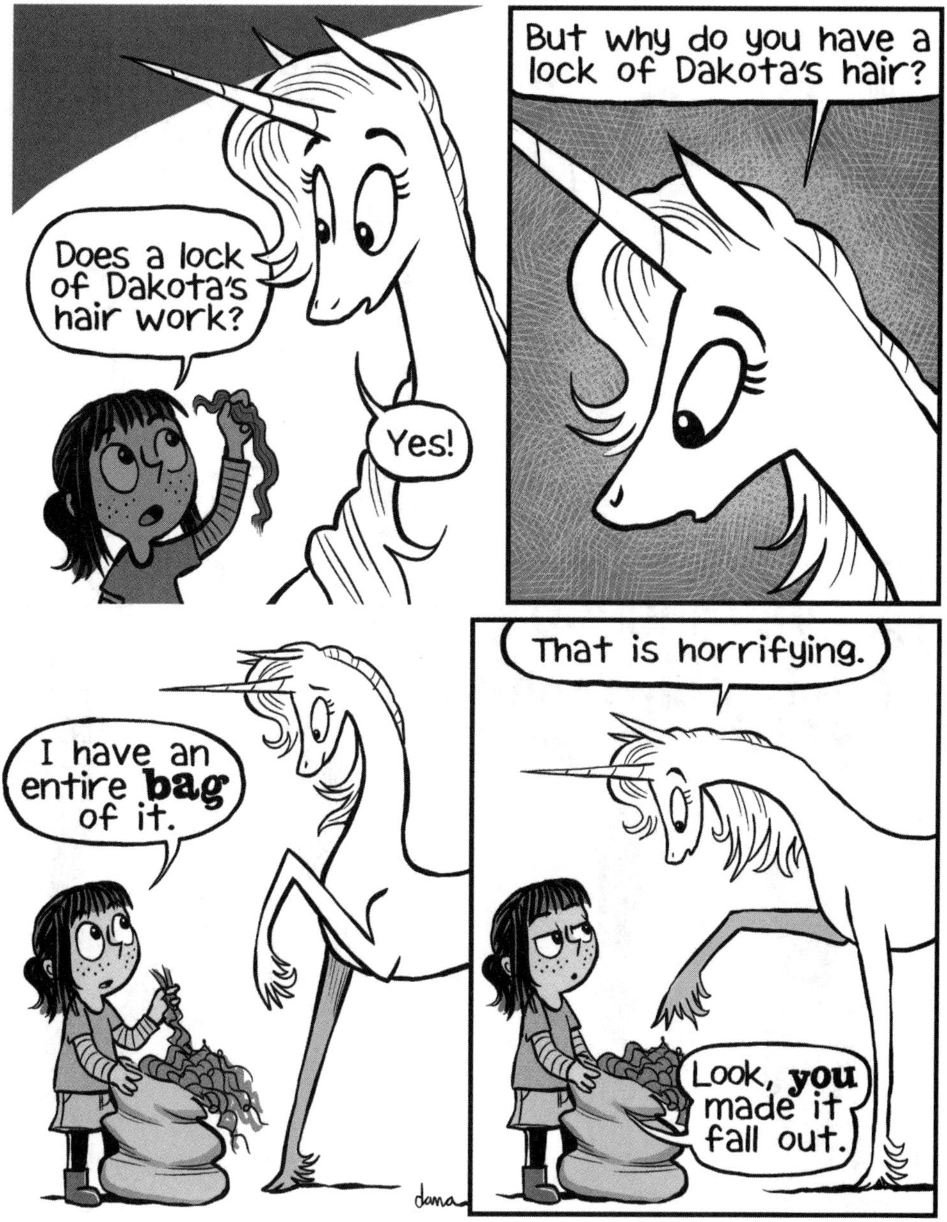
Does a lock of Dakota's hair work?
Yes!
But why do you have a lock of Dakota's hair?
I have an entire **bag** of it.
That is horrifying.
Look, **you** made it fall out.
dana

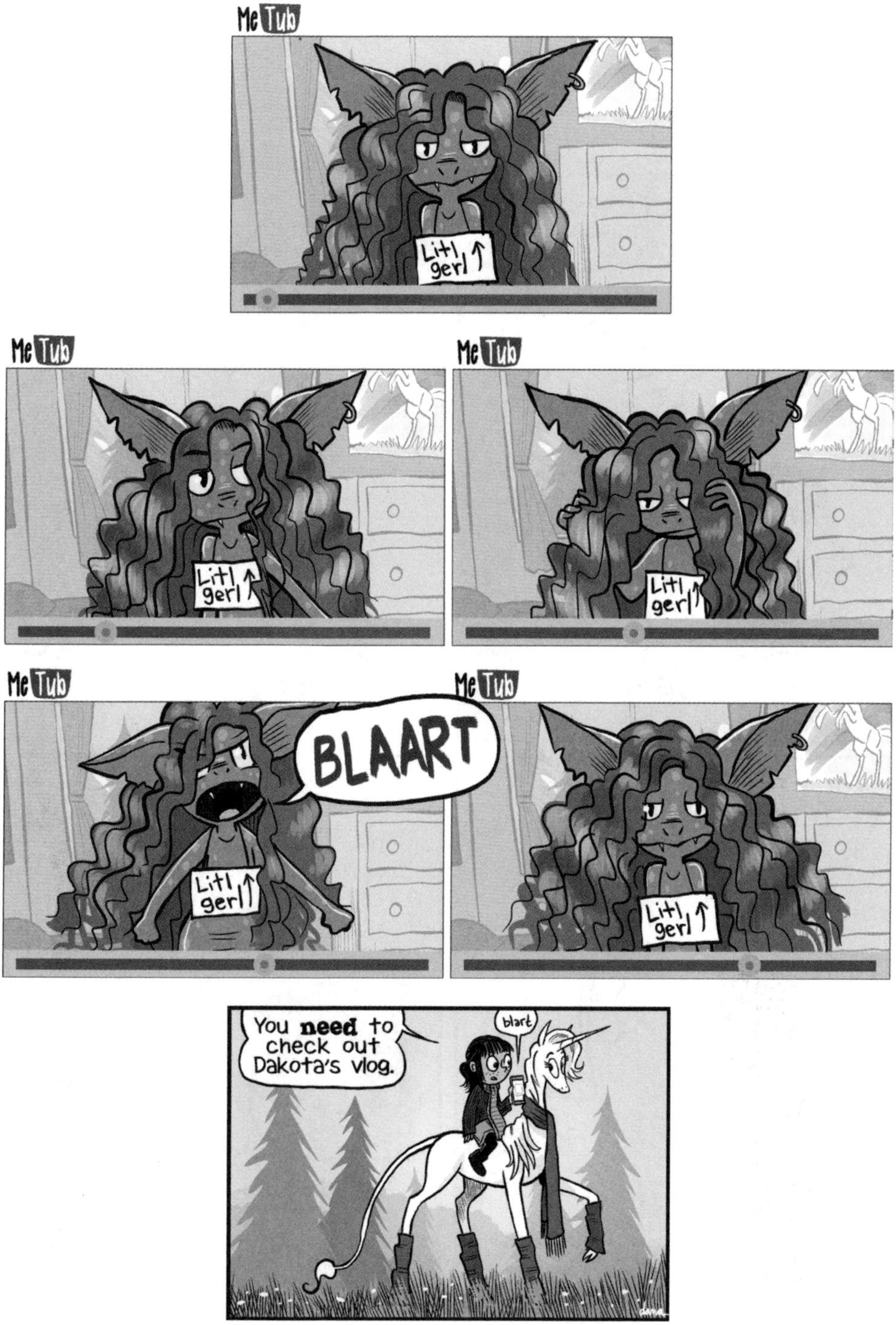
Me Tub
Litl gerl ↑
Me Tub
Litl gerl ↑
Me Tub
Litl gerl ↑
Me Tub
BLAART
Litl gerl ↑
Me Tub
Litl gerl ↑
You **need** to check out Dakota's vlog.
blart

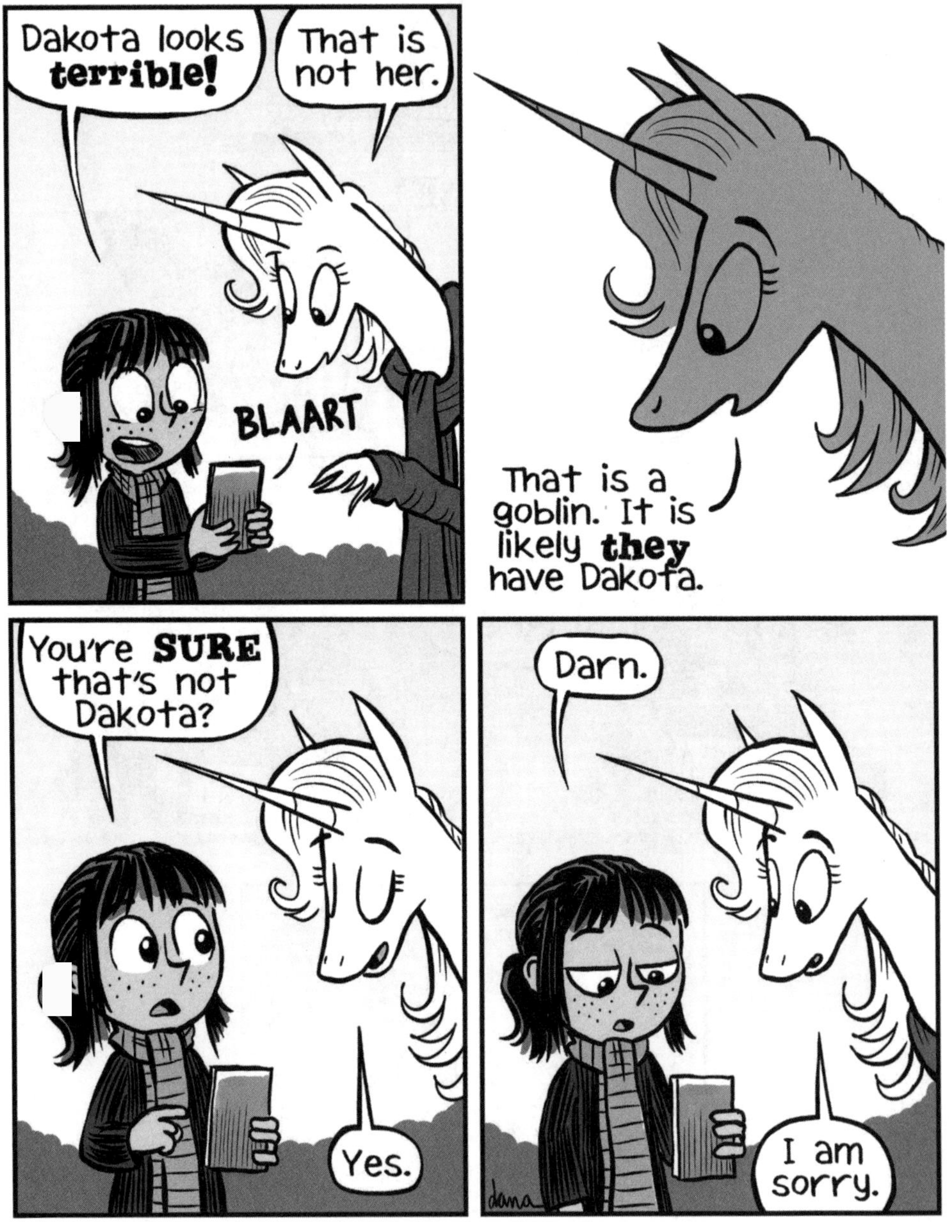
Dakota looks **terrible!**
That is not her.
BLAART
That is a goblin. It is likely **they** have Dakota.
You're **SURE** that's not Dakota?
Yes.
Darn.
I am sorry.
dana

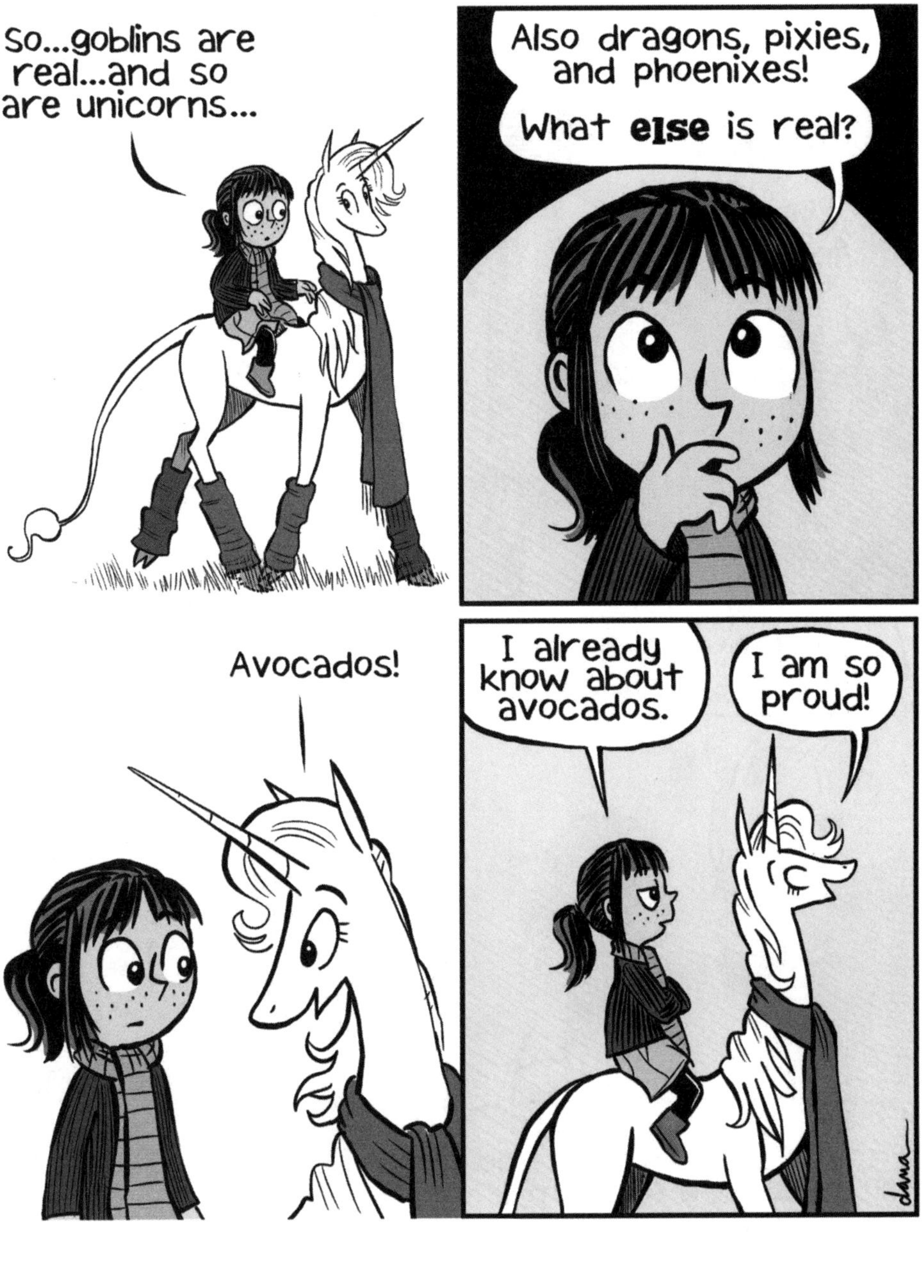
So...goblins are real...and so are unicorns...
Also dragons, pixies, and phoenixes!
What **else** is real?
Avocados!
I already know about avocados.
I am so proud!
dana

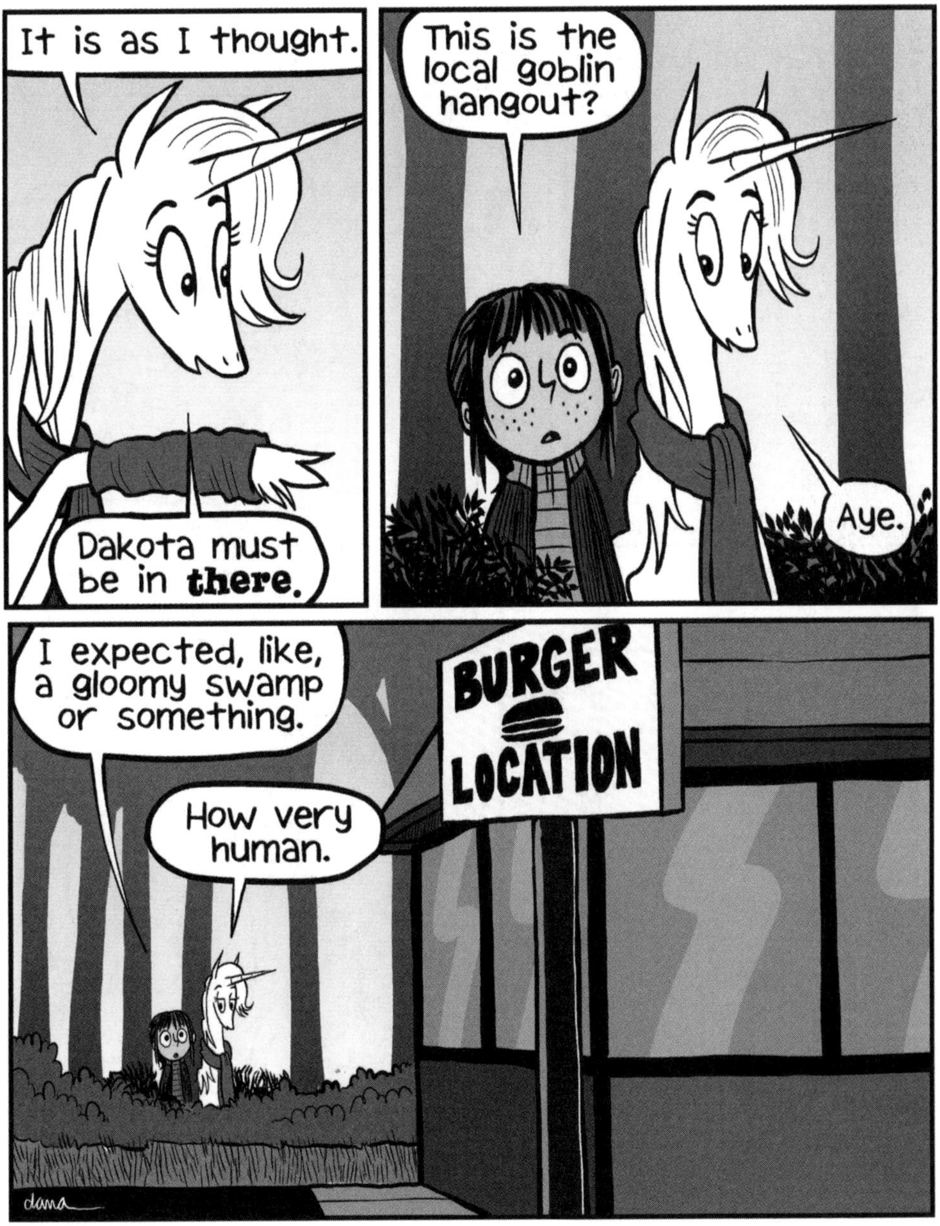
It is as I thought.
Dakota must be in **there**.
This is the local goblin hangout?
Aye.
I expected, like, a gloomy swamp or something.
How very human.
BURGER LOCATION
dana

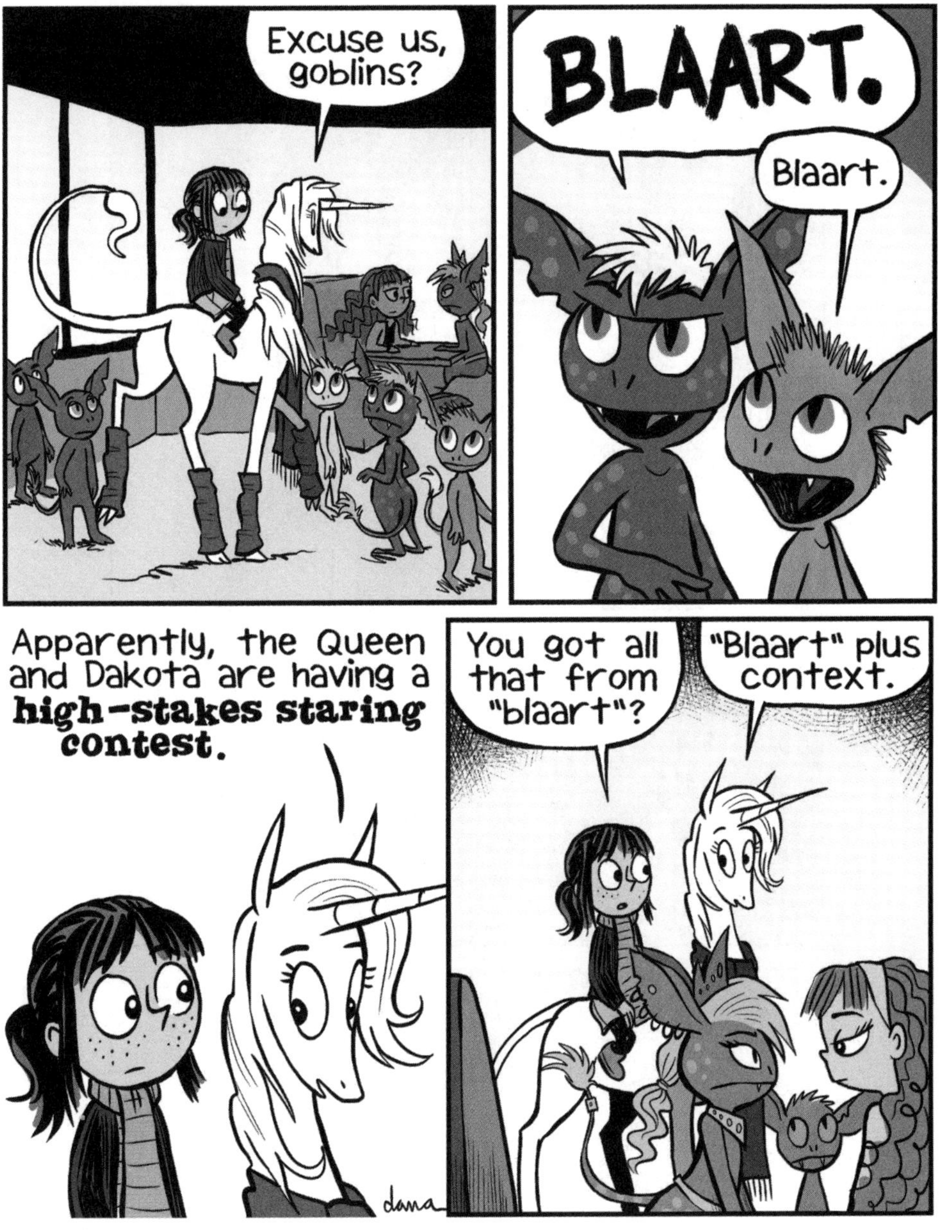

Excuse us, goblins?
BLAART.
Blaart.
Apparently, the Queen and Dakota are having a **high-stakes staring contest**.
You got all that from "blaart"?
"Blaart" plus context.
dana

A DAY IN THE LIFE OF A GOBLIN POSING AS A KID

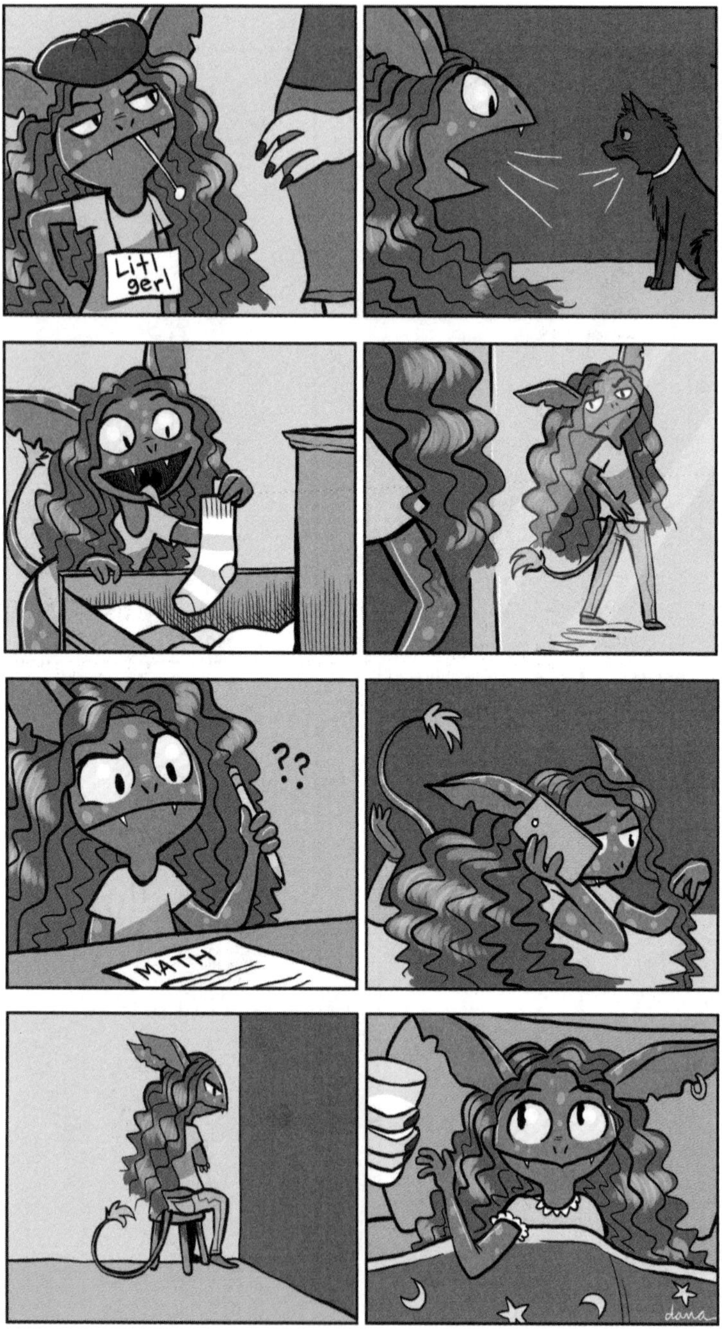
Litl gerl
??
MATH
dana

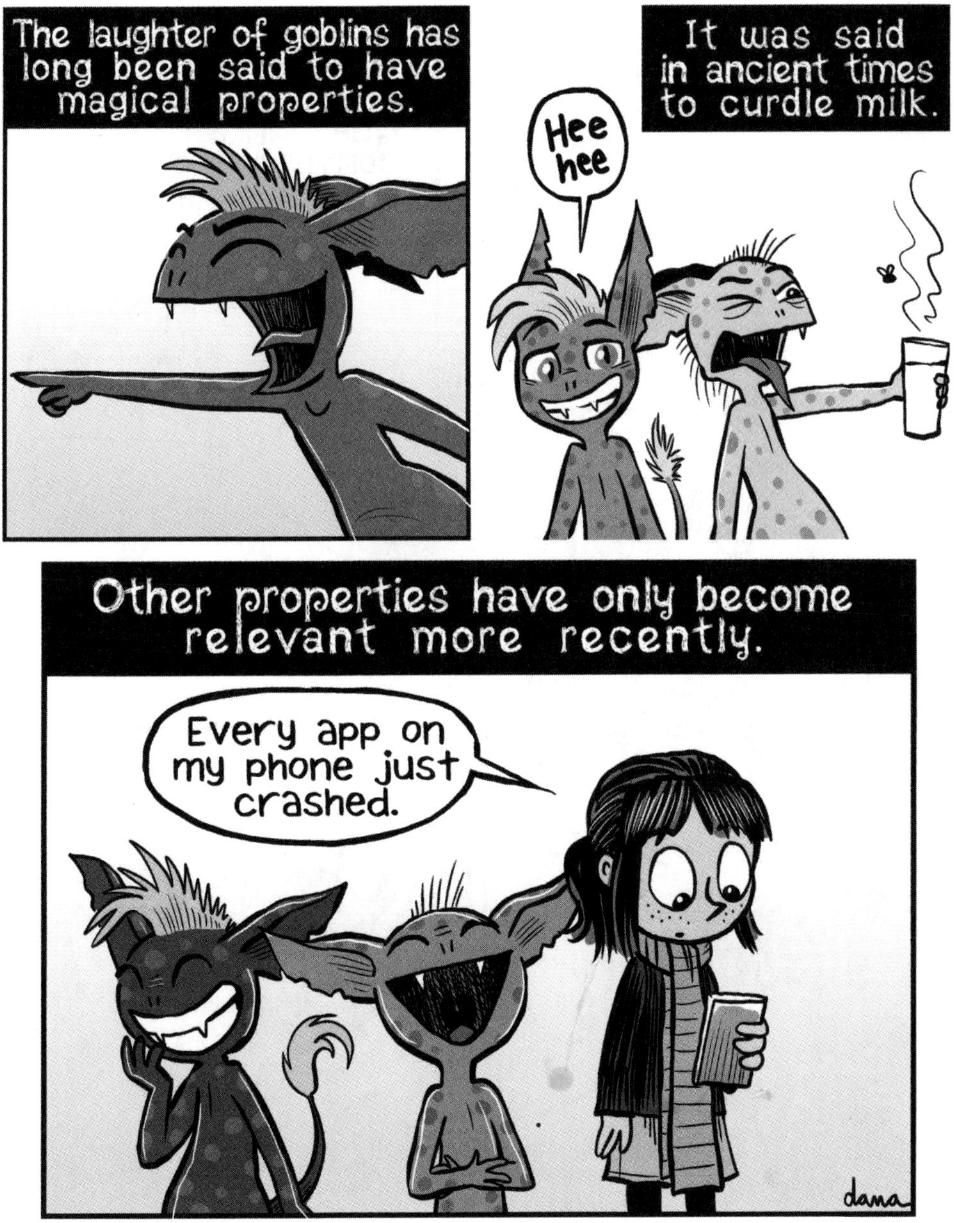
The laughter of goblins has long been said to have magical properties.
It was said in ancient times to curdle milk.
Hee hee
Other properties have only become relevant more recently.
Every app on my phone just crashed.
dana

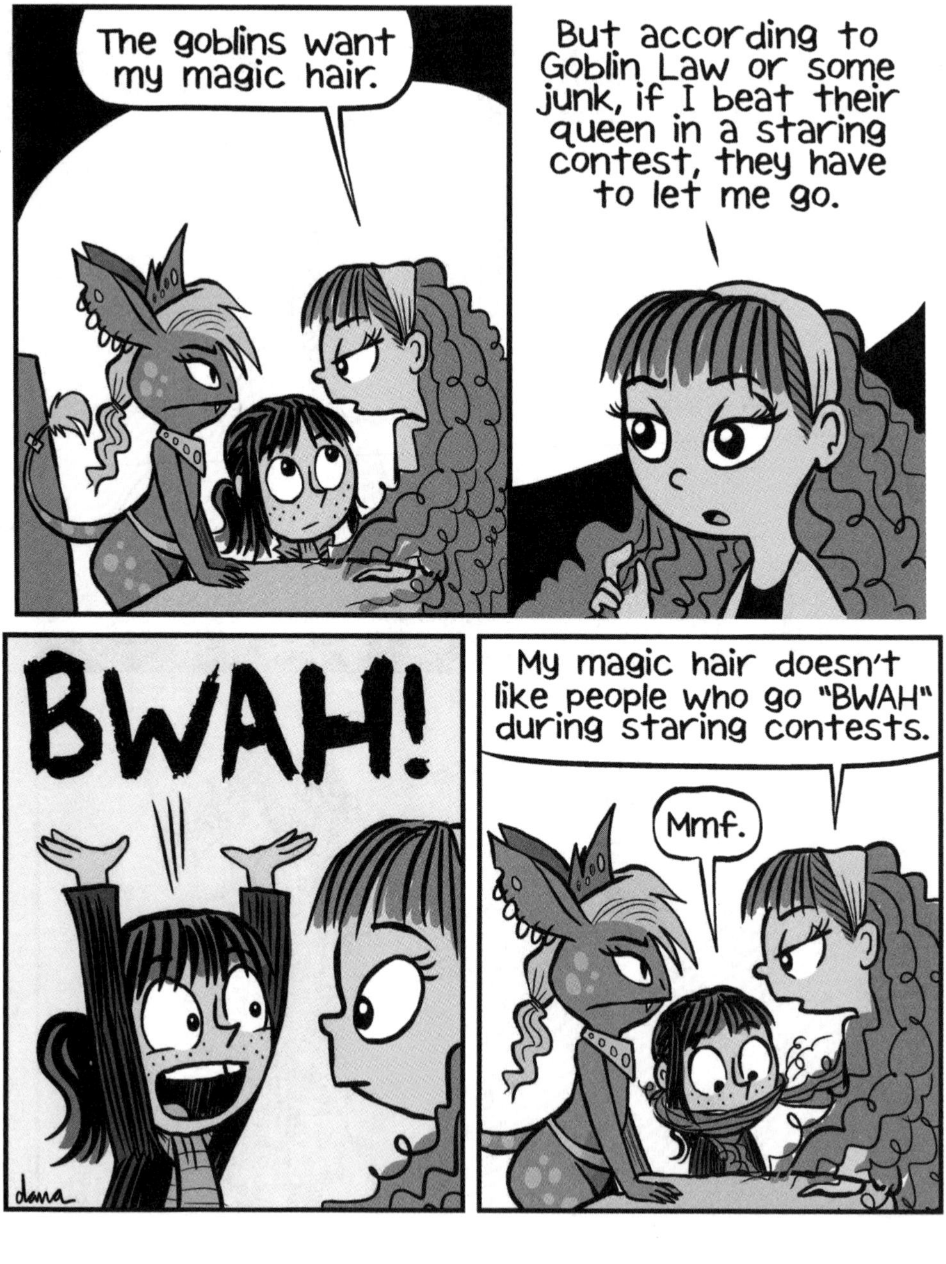

The goblins want my magic hair.
But according to Goblin Law or some junk, if I beat their queen in a staring contest, they have to let me go.
BWAH!
dana
My magic hair doesn't like people who go "BWAH" during staring contests.
Mmf.

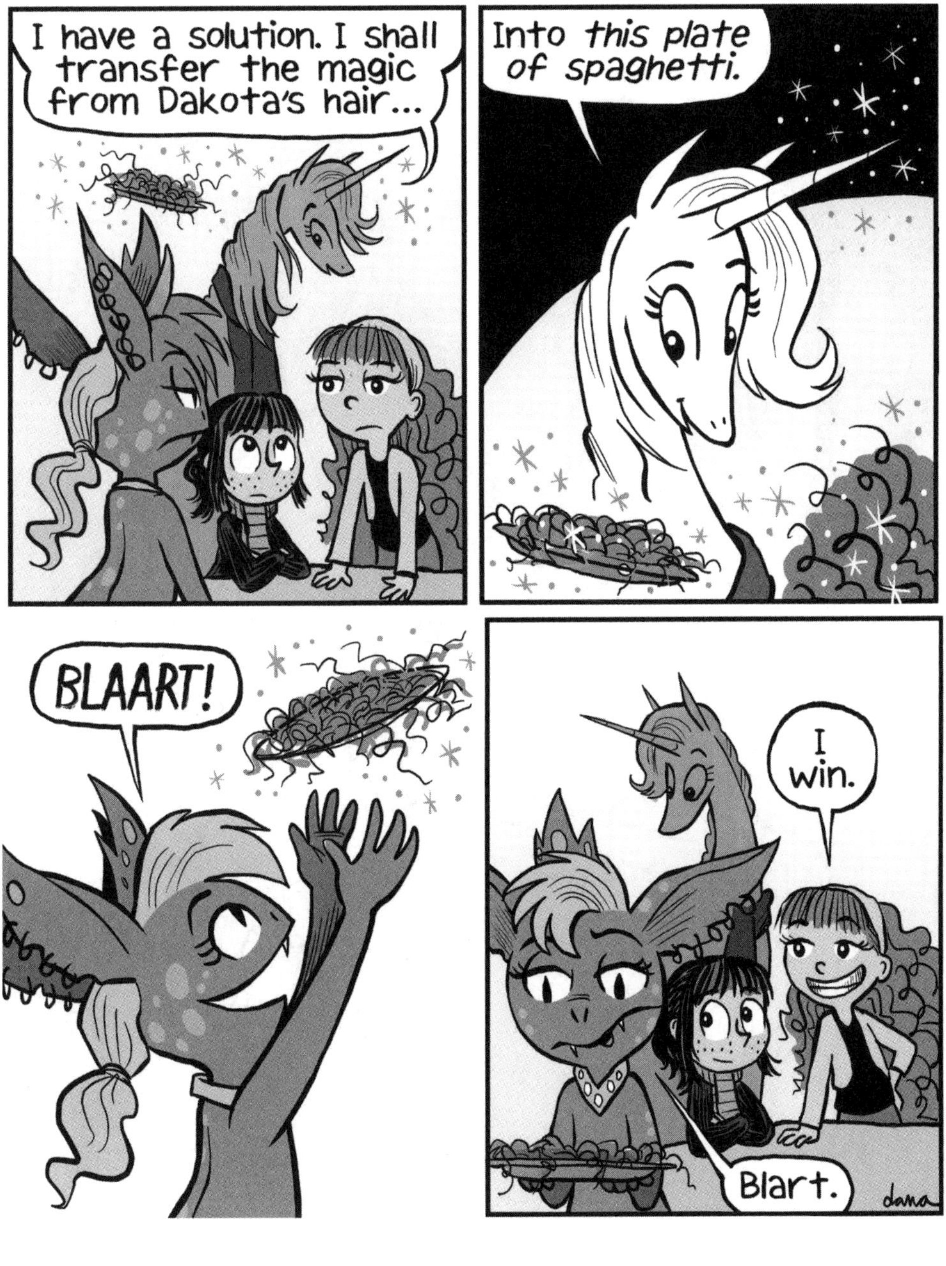
I have a solution. I shall transfer the magic from Dakota's hair...
Into *this plate of spaghetti.*
BLAART!
I win.
Blart.
dana

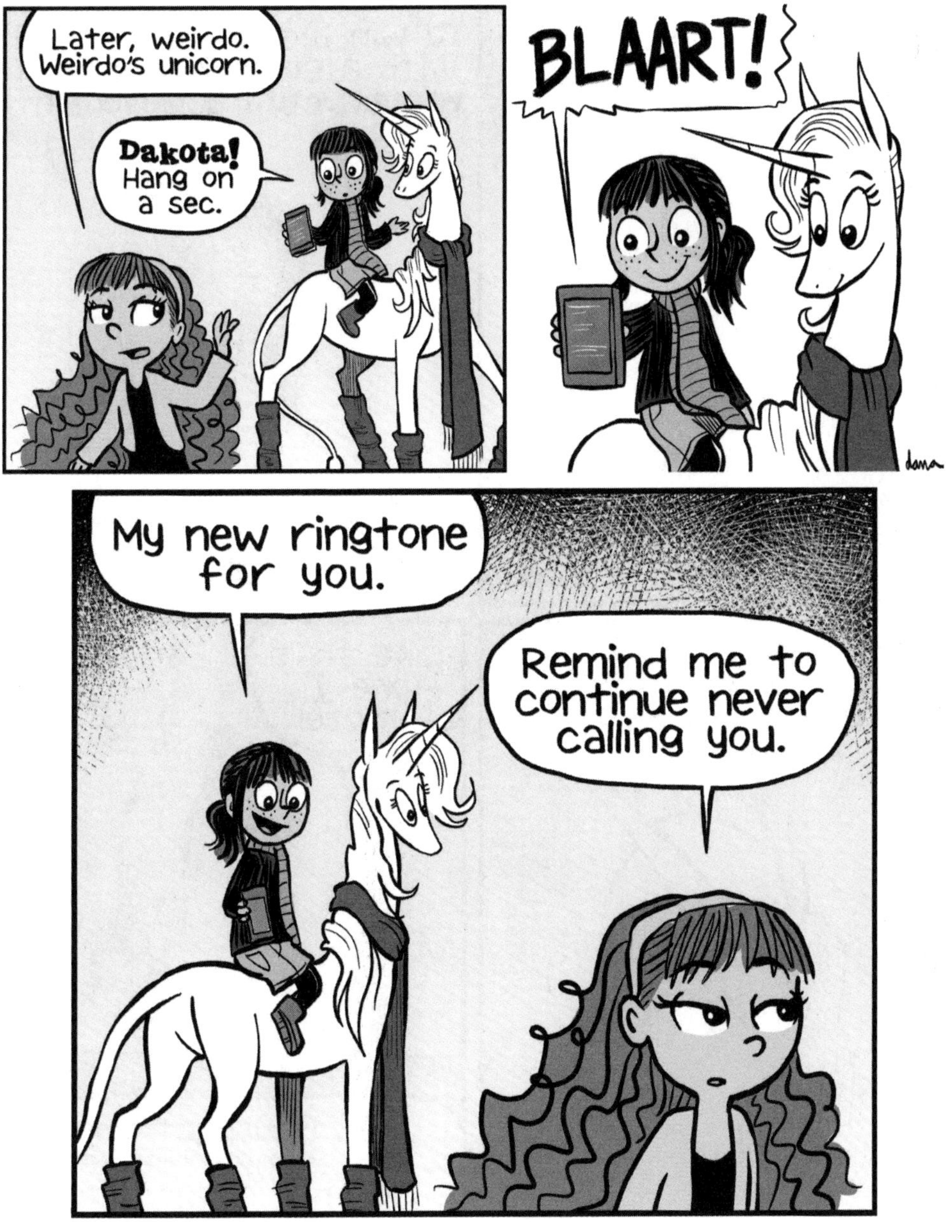
Later, weirdo. Weirdo's unicorn.
Dakota! Hang on a sec.
BLAART!
dana
My new ringtone for you.
Remind me to continue never calling you.

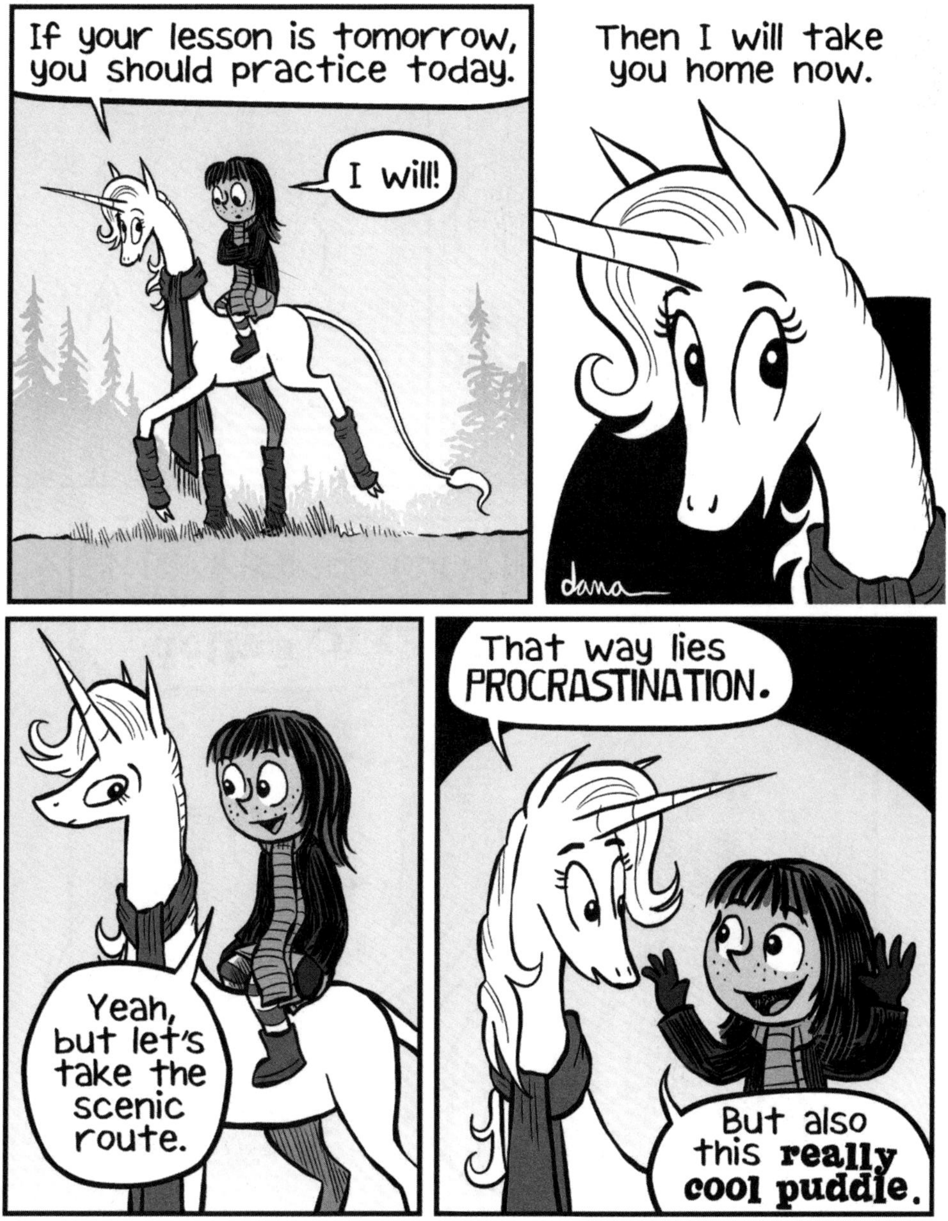

If your lesson is tomorrow, you should practice today.
I will!
Then I will take you home now.
dana
Yeah, but let's take the scenic route.
That way lies PROCRASTINATION.
But also this **really cool puddle**.

Let's Draw Some Supporting Characters

There are more characters than just Phoebe and Marigold! Here's a look at how I draw some of them.

Dakota and Max

Like Phoebe's, Dakota's head is based on a circle.

Max's is more of an oval.

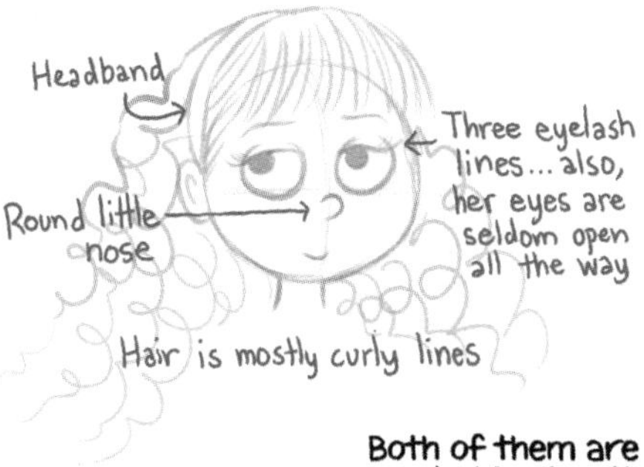
Headband
Three eyelash lines... also, her eyes are seldom open all the way
Round little nose
Hair is mostly curly lines

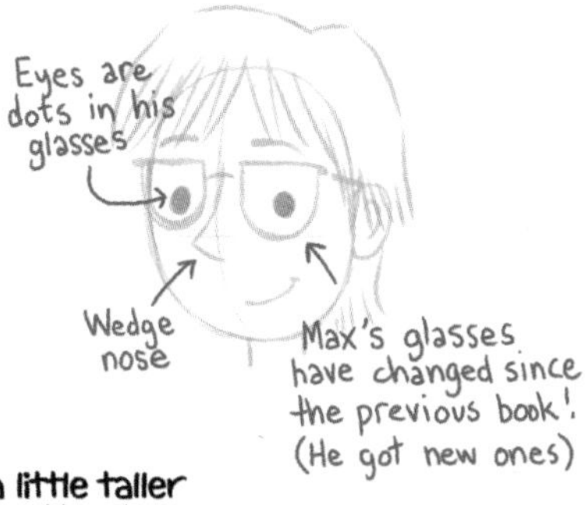
Eyes are dots in his glasses
Wedge nose
Max's glasses have changed since the previous book! (He got new ones)

Both of them are a little taller and skinnier than Phoebe.

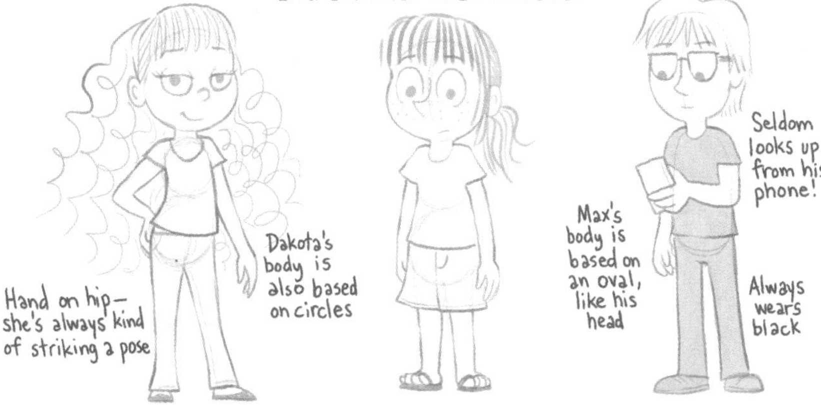
Dakota's body is also based on circles
Hand on hip— she's always kind of striking a pose
Seldom looks up from his phone!
Max's body is based on an oval, like his head
Always wears black

Todd the Candy-Breathing Dragon

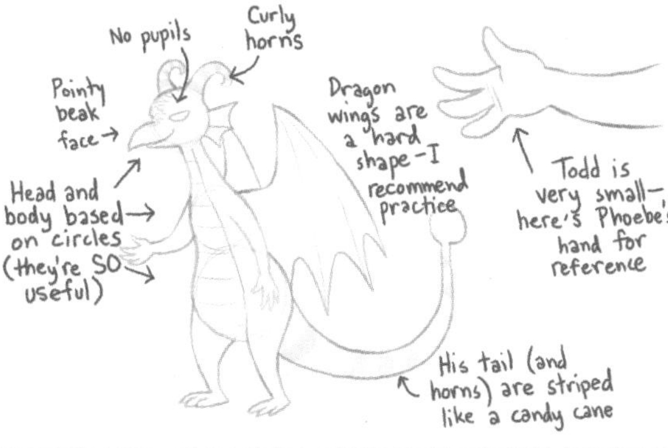
No pupils
Curly horns
Pointy beak face
Head and body based on circles (they're SO useful)
Dragon wings are a hard shape—I recommend practice
Todd is very small— here's Phoebe's hand for reference
His tail (and horns) are striped like a candy cane

Florence Unfortunate Nostrils

Florence looks a lot like her sister Marigold Heavenly Nostrils in some ways, but there are also some big differences.

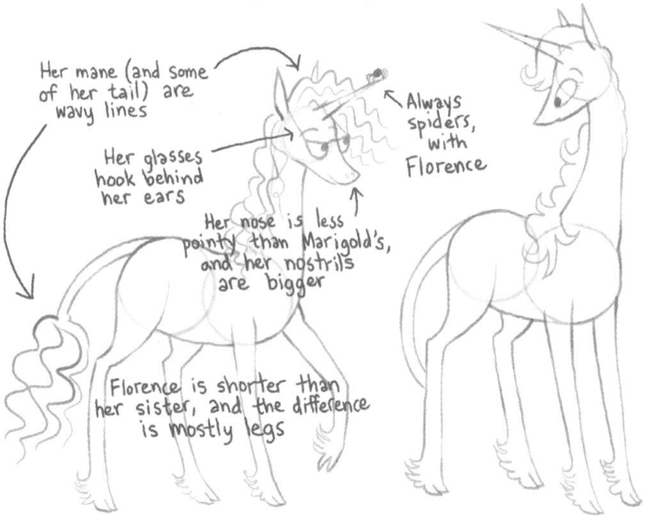

Her mane (and some of her tail) are wavy lines
Her glasses hook behind her ears
Always spiders, with Florence
Her nose is less pointy than Marigold's, and her nostrils are bigger
Florence is shorter than her sister, and the difference is mostly legs

Goblins

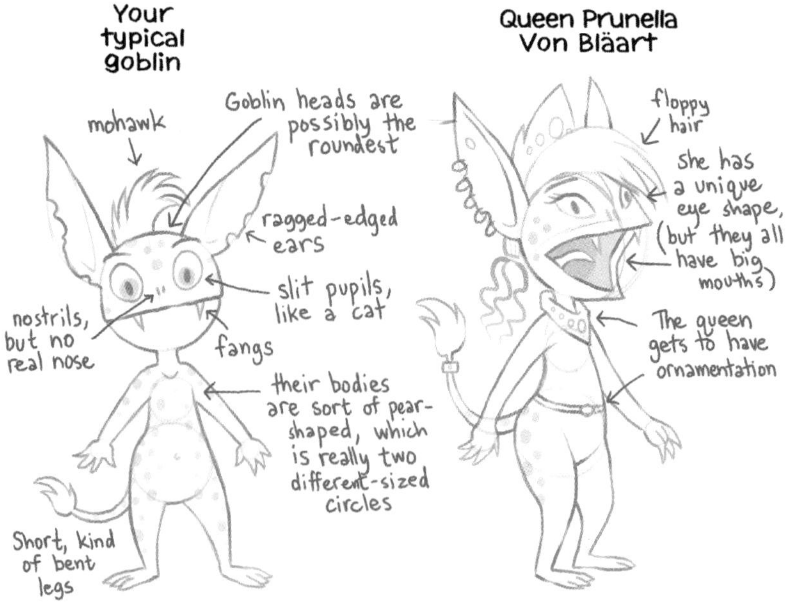

Your typical goblin
mohawk
Goblin heads are possibly the roundest
ragged-edged ears
slit pupils, like a cat
nostrils, but no real nose
fangs
their bodies are sort of pear-shaped, which is really two different-sized circles
Short, kind of bent legs
Queen Prunella Von Bläart
floppy hair
she has a unique eye shape, (but they all have big mouths)
The queen gets to have ornamentation

Goblins come in different heights, shapes, spot patterns...they probably vary as much as humans.

Questing Mix

Marigold might be able to survive on grass when she and Phoebe go on their quest to save Dakota from the goblins, but Phoebe will need something to snack on, and you will too! This special trail mix is easy to take along or to share with friends.

INGREDIENTS:

½ cup peanuts or other nuts

½ cup mini pretzels or 1-inch pieces small pretzels

½ cup semisweet chocolate chips

½ cup dried cranberries or cherries

¼ cup Goldfish crackers

¼ cup raisins

¼ cup sunflower seeds

INSTRUCTIONS:

In a large bowl, combine all the ingredients and toss to mix well.

The trail mix will keep in an airtight container at room temperature for at least 2 weeks.

Makes about 8 servings, about 3 cups.

Alice and the Unicorn

Not surprisingly, the unicorn makes an appearance in the works of Lewis Carroll, creator of the most delightful whimsy of the Victorian age. In *Through the Looking Glass and What Alice Found There*, Alice encounters a unicorn in a passage that captures the essential paradox of the legendary beast:

> ". . . He was going on, when his eye happened to fall upon Alice: he turned round instantly, and stood for some time looking at her with an air of the deepest disgust.
>
> 'What—is—this?' he said at last.
>
> 'This is a child!' Haigha replied eagerly . . . 'We only found it today. It's as large as life, and twice as natural!'
>
> 'I always thought they were fabulous monsters!' said the Unicorn. 'Is it alive?"
>
> 'It can talk,' said Haigha solemnly.
>
> The Unicorn looked dreamily to Alice, and said, 'Talk, child.'
>
> Alice could not help her lips curling into a smile as she began: 'Do you know, I always thought Unicorns were fabulous monsters, too? I never saw one alive before!'
>
> 'Well, now we *have* seen each other,' said the Unicorn, 'if you'll believe in me, I'll believe in you. Is that a bargain?'"

Andrews McMeel Publishing
a division of Andrews McMeel Universal
1130 Walnut Street, Kansas City, Missouri 64106

www.andrewsmcmeel.com

16 17 18 19 20 RR2 10 9 8 7 6 5 4 3 2 1

ISBN: 978-1-4494-8350-0

Library of Congress Control Number: 2015954011

Made by:
RR Donnelley & Sons
Address and location of manufacturer:
1009 Sloan Street
Crawfordsville, IN 47933-2743
1st Printing—8/5/16

ATTENTION: SCHOOLS AND BUSINESSES
Andrews McMeel books are available at quantity discounts with bulk purchase for educational, business, or sales promotional use. For information, please e-mail the Andrews McMeel Publishing Special Sales Department: specialsales@amuniversal.com.

amp! COMICS for kids

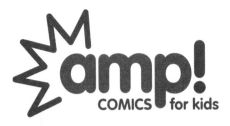

Check out these and other books at ampkids.com

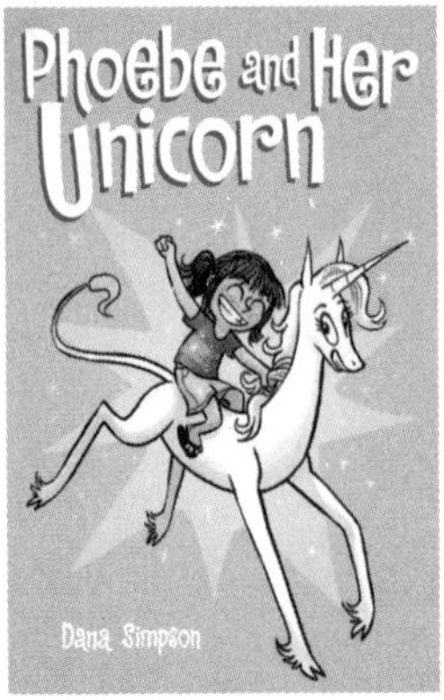
Phoebe and Her Unicorn
Dana Simpson

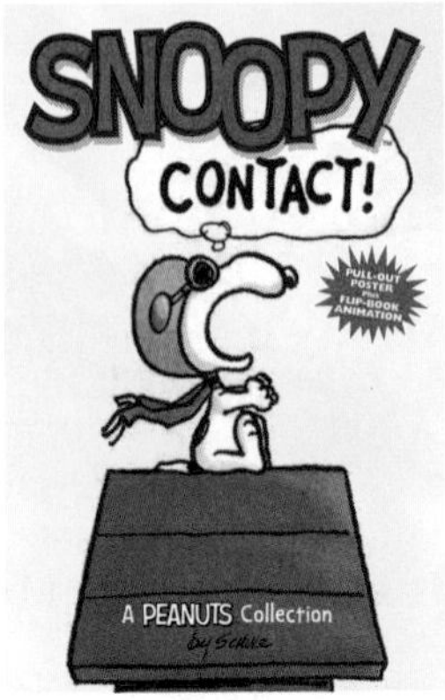
SNOOPY
CONTACT!
PULL-OUT POSTER Plus FLIP-BOOK ANIMATION
A PEANUTS Collection

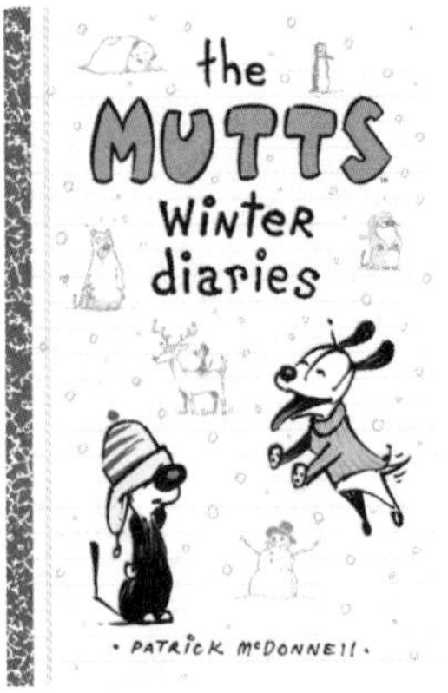
the MUTTS Winter diaries
PATRICK McDONNELL

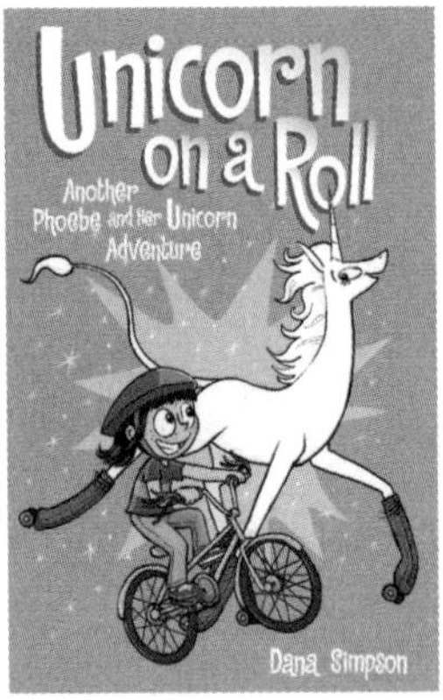
Unicorn on a Roll
Another Phoebe and Her Unicorn Adventure
Dana Simpson

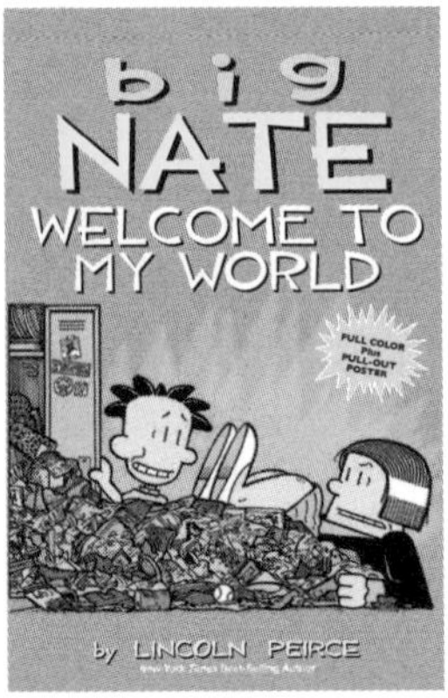
big NATE
WELCOME TO MY WORLD
FULL COLOR Plus PULL-OUT POSTER
by LINCOLN PEIRCE

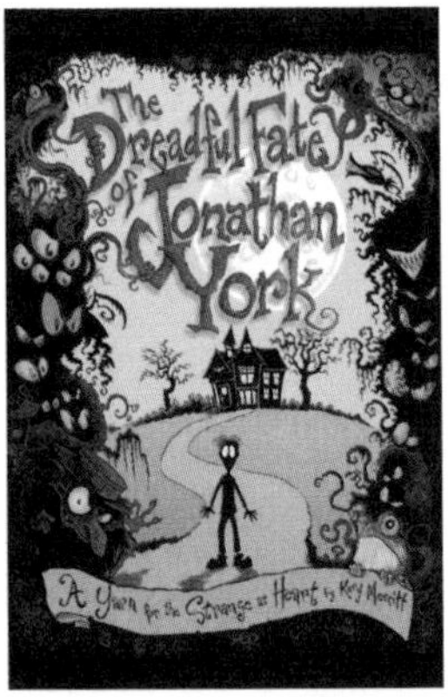
The Dreadful Fate of Jonathan York

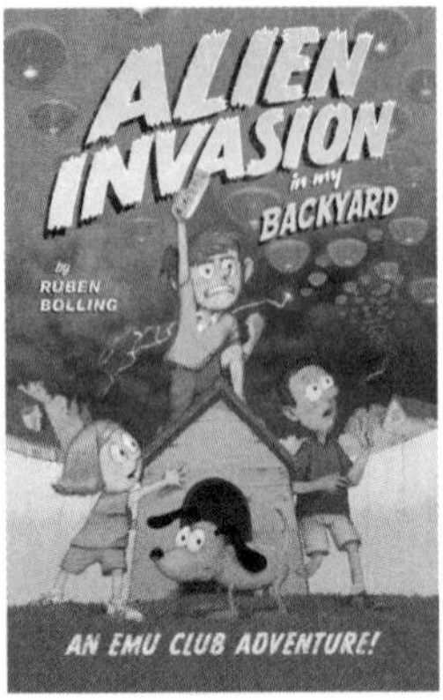
ALIEN INVASION in my BACKYARD
by RUBEN BOLLING
AN EMU CLUB ADVENTURE!

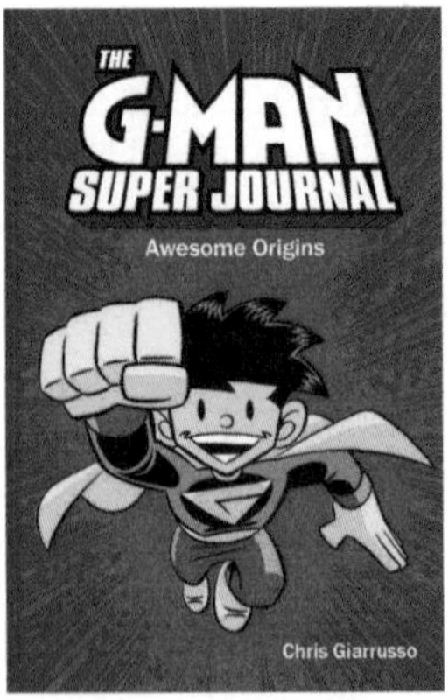
THE G-MAN SUPER JOURNAL
Awesome Origins
Chris Giarrusso

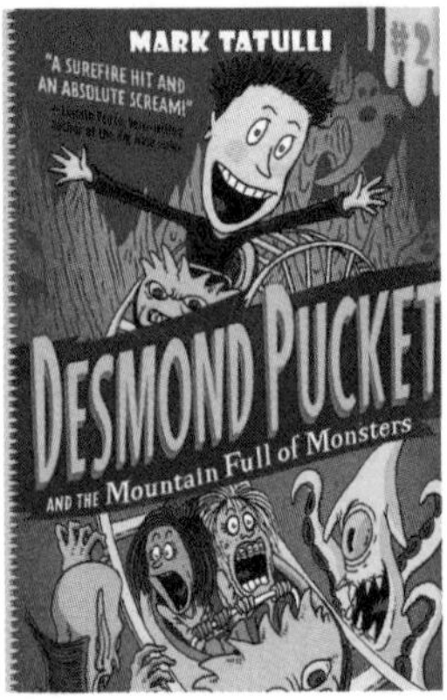
MARK TATULLI
"A SUREFIRE HIT AND AN ABSOLUTE SCREAM!"
DESMOND PUCKET
AND THE Mountain Full of Monsters

Also available:
Teaching and activity guides for each title.
AMP! Comics for Kids books make reading FUN!